KISS OF THE
TSUNAMI

RACHEL RIVERS PORTER

KISS OF THE TSUNAMI

Rachel Rivers Porter

Cover design by Phil Tee

Printed and bound by
Ashford Colour Press Ltd, Gosport, Hants. PO13 0FW

+++

First published 2016
by Rivers Porter Publishing, Great Britain
riversporter.com

Paperback: ISBN 978-0-9956570-0-7

+++

REVIEWS

'A unique and accomplished novel with excellent, moving writing. Kiss of the Tsunami is a sensitively written, authentic and emotive story of two teens from very different cultures swept up in a horrific event – the 2004 Boxing Day tsunami. The author has done an excellent job of creating two narrators with very unique voices. I really enjoyed this novel and think the writer has a lot of promise.'

Chicken House Reader's Report

'A heart-rending story with a serious message. Rachel Rivers Porter is an exciting, original new writer.'

Bea Davenport, author

'Rachel Rivers Porter is one of the successes of Penguin Random House Writers' Academy. It was a fantastic achievement being long-listed by The Times Chicken House Children's Fiction Competition.'

Rebecca Watson,
Penguin Random House Writers' Academy

ACKNOWLEDGEMENTS

I am very grateful to the team of people around me, without whom this novel could not have been published.

Penguin Random House Writers' Academy for its fantastic 'Constructing a Novel' course.

Barbara Henderson, The Writers' Academy tutor, whose wisdom and helpful advice have been invaluable.

Chicken House Publishing, for long-listing 'Kiss of the Tsunami' and providing an inspiring Reader's Report.

'The Random Penguins,' a talented and supportive group of writers.

Seymour Jacklin Editorial Services, for astute, detailed feedback.

Phil Tee, who kindly designed the beautiful cover.

Andrew Grant, for generously giving his time and expertise to help prepare the e-book.

Sandra Bell, Judith Grant and Carrie Clay, whose encouragement and motivation have kept me going.

Jane Robson, Heather Mellars, Tayo Adewumi, Helen Hunter and Jill Jackson, for all those fun coffee and cake chats.

My brothers, David and George, for enthusiastically listening to my stories when we were young.

My children, James, Michael and Rosie, for making me smile each day and for technical support when the computer wouldn't obey me!

My husband Stuart, whose hard work in formatting the manuscript, has made my dream become a reality.

And a special thank you to the many people whose documented experiences of the tsunami have enabled me to create an authentic story based upon the horrific events of Boxing Day 2004.

DEDICATION

This book is dedicated to all those affected by the 2004
Indian Ocean Tsunami.

Also to my parents, Alec and Audrey,
whose faithfulness and kindness have blessed me
and many others over the years.

CONTENTS

PART 1 – DREAMS

PART 2 – TSUNAMI

PART 3 – AFTERMATH

PART 4 – DESTINY

EPILOGUE

The Laboon once swallowed whole villages.
When the crabs crawl to the forest
and the birds stop singing
and the tide disappears into the mist,
you must run.

Moken folklore

PART 1 – DREAMS

"The ocean is my universe;
I was born with the sound of the waves in my
ears and the smell of the sea filling my body.
And the ocean is still inside me."

– Papa

1. Sea Gypsy

25th December 2004

MARTI

I'm going to tell him tonight. I've had a lifetime of being nobody and it is too long. I can't live his dream, floating between islands. I may just be collecting garbage and cleaning the hotel pool, but it's better than spending every day under the sea.

The sun is low in the sky and my stomach is grumbling. Having finished sweeping the paths and picking up stray cans and empty fast-food trays, I walk to the kitchen, drawn by the spicy smell of curry. With luck, the Thai waiters will be stuck in the dining room and won't see me.

As soon as I open the door, they slither out like eels from crevices in coral reefs — eyes glaring, mouths twisted. Chaow throws his arms wide and his empty tray clatters on the floor. "Watch out; it's Fish Boy!"

Virote arches away from me like I'm infectious. "Dirty Moken scum! It should be thrown back in the sea!"

Forcing my chin up, I place my legs wide. Sometimes I need to know the ground is safe beneath my feet. Chaow is tall, his cheeks hidden behind stubble.

Virote stands in his shadow, one nostril raised like he thinks the world owes him something. His eyes narrow. "Lost your tongue?"

"It can't speak," says Chaow, "like a dumb fish!"

"You are slimier than the ones I've gutted," I say calmly. Breath grates between his teeth like it's stuck, then he glances at his friend. Virote tips his head back and gargles. I know what's coming, and try to dodge, but they block me either side. Arching back, I avoid Chaow's fist. Then pain shoots into my cheek as Virote slams me against the fridge. The smell of garlic hits me. His eyes glint as he leans over me and I'm forced to watch the globule of saliva oozing down my shirt.

When they've gone, I stab a knife into a bowl of prawns. I can't wait to escape. I'm fed up with the rubbish they spew at me. I'll fly away like the tourists and order cocktails and four course dinners every night. I'll sleep in smooth, white sheets, not palm leaf matting. White bodies arrive with bulging suitcases, fat wallets and shiny sunglasses. A week later, a sea of tanned faces leaves after their sunshine fix. I want their electric world. Papa says the spirits will destroy us if we play around with technology, but I've been watching Rune's TV most evenings and nothing bad has happened yet.

I spit out a hard bit of prawn and spear another right through. Papa will be angry when I tell him, but he can't stop me, because he never joins the flotilla now. Grandad still lives on the Kabang and the ocean is his companion, while Papa sits there like a pile of fish guts, mucus dripping down his nose. Wasting his life.

Even Coral thinks that Papa is lazy, although she's too respectful to tell him. My beautiful older sister tries to smooth out the ripples in people's lives, like the ocean when the wind holds its breath. Everyone loves Coral. I've seen the way men look at her, wanting her, but she will be married soon. I'll miss Coral when I leave, and little Petal and Mama. I'll miss Grandad: he's so wrinkled, his face looks like a sponge when he laughs, the crinkles creasing in and out. But I won't miss Papa.

2. Christmas in Paradise

KRISTA

How does Dad expect me to smile when I've been sitting next to The Woman for the past six and a half hours? She's like an excited little kid and won't stop talking. "First time I've been to Asia... exotic markets... delicious food... never been further than Ibiza before..."

Nor have I, but I'm not telling the whole world. I've only travelled to Chamonix on a school ski trip. Our family used to go to Scotland on holiday — to the same place, this big old stone house near Loch Lomond and The Trossachs National Park. We went up there when Mum died, just Dad and me. We walked and sailed on the loch, and bagged four Munros. Climbing the mountains was hard work, so it stopped you thinking for a bit. Then the pain would come back, tearing me inside like a digger stripping off the surface of a road. Scarred, raw, exposed.

I kept thinking I'd see her, that she'd walk through the door or be at the end of the phone. Some days we talked about her, funny things that we remembered, but mostly it was too painful. It still is. But Dad and I were there for each other and it helped. Sitting on the thick carpet by the log fire, watching the flames chase each other. Thinking. Dreaming. Wishing Mum was still alive.

I wanted Dad to sit next to me on the plane, but The Woman sank into the middle seat, saying as it was a long flight, it would be fun to chat to both of us. For the first half an hour, I did my best to answer, but she flaps her arms when she talks, and unfortunately, the exotic fragrance she bought from the Duty Free, doesn't disguise sweaty armpits. I'm pressing against the aeroplane window but she doesn't get the hint; her head is moving from side to side like she's umpiring a tennis match. I know she's trying to include me, but it feels like she and Dad are on the same side and I'm on the other.

"Christmas in Thailand!" Dad had announced last month, throwing a travel brochure on top of my Maths revision file. "Just think of it, Kris: beautiful sandy beaches, clear blue skies…" His fingers ran along the glossy photos, brushing the coral reef. "We'll have the time of our lives!" He grabbed my hand across the table. "The scuba diving is amazing, but if you don't want to explore the underwater world, Jo says she'll keep you company." He let go of me to touch The Woman's cheek. "Isn't that right, love?" I sank back into the seat, trying to control my disappointment, but Dad just smiled. "Phuket is wonderful, Krista, I know you'll love it!"

I know I'll hate it. My step-mum is smiling at Dad with flushed cheeks, matching her dress. Red for "danger" and "stop" — like I wish she had, before she'd got a job as Dad's secretary and he fell for her. How can he forget about Mum; how can he move on as if nothing has happened, as if she never existed?

I told Dad that Granny had offered I could stay with her and Grandad, but he said the holiday wouldn't be the same without me. Then I mentioned that it clashed with Izzie's New Year's Eve party, but he ruffled my hair like a pet dog's and said there'll be other parties.

"Not like this one: everyone's going!"

When my step-mum suggested we postpone the trip until the summer, I felt guilty because the real reason I don't want to go is because of her. True, I don't want to miss the party — Izzie's Mum has organised all this cool stuff. And Jack will be there. But it's not that big a deal; I see him every day at school. He's been hanging around with our set this term, and Izzie thinks he fancies me.

Like Dad fancies Jo.

My stomach tightens as I remember their wedding. They looked so happy, and I smiled through it all. My new step-mum hugged me and said I looked like a beautiful slim model in my bridesmaid dress. I felt ugly, all hard and wrinkled inside like a walnut. I danced with my cousins and laughed at Dad's jokes, but inside I was crying. When he hugged me before they drove away on honeymoon, I didn't want to let go. I felt like I was losing Dad as well as Mum.

They had no idea how I was feeling, no-one did. Except Granny, maybe. She lent me her handkerchief, the special one with the embroidered roses and said I could wipe away the happy tears. But when she looked into my eyes, I knew she knew they weren't happy tears. Granny has lost Mum too, but with her work at Isabel Hospice, she has found a way to move on. It's me who is stuck, unable to say goodbye.

Perhaps Jo suggested moving the holiday to the summer because she felt awkward and knew we both needed some space. Dad waved the brochure, brushing away her idea. "Too late. Went online this morning. Got a last minute deal!"

"But Dad…"

"But nothing. Just think of it: 'turquoise waters in sheltered coves, mountains rising out of emerald seas, stunning waterfalls'… "

15

But Mum isn't with us, so how can I enjoy it?

"Come on Kris, it's a trip to Paradise — nothing can beat that!"

"A sleepover can. I'll be the only girl not there. I'll miss out on everything!"

He didn't fall for it; my words were like waves washing over a rock. Now we're millions of miles from home. Why did we have to fly halfway across the world? Dad thinks it's going to be the holiday of a lifetime, but how can it be without Mum? I know he's got a right to be happy again, but it hurts seeing my step-mum acting like she owns him. I can see that she wants to be my friend, but she's trying too hard. I'm fifteen and a half, not six. And she has only been married to Dad for four months and thirteen days — she doesn't know me, not even around the edges.

I smell a fresh waft of flowery perfume and feel a touch on my arm. "I wouldn't worry too much about missing the party, there's plenty of time." I twist my shoulder, trying to avoid Jo's frizzy hair, but she leans closer. "You'll meet lots of nice young men soon enough, don't you worry!" I can't believe she's just said this. The man in front will think I'm a freak who can't find a boyfriend. Anyway, if I want to talk to someone about guys, I'll tell Izzie – I've known her since primary school. I look at my watch. We're six hours ahead of the UK, so right now she will be opening her presents while her mum is preparing the Christmas dinner.

My step-mum is rabbiting on about how kind Dad is and how wonderful it is *"not to be alone after all these years."* I can feel the hard ridge of the window as my cheek squashes against the glass. If I need a nose job after this, I'm suing her! And as for suggesting I might find a friend at the hotel, *"another teenager I would rather spend time with"* she's just trying to get me out of the way so she can be with Dad. I don't want to meet a random guy, I want to be with Jack.

Somewhere above the ocean, she gives up talking to me. Dad leans closer to her; I can see their knees touching like they're magnetic. The plane is packed, the usual jumble of voices and coughs and kids moaning, but I feel so alone. I pull on a set of earphones and try to zone out.

When the pilot announces we're beginning our descent, I can't help feeling a twitch of excitement. I fasten my seatbelt and watch the world growing larger, then suddenly we're down and a buzz of noise fills the plane. Vehicles are whizzing around the tarmac like toy cars, ready for a quick change-over. The aisle is filling up with people eager to get out. Dad unfolds his body and steps into the aisle, almost hitting his head on the ceiling. I can't move as Jo is wriggling her bottom onto the aisle seat – wish she was wearing trousers.

Dad doesn't seem to notice her dress has floated halfway up her thigh and offers his hand, pulling my step-mum towards him. Smiling over her shoulder, he beckons me to hurry. "Or are you staying the night on the plane?" He tosses me an in-flight travel magazine. "Put that in your bag, Kris; there's some useful tips about snorkelling."

"I'd rather see baby turtles hatching on the beach; they look cute on TV."

"Yes, that would be amazing," says my step-mum, jumping into our conversation.

Sliding into the aisle, I fix my eyes on Dad. "Can we see them?" I tug his arm. "And will you take me elephant trekking in the rainforest?"

"Like that time at the zoo?" Dad asks, his eyes crinkling at the edges. I relax, remembering the bronze elephant statue I'd stood on when I was about five or six. Mum was holding my hand and we were laughing into the camera. I look deep into Dad's green eyes and it's like there's this secret bond between us again.

Then The Woman laughs, stealing our closeness. Dad goes back into being The Woman's Husband. He points at the overhead compartment. "This bag is yours, isn't it, Jo?" He lifts down the purple flight case, then looks at me. "I'll get yours down too, Kris, we mustn't keep people waiting."

"It's fine, I can manage." But my bag is stuck between two flight cases. I'm attempting to lever it out when something hard jabs me in the shins and I hear an impatient passenger telling me to hurry up. *What do you think I'm trying to do?* I tug one of the straps and the next second, I'm holding the frayed end in my hand. I hear a groan and can't help smiling to myself. The guy shouldn't have been hassling me — now he'll have to wait even longer to get past.

Dad is apologising for me, while I am pulling the other strap, but it's like someone has super-glued the bags. I'm about to ask for his help, when I see him leaning towards my step-mum, whispering in her ear. And I feel left out. I know it's stupid, but we were on the same wave-length a moment ago. Swivelling around, I yank the strap, then the bag shoots towards me. I duck and a split second later, hear a high-pitched, "Ooh!"

I feel sick: Jo was in direct firing line. She is rubbing her shoulder, and I know she thinks I did it on purpose. So does Dad. I'm trying not to show I'm hurting, but inside, worry lines are crossing over themselves and tangling in knots.

Dad's eyes aren't twinkling now, or even blinking: he's looking at me with a serious expression. He blocks the man who is trying to barge through an impossible gap, and bends down to kiss Jo's cheek. "Alright, love?" Her mouth stretches and she nods. When she doesn't complain, it makes me feel guilty even though it was an accident. I'm suddenly cold and feel like curling up in a little ball. I pick up the broken bag and clutch it to my chest.

Lifting both their flight cases, Dad shuffles along in the queue moving towards the cabin door. My step-mum smiles at me as if nothing has happened and looks over her shoulder, hand on hip, attempting a celebrity pose. "You're getting so tall, Krista; I'm sure I couldn't reach the luggage rack at your age." *You still can't!* I think but I bite back the words. She laughs. "I was always the smallest in my class at school and then I go and marry your Dad who is six foot three! Funny, isn't it?"

Why does something that one person thinks is funny make you want to cry?

I wish you had never met my Dad! The thought whizzes into my mind before I can stop it. I don't mean it — she's trying to be kind like Dad said — it's just that I still miss Mum so much. I watch my step-mum as she follows Dad, disappearing down the gangway. I wish, just for a moment, they could see into my mind, see how I really feel. Everything's happened so fast. The Woman jumped into our lives and created these ripples that won't stop getting bigger. Mum used to say when something hurts, "it's getting better." She was wrong.

It feels like I'm stepping into a sauna as I walk down the gangway. For a second I can't breathe. England has gone and Thailand is on the tarmac, hitting me with heat.

3. Girl with Golden Hair

MARTI

I'm sweeping the hotel path when another batch of tourists spills out of a bus. And I see a girl with golden hair. She is slim, almost as tall as me and has the longest legs, topped with skimpy denim shorts western teenagers often wear. I try not to stare at the frayed edge topping her thigh. Liar. Of course I look.

Cases fill the pavement, but the girl stands on her own, hair flowing over her shoulders as she digs flip-flop toes in the dust, tracing a circle. I wonder what she is thinking and if I will see her again. But why would she pick a pebble when she could find a pearl? Sea gypsies have no chance with white girls, especially pretty ones.

She disappears into The Green Turtle Hotel and I stay outside where I belong. One day the winds may change and I may be upon another shore, but today, I must work. Tourists will be celebrating way into the night and there will be mountains of rubbish to clear.

The moon has sailed high into the sky when I am free at last. Rune is still on duty in reception, so I tap on the window. His eyes twinkle like the sparkling lights draped above his desk. Looking around to see if anyone is watching, I tiptoe into the lobby. "Sorry I'm late."

"What's your excuse this time?" he asks, smiling.

"A kid tipped a packet of crisps into the pool."

Rune laughs and raises his eyebrows.

"It's true! You know what the manager is like — he wouldn't let me go until I'd collected every last bit."

"It's a hard life!" My friend stretches his leg under the desk, then leans on his elbows. "I know, you've also got to dispose of the waste and keep the paths immaculate."

"Clean as the sand after a new tide," I say.

Rune points to the plastic tree perched on the counter, then taps his watch. "Smile Marti; it's Christmas!" I stretch my lips, but I'm tired after working a ten-hour shift with just one break. Alcohol turns people into different versions of themselves: some expand and others contract. When they lose control, I don't like being in their way. Rune doesn't practice Christmas, but the festival is good for business. And what is good for business is good for me. Money is the road to freedom.

People wouldn't know anything is wrong with my friend as he sits behind the desk. He smiles. "Never mind, it's nearly New Year. You've learned so much: your Thai and English are nearly fluent. You never know what might lie ahead."

"Sometimes I think I'll be stuck here forever."

"Would that be so bad?"

"Are you joking? You know my dreams."

The street is noisy. A group of young men sway around a bar, singing — if you can call it that. My grandma used to sing soft melodies of the ocean, but these guys are shouting out the tunes in a storm of voices, all sounding the same. We pass a nightclub, dance music pouring into the night air. Couples cling together and women beckon to us on street corners.

Rune buys two rice and vegetable wraps from a street vendor, then we walk closer to the shoreline to find his bungalow, hidden behind the guests' larger ones. He leans on the wooden veranda, his forearms resting on the bar for support. My friend is small boned as a girl, but his grip is surprisingly strong. "So, have you decided?" he asks, nodding his head.

I stare into the darkness thinking of my family. How can I tell them I'm leaving? As I'm searching for an answer in the stars, a tiny arrow shoots across the sky then disappears. I turn to face Rune. "When the tide flows out, I will talk to Papa." I look into the cosy living room, lit up with bright light. "But I can't promise anything. Papa is like a tree with deep roots; he does not easily sway."

Rune's cheeks fall. "Staying here would make life much easier, saving an hour's walk twice a day."

"But I'll be disowning my family."

His eyes hold me without blinking. "Everybody has to leave sometime."

The bungalow is close to the hotel, so I could sleep in a proper bed and there would be electric lights and a fridge. I wouldn't be so tired from trekking around the bay to our hut. I've made up my mind, so why am I hesitating?

The TV starts talking to us in a fast voice. My family don't have electricity. Papa says technology is evil and hates me working at the hotel. But I'm not sinking into their culture — it's just a way out. If he thinks I'm talking and walking with the manager and the staff, he's wrong. I am under their feet: *"Fish Boy do this!… Fish Boy get that!… Clean up Fish Boy!"*

Papa says our ancestors will be angry if I stop diving. But their fury should be against those who treat us like 'Basement people.' I want to save money and move to a place where they do not say *"Dirty Islander"* with spit running round their mouths – where people treat me like I'm human, like Rune does.

He hands me a coke and I watch as he lifts his left leg with both hands, then slides his feet under the table. Rune never complains, although I see his forehead crease when he doesn't know I'm watching. He looks up. "So, am I getting a lodger?" I shrug my shoulders and he continues. "I wouldn't charge much, you know, just for food. It would be nice to have someone around." His eyes meet mine. "It gets quite lonely here at times.

"But there are so many people with the nightclubs and bars…"

He sighs. "A crowd is sometimes the loneliest place to be."

I hear the whisper of the waves, but I can't see the ocean; she has been eaten by darkness. I've often wondered why Rune hasn't married: he's old enough to be my father and he's so kind that girls must have liked him once. When we first met outside the hotel, he spoke to me, then, on the next full moon, he offered to teach me Thai. He gave me a new name, Sumart, so I could fit in better. Then he taught me English and I became Marti.

I feel hands on my shoulders. "The boss has been working you too hard." I turn to see shadows on Rune's face, as moonlight catches his cheeks. It's like he knows me sometimes.

"I'm sick of being made to entertain kids by doing tricks in the pool," I burst out. "They treat me like I'm a toy."

As Rune smiles, it looks like a bird's footprint is printed at the side of each eye. "You shouldn't be so attractive, Marti, all the girls like you."

"No they don't."

My friend purses his lips and puts on a high voice.

"Marti, help me get on this lilo... Marti, show me how to dive... Marti, rub my back with suntan cream!"

Wrinkling my nose, I shake my head. "They are western. I can look, but not touch. As soon as I come together with a girl, we are married." I look at him. "And I have to marry a Moken girl."

Rune starts to say something, then snaps his mouth shut. We sit in silence, until he says it's late and gives me a torch. My people don't do time — we work by the tides and the moon. But I'm learning not to judge everything by how far the sun has climbed up the sky. "I'll see you tomorrow then," I say.

"Happy Christmas!" I hear Rune's voice floating down the beach as I walk into the night.

4. The Woman

KRISTA

The dream was so real. I screw up my eyes, trying to hold onto Mum's image. She was in the garden telling me something important. Her words fade into nothing, but I can still smell the roses.

It is pitch black. My watch says 11.32pm in luminous green. I've only been asleep for an hour – why did I wake so soon? I turn onto my side, trying to get comfortable, then hear something fall onto the floor. Switching on the light, I blink as my eyes adjust. I know the small gift is from Dad as he's not hot on packaging. The flimsy paper rips at the first touch. Staring at the plain wooden box, I feel let down. But when I open it, a lump jumps into my throat. Nestling in faded purple velvet is a golden chain, curled around a locket.

And I'm back with Mum, watching the locket dancing as she tips back her head. Mum was always laughing, except in the last few weeks. But she still smiled, even then. She never gave up. Except when life gave up on her.

The thick, linked chain uncoils and falls through my fingers; I'd forgotten how heavy it is. The catch slowly opens like a spring flower.

And she is smiling at me. Like she's here, she's alive and she's saying, *"Krissie, I love you and I always will."*

Tears drip onto the locket, and I wipe it with my pyjama sleeve. Mum never liked water; it was the one thing she was afraid of. Closing my eyes, it feels like four years have disappeared. I'm laughing with Mum and Dad, playing in the garden. A cluster of yellow roses is trailing over the fence.

A long sigh deflates my body and the roses disappear. I wish I could hug Mum and tell her what The Woman is like. She's always asking me questions and wanting to know what I think about things like she's a teacher, which makes me back off. As soon as we landed in Dubai for our four-hour stop-over, she dragged me around all the boutiques. I realise she was being kind, and for someone who wears frumpy clothes, she had surprisingly good taste – the denim jacket is cool – but she can't just buy me some designer brands and expect everything to be fine.

I trace Mum's tiny face with my forefinger and touch her smiling mouth. "I've tried to be happy for Dad, I guess he's got a right to get remarried, but it feels wrong – like he's betraying you." Mum's face suddenly goes blurry. "Don't go, I need you!"

I blink away the tears. When I glance at Mum again, she still looks happy. Like Dad is. I'm glad that he's found his future, but I need to know he hasn't forgotten the past: our family, our life together.

Accept her.

"Did you put that thought in my mind, Mum? Are you saying it's ok for Dad to be happy with someone else? But this is supposed to be my family holiday, not another honeymoon."

A light breeze touches my cheeks. I notice the edges of curtains swaying and can't help sighing. When our taxi left Phuket International Airport, I tried to blot out my step-mum's voice by staring at the scenery, but her constant chatter made it impossible. After about half an hour, we reached Phuket town, a mixture of tall white buildings and shabby shop signs. The streets were packed with motorbikes skidding through traffic, car horns blaring and people everywhere. I was pleased when the taxi driver got through the queues and we headed south.

The air smelt fresher and the hills were covered in vegetation. The best part was seeing a monkey sitting on the roadside. "What does it expect, a lift?" Dad said. He leaned out of the window. "Do you fancy a ride in the front? I could do with stretching my feet; haven't been running for two days!" The monkey lifted its arms and it was funny until my step-mum started laughing like a hyena.

To distract her, I got out my phone and tried to zap random shapes which darted around the game. But out of the corner of my eye, I noticed Jo looking down at her hands and twisting her wedding ring around her finger. I knew I'd been mean and tried to think of something to make her smile again, but the words stuck in my throat. Then the moment was gone. She took her camera out of her bag and rolled down the window.

The taxi hovered while she took hundreds of photos. How many pictures of rainforest do you need? I could hear the driver tapping the steering wheel like he was playing the piano. Then he swerved around the corner and we were hanging above the ocean. It stretched either way right into the distance, dotted with small islands. My step-mum was busy saying *Wow!* in different ways, but Dad and I were gazing at the amazing colour of the water in the bay: sapphire like Mum's engagement ring, which I keep in my jewellery box.

Brakes screeched as we descended into a wide bay, with hotels fringing the sea. After the peace of the forest, the noise of the resort hit us: people shouting and selling souvenirs in small shacks. Brightly coloured silks and wall hangings lined the streets. I saw Jo's eyes light up and knew she would drag us back. I was right.

Our thatched bungalow is right next to the beach, shaded by a palm tree. Bright pink and red bushes grow at the front, like they are saying hello. It is painted white and has two bedrooms, a shower room and a huge lounge overlooking the sea. The waves were lapping at the shoreline when we arrived and the beach was packed. Dad and I wanted to relax, but as soon as we had dumped our cases, Jo was keen to hit the streets. I was forced to tag along, because they think I can't cope on my own.

"I'd rather we stick together, Kris," said Dad. He tapped the guidebook. "Their advice is to keep your valuables close to you. And you," he winked at me, "are my most valuable possession!" I was about to argue that I'm not a possession, when I saw my step-mum's face. Now perhaps she will know there is a corner of Dad's heart she cannot touch.

In the market, Jo bagged a Chinese silk blouse and a sparkly scarf, because the guy convinced her each strand was dyed a different colour. Dad tried to put her off, saying it was probably polyester, but she said real silk has little bumps along the thread. Then she went crazy over some patterned ceramic pots, but couldn't decide on her favourite, so she bought all three!

While they were being wrapped, Dad winked at me and we escaped to a craft stall. He picked up a wooden boat in his arms. "I think this is a Kabang, one of the sea gypsy fishing boats." The model felt smooth, like someone had spent a long time making it, but there was an indent at each end as if they had carved into it too much. Dad laughed at me, as he paid the street vendor. "I think the indigenous Moken people know more about boat building than we do!" Sea gypsies sound cool, but

I'd be scared to be on one of their narrow boats; it would be too easy to fall in.

We wandered past a stall full of exotic looking fish and trays filled with mussels. Then I spotted the henna artist – I've always wanted my hands painted. I was waiting in the queue when Jo turned up posing in a batik sarong and said it was getting late and she was hungry. The pots of handmade noodles and crispy fried shrimps smelt delicious, so I persuaded Dad to buy some, but my step-mum wanted to eat in our hotel restaurant, not "cheap street food." I could tell Dad fancied the noodles, so we took turns in dipping the plastic fork into the container as we walked back to the hotel. Palm trees lined the wide pavement and although it was getting dark, the beach was still crowded with people celebrating. Fireworks were popping, crackling and whistling.

From the restaurant window, I watched rockets turning the sky red, green and gold; while Dad scoffed another meal. He said he needed to keep up his strength for his early morning run. My step-mum thought it would be tough, jogging along the beach in the heat; but he's doing this in memory of Mum, so I wished The Woman would keep quiet. Dad's running a half-marathon for Macmillan cancer support in March, so he takes every chance he can to put in the miles. Then he promised he'd buy me a drink at the beach cafe tomorrow, just the two of us.

I cradle the locket in my hand and stare at Mum's face. She's still smiling. Sighing, I press the tiny lid shut. It closes with a gentle click. *Like a last breath.* Then I slip the chain around my neck. If Mum was alive, there would be no other woman; Dad wouldn't push himself so hard and we'd be a proper family again.

5. Decision

MARTI

Clouds have stolen the moon when I reach our hut. Slipping the torch into my shorts, I wade into the water, feeling for the wooden steps with my feet. When I am standing on the balcony, I look into the black ocean. Even the stars have gone to sleep.

Rune is right: instead of walking back around the headland, I could be relaxing in his bungalow. No longer would I have to climb the hill to avoid the swampy mangroves. It's always late when I return and trees dissolve into mist; although when the moon is smiling, you can see the faint outline of the seashore. Long sandy beaches may lure tourists, but I'd rather see the bright lights of the city. I'll be on my way up, not stamped down. I'll own a real bank account like Rune and send Mama money, so she can stop weaving baskets to sell in the market.

Despite the warning noises in my head, I have made the right decision; I'll tell Papa I'm leaving when light touches the sky. Turning my back on the ocean, I close the door.

I'm woken by coughing. A knot forms in my stomach. I hate that rasping choke, hate what it's doing to Papa and hate the anger that shoots up inside me. Why won't he ask the elders for help, if it's this bad? I try to block out the sound, but every time he barks, my body tenses. Sleep is impossible.

Turning on the torch, I rip aside the dividing curtain. Mama is gently snoring and her face is relaxed, but shadows cling under Papa's eyes and his lower jaw is drooping. He blinks as the beam of light shines on his face, then a cough shakes his chest. I step back, seeing mucus dribble down his chin. "Why do you always have to wake me? I'm going to work when the sun rises, even if you can't be bothered."

Blurry red rimmed eyes look up. "Is that what they call it? You should be diving, not wasting time at that hotel." He spits the last word like it's a disease.

"I'm earning money. You need it to buy fuel for the outboard motor; you should be pleased."

"That my son is dishonouring his ancestors and the spirits?" Papa is whipping himself up into a thunderstorm. He opens his mouth to shout at me again, but starts choking as if sandpaper is scratching his throat. Mama moans, moving in her sleep.

My fingers clench around the torch as I try to control my voice. "Can't you see I'm trying to help? I buy rice with my wages, don't I?"

"We have always traded stingrays for rice. Mother Ocean gives and we only take what we need."

"So when did you last dive?"

Papa raises his shoulders and his body expands, then shrinks as he breathes out like the wind. "The ocean is my universe; I was born with the sound of the waves in my ears and the smell of the sea filling my body." He taps his chest. "And the ocean is still inside me."

Ignoring his outstretched hand, I fold my arms, staring into grey eyes that once danced with reflections of the sea. Now Papa is lying like a beached eagle ray. He tips back his head, looking at me. "I'm so tired, Sky, I can't fish."

"Marti! My name's Marti now — I've told you before!" I spit out the words, as he spits out phlegm.

Mama's eyes blink open, but Papa ignores her. I know what's coming. "At least I haven't turned my back on my culture," he rasps.

I glare back. "The world is changing — we need to change with it!"

"If we forget our traditions, we become less than ourselves. Our forefathers passed down knowledge which we should treasure…" he coughs, shaking his finger at me, "not ignore."

"But you let Coral work at the snack shack…"

"Only until she is married. Then when she has a baby, she and her husband will…"

"Build their own Kabang, yes I know. But there are fast boats now; I've seen them moored by the hotel. Shiny new hulls, they fly over the waves…"

As Papa tries to stand, the palm matting crinkles under his toes. I shine the torch on the woven strands, then hear Papa growl, his low voice sounding like a warning. "If more big boats come, what do you think will happen to us?" When I lift up my chin, Papa's eyebrows join in a thick line. "You are no sea gypsy! Go and join them if you want, but soon they will drag their nets right across the ocean and harvest all the fish in the sea!"

Before he can reel me in, I slither down the steps, then, one splash later, I'm underwater. Launching into darkness is better than facing Papa's disapproval. Too late, I remember I'm still gripping Rune's torch. Rising to the surface, I shake the hair out of my eyes and flick the switch. It's dead. The ocean is black, then the moon sails out behind a cloud, shining a path across the water. When I see the Grandad's Kabang, I start swimming.

The wooden boat sits low on the water, like it

belongs. A few more strokes and I'll touch the side. I remember standing tall, trying to touch the roof with my fingertips, when I was young. We would sail from island to island, drifting with the tide. Coral and I enjoyed splashing oars in the water, thinking we were stronger than the sail. Mama would be weaving baskets, while Papa would steer. When we anchored, they would take turns in diving for fish and teach us what to do. The underwater world was our kingdom.

Hoisting myself onto the curved wooden hull, I try not to wake Grandad. But he always sleeps with one ear ready to hear the wind and waves. As I strip off my wet clothes, he is crouching under the canopy. He doesn't look surprised to see me.

"The spirits brought you here, Sky," he says, handing me a rough towel. "The Kabang is your destiny." Grandad smiles, the gap in his teeth looking like a cave in the moonlight. "Welcome home."

6. Boxing Day

26th December 2004

KRISTA

Someone is outside; I can hear the door rattling. The room suddenly feels oppressive, like air heavy with thunder. Hugging the duvet, I scrunch into a ball and hide. Breath is hot on my chest. My heart is hammering to get out. I'm suffocating.

Arching my back, I claw the duvet aside and open my eyes. The bed is shaking and for a split second, it sounds as if a train is roaring across the ceiling. Either I'm going crazy or I'm stuck in a nightmare. When the door creaks open, I scream.

Dad laughs. "I'm not that scary am I?" He bends down and sits next to me on the bed. "There's nothing to worry about, the earth's just having a little shake up." He rubs my shoulder, then opens his arms. My cheek squashes his shirt, but it's the kind of hug when you know nothing bad is ever going to happen.

The roaring dies away; the floor stops moving. Dad uncoils his body and towers above me, his green eyes twinkling. "You okay?" he says. "Honestly, love, it was only a minor quake, no big deal." He points to his watch. "Eight o'clock. Two minutes out of your life isn't much, is it?" I nod and the locket swings against my pyjama top.

Dad's eyes sparkle. "I see you've found your last Christmas present."

"My best present!"

"Mum wanted you to have the locket on your 16th birthday, but I know life hasn't been easy for you recently." As Dad looks at me, I can feel my lip wobbling. He touches a strand of my hair. "It must have been difficult sometimes… adjusting." I look at my fingernails and blink away a tear.

Dad kneels so his eyes are level with mine. "I miss her too, you know. I always will." He strokes my cheek. "But she'd want us to be happy, not to live in the past. So let's do our best to make this holiday memorable, eh?"

"I'll try."

Twenty minutes later, as I'm pulling a long beach shirt over my bikini, the floor shakes again. Dad knocks on my door in his sports gear and I run straight into his arms.

"What's this?" he says, swinging me round like he used to. "I told you not to worry, it's only a slight aftershock." He lifts me down and then holds my hands with outstretched arms. "Listen, I'm taking my phone and I'm not attempting my usual ten miles; I'm only running as far as the mangroves. You know I've always wanted to see them; first-hand knowledge is invaluable for teaching."

"I thought your lectures already were amazing?"

Dad grins. "Really?" He pushes his shoulders back and puts on a posh voice. "The mangroves prevent erosion, by absorbing the energy of the waves..."

"The sea's natural bodyguard, yes, you've told me before."

"And I thought you were never listening!"

I can't smile like I usually do when he teases,

because I'm worried about more aftershocks. His chest falls as he leans towards me. "Krissie, I wouldn't go out if there was any danger, you're too precious."

"Am I?" I ask in a small voice.

Dad looks surprised. "Just because I'm married now, I don't want you ever to think that I love you less." His green eyes seem to reach deep inside me, as he speaks slowly. "I couldn't love you more!" I snuggle in his arms, feeling totally happy and peaceful, something I haven't felt since Mum died. Then he swings me up in the air, like he did when I was a little kid. I scream, but it's a good scream when you're having fun. When Dad puts me down, he holds my gaze for several seconds. "Minor earthquakes are common in Thailand, love, there's no danger. Trust me." Kissing my cheek, he smiles.

"Trust me, it will hurt less as the weeks go by," Dad said when Mum died, and he was right. Except it took many months — nearly a year — before I stopped crying into my pillow and the pain stopped cutting me in two. I can think of her now and remember the good times, but I can't remember the sound of her voice.

Waving goodbye, I watch him shrinking into the distance. Little dots of colour are already filling up the beach. Through gaps in the palm trees and red umbrellas I see bright blue skies, a perfect postcard view.

7. Coral

MARTI

Sometimes I know she's there even before I see her. She is kneeling, her back to me, searching for early morning shells. Jumping over the small waves, I step onto the sand. I'm trying to creep up and surprise my sister, but before I can reach her, she spins around.

"Marti!" Coral throws a shell at me, but I dodge. In one smooth movement, she glides to her feet, then hugs me. "Where did you disappear to?" I point to the Kabang.

"You stayed with Grandad? Marti, you can't hide away from everything!"

"What have I done now?" I ask, spreading my palms to the sky.

"I heard the argument."

"I didn't know you were there."

My sister raises her eyebrows. "Where else would I be? I was lying in the next room, hoping Petal wouldn't wake. You and Papa were like two sea lions roaring at each other."

"But I had to tell him... I can't live his life any longer."

"Papa is sick; he's like a fish without water." Coral touches my arm. "Don't you think that he longs to dive again? We have no stall in the Fish Market, while Cloud and his brother often sail their longboat to the town and

37

sell their catch. Rock lobsters and sea cucumbers fetch a good price…" Her fingertips press tighter as she looks into my eyes. "And their Mama is wearing a new dress."

"So that's what you want!" I tease. "Alright, I will buy you something."

"No, not for me. Petal is growing fast; her clothes have holes."

My smile disappears. Coral is always thinking of others, but when did I last spend time with my little sister, or even notice what she was wearing? I press a stone into the sand, twisting it with my heel. "I'll try to earn more money."

"But only what we need." Coral gestures along the beach. "In the town I hear words like 'tomorrow' and 'future,' but each new tide brings gifts; we do not need to store up like there is no more treasure in the ocean."

She brushes past me, then tickles the sand until she finds the stone. "We are children of the sea. Papa looks to you, his son, to follow his dreams, to embrace the ocean." She raises her arm towards the waves, but there is no splash; the stone lands on the beach. Her face falls. "Why won't you dive any longer?"

"I dive for coins to entertain the guests!"

She doesn't smile. "That's not what I meant and you know it. How can a little pool compare with all that?"

I follow her gaze and stare at the horizon. The ocean swirls around my mind. Freedom. No walls. No Virote and Chaow spearing me with words. I could be gliding through the reef, brushing my fingers through the swaying seaweed. Singing to the dance of the ocean.

"Marti?" I look up. My sister's oval eyes hold a question under her arched eyebrows. "Where were you?"

I shake my head. "I need to go – if I'm late, the manager won't pay me."

She takes my hand and presses it. "Speak to Papa.

Please don't leave it like this."

"I didn't say I'd never help, but I'm sleeping over at Rune's." Coral sighs, so I look into her eyes. "I'll bring Papa some oil and rice tonight."

"And you'll stay?" As she nods, her shell necklace tinkles around her neck.

Without realising, I have bent my knees, so my head is level with hers. "You know what he's like when we spend too much time together…"

"A sea lion?"

"More like a shark thrashing in the water!"

Coral laughs. "Like someone else I know?"

"I don't know who you mean!"

When I leave her, I'm still smiling. She is sifting through the sand looking for treasure that the ocean gives us every new tide. If she finds some large shells, she'll polish them, then string the smaller ones into necklaces. I have agreed to meet her in the snack shack in my break. The flimsy shed sits on the edge of the beach, near a site where a new hotel is growing.

I've seen the way the workmen men stare at my sister. They stand on scaffolding, like monkeys in the mangrove forest, looking for anything that moves. Young guys in tribes roam the beach, hunting. And fat older men with overhanging bellies crawl around like crabs. I saw one trying to touch Coral's glossy black hair and licking his lips. I know what they want. But, as long as I'm working close by, I can look out for my sister. I'd die rather than let her be hurt. People gather around Coral like bees buzzing around a flower, so I know when she's selling her jewellery. I always find her.

8. Attraction

KRISTA

Breakfast was noisy in the hotel, everyone talking across the tables. Last night, there were invisible barriers between people, even though it was Christmas, but now everyone's buzzing about the earthquake. Except for me. As my step-mum still hasn't emerged from the bungalow, I'm going to find a postcard — Izzie said she'll kill me if I don't send one.

I walk along the neat path towards the hotel reception where we checked in yesterday. There are little lights edging the path; it's really pretty. In the lobby, I ask the receptionist where I can buy a postcard. He stands up slowly and I see his leg dragging behind, strapped with brown clasps. He smiles, saying he'll add the cost to Dad's bill.

The views are stunning: turquoise water and steep green hills, but I prefer the photos of animals. I choose a picture with an elephant turning its head to look down at its calf and linking trunks, as if encouraging it to walk faster. I flip it over and scribble a message.

Hi Iz,

I bet the elephant's saying: "Are we nearly there yet?!" We arrived yesterday and I'm gutted I'm missing your party. It's beautiful here with palm trees and the sea looks amazing- but you know I'm not into swimming, so I'm going to hit the beach and come back with a serious tan!

Kris xxx

ps. Remember what I said about Loren...I know she fancies Jack, so don't let her get her hands on him!

The receptionist says I can leave the card on the desk, but I'd rather explore and find a postbox in town. I'm not meeting Dad for a couple of hours, so there's plenty of time.

+++

MARTI

She's wearing a loose beach shirt covering her body, but I can see the outline of her bikini — black as night. Seriously cute. Her body is slender like a young tree and she's leaning forward shading her eyes like she's trying to find something. I know my job is picking up the rubbish, but if a guest needs help, surely I'm allowed to approach her? I scrape a bottle of coke along the ground, trying to get her attention. She doesn't move, so holding the bottle like a spear, I throw it over her head into the bin.

The girl jumps and looks around like Petal when she's scared: one hand on her chest and the other covering her mouth. As she moves, something flutters onto the path.

And I'm there. "Can I help you, Miss?" I bend down and pick up the postcard, one of the usual views of the bay. Turning it over, I see lines of neat writing.

"Interesting, is it?" Her English is clear and easy to understand. So is her body language: her neck stretching and her chin jutting out as she stares at me. I offer the card and golden hair swings around her shoulders as she leans towards me. For the tiniest second, her fingers touch mine.

A sunset floods her face. "Er... thanks," she says, her words broken up as if they are swimming through a net. Both of us stand there like we don't know what to do.

I ought to go, but this could be my only chance to talk to her. "Were you looking for something; can I help you, Miss?

"Yes. No. And stop calling me Miss!"

"What should I call you, then?" I dare to ask.

The sunset deepens as she glares at me. "Nothing!"

"Ok, Miss... Nothing," I say and can't help smiling.

She looks down, but her lips are dancing – I know she's trying not to give in. She covers her mouth and pretends to cough. "I was just trying to find…"

"Where to post it?" I finish the sentence for her, feeling pleased that my English is this good now. If it was last year, I'd be stuttering over the words and there'd be no way I could hold a conversation with anyone in English, let alone a beautiful girl.

"Could you, I mean, would you show me where to post it please?" the girl asks and I feel suddenly taller and more important.

"Sure, over there," I say, pointing in the direction of the road. She starts walking and I bite my lip. *How stupid can you get? You had the chance to walk across the grass with her and you let her go!*

Shoes scrape the sandy path. Thin flip flops with little bangles attached. I look up, my heart thumping. "Can I help you, Miss?"

This time the girl smiles and I feel like I've just caught the best fish of the day.

"I, er, wasn't exactly sure which way you meant when I get out of the hotel grounds: left or right?" This time I don't make a mistake. After a quick look around, I lead the girl to the edge of the manicured lawn. The Green Turtle is a seafront hotel, one of a line of hotels perched between the town and the ocean. Once you leave the grounds, there is a wide pavement running alongside and palm trees to shade tourists while they are shopping.

I explain where the girl can post the card, although she could have just left it at Reception with Rune. When we reach the road, a truck rumbles past with a queue of vehicles jammed behind. Two guys on scooters are weaving in and out. As soon as there is a gap in the traffic, the girl puts her foot into the road, but I hear a taxi hooting and pull her back. For the second time, the postcard falls to the ground. I lean down, but she does too, and we collide.

My head is hurting and I'm sure hers is too, so I hold the girl's arms to steady her as we stand up. We are facing each other, so close only a tiny fish could swim through. I swallow several times. "I should have been more careful." I see the girl's pink lips move but her reply is lost in the noise of the traffic.

She moves away from me and examines the postcard, rubbing it with a slim finger. Then she wrinkles her nose. "Izzie won't think much of this now! I'll have to send her another one."

"It's not that dirty."

"You don't know what she's like."

"But if it's going a long way…?"

"Yes, to Cambridge..."

"It might get scratched on the journey — she'd never know."

A smile curves the girl's mouth and she nods, then curls a lock of hair around her finger. "Maybe you're right. I can't be bothered to buy another one. I want to sunbathe before it gets too hot."

Trying not to think of her bikini, I ask her if

Cambridge is in London. "I've heard of St Paul's Cathedral and The Tower Bridge, but I haven't heard of Came Bridge."

Her eyebrows jump up as she leans forward. "In *London?* Cambridge is only one of the oldest cities and one of the best universities in the whole country... in the whole world!"

Light is sparkling in her eyes, but I feel like diving into the ocean, where I can hide. *Don't be stupid, Marti, you had no chance anyway.* I head back into my life and leave her standing on the edge of the road.

+++

KRISTA

Sinking onto a reclining beach chair by the pool, I close my eyes. Another hour before I meet Dad in the beach cafe. I wish I had someone to talk to, but Jo isn't here; she must be exhausted. Now that I'm alone, I miss hearing her excited voice. I know I got a bit moody on the journey when she wouldn't shut up, but at least life is never dull when she's around! Dad's right: I need to make more of an effort to get to know her properly.

I've got no friends here. Even that lad didn't want to stick around. It took ages to cross the road as half the world's scooters seem to live here. After I posted Izzie's card, I couldn't face exploring. I hope it reaches her before the New Year's Party and she phones me. But it's not the same just hearing about it, you miss all the little jokes and guys teasing you. Like Jack.

Instead of Jack's face, I see the Thai guy's brown eyes in my mind. When we were talking, it was the way he looked at me, my heart started racing like I'd been running or something. His voice is deep — must be seventeen or eighteen. This is crazy, there's no way I'm falling for some random guy on holiday. Especially a six foot tanned guy who probably chats up all the girls. I've got Jack. He may be thousands of miles away, but I'm sure he likes me. We've got lots in common and we both like the same football team, Tottenham Hotspur. Perhaps he'll take me to see a game on our first date. I try to picture what I'd say to him, but all I can hear in my mind is a soft amused accent, "Can I help you, Miss?"

I squeeze my eyes tighter and concentrate on listening to the sound of the sea. Dad wants us all to go kayaking, but I don't fancy falling in. I'd feel safer on a yacht soaking up a tan, while we explore hidden islands.

A shadow passes over me, and my forehead wrinkles. I open my eyes. *It's him!* Hands on hips, hair flopping across one eye, trying to look cool. My lips suddenly feel numb like I need a moisturiser. He is smiling at me and I force myself not to blush. Not sure I succeed.

"I guess you've just arrived as you're not tanned yet," he says. I ignore him. How dare he imply I'm pasty white? So what if his skin is a lovely dark colour and his brown hair has reddish blond highlights as if it's been bleached by the sun. His mouth curves and light dances in his chocolate eyes like he's laughing at me. I fold my arms across my chest and stare back. Then wish I hadn't, because he looks really fit. He holds up his hands and I can't help admiring his muscular arms as he leans back. "I didn't mean to offend you... Miss." He says the last word after a slight pause and I know he's teasing me.

While he's talking, I tuck up my knees, feeling a bit exposed, but the sun lounger rocks and I nearly fall off. I hear the lad chuckle. "Do you want any help?" Tingles of fear run through me as I remember Dad's warning about talking to strange guys. I hate the jets of excitement making my voice sound breathy, as I tell him to leave me alone.

+++

MARTI

She has pulled down the white beach shirt so it skims her knees and closed her eyes, shutting me out, but I can't help looking. Her chin is like the curve of a shell, with a delicate blush inside. There's something about her that reminds me of Petal when she got lost in the mangroves. The girl with golden hair holds her head up high, yet I feel she could easily fall. I'm about to ask if she found the postbox, when a group of giggling girls cluster around me.

"Marti, are you diving today?" asks the fat one. Reaching into her sparkly bag, she pulls out a purse, and then she scatters coins into the pool, splashing like a shoal of anemone fish. I glance at the hotel entrance and the manager nods, so I kick off my shoes. Usually he ignores me like rubbish, but when it suits him, he shows me off like some kind of exotic side-show: his pet sea gypsy.

The pack prowl towards me. "If you can hold your breath for over three minutes, you can keep the money!" Glancing at the girl sitting on the sun lounger, I rip off my shirt — with luck, she'll be impressed.

It's easy to scoop the coins off the bottom of the pool; I've been free diving all my life to depths of twenty metres. Another shower of coins drifts down, so I slide along the bottom, collecting them. When I surface, the tigers are leaning over, showing their teeth and most of their flesh. I feel a bit sick. I sneak a look at the pretty girl on the sun lounger and, when our eyes meet, a sunset colours her cheeks again.

Kicking my feet, I glide to the poolside, then uncurl

my fingers like a starfish, revealing the coins. But the girl isn't there. Heaving myself out, I see her walking across the lawn, towards the beach. The large girl brushes against me, jingling her purse. Sighing, I dive back into the pool — Mama needs the money to buy Petal a new dress.

The sun is higher in the sky when I escape the ambush. I'm standing at the edge of the hotel garden, with only a sandy path and a small sea wall between us and the ocean. The resort is in a large bay fringed by mangroves, with rainforest in the hills. Hidden behind the tip of the headland are the Moken huts and Grandad's Kabang. Mama and Papa stay in our hut most of the year now, but Grandad was born on the ocean and he will die on the ocean. That's what he says.

My feet take me across the grass to the sea wall. The beach is filling up with youth and beauty. And somewhere in the mass of people is a girl with blue eyes and golden hair.

PART 2 – TSUNAMI

It's amazing: the tide's gone way out.
How could all that water just vanish?
Either I've been stuck in a time-warp,
or someone's pulled the plug out of the sea.

– Krista

9. Wall of Water

KRISTA

I'm sweating and the locket is sticking to my chest. I waft the long blouse, freeing the chain, and the gold oval sparkles in the sun. Turning my back on the sea, I spot the beach-side café where I'm meeting Dad. Hope he's there; it will be the only time I have him to myself today. Kids are streaming down the beach, so I zigzag to avoid them; you'd think they'd never seen the sea before.

Skirting a red umbrella, I see a man smoothing lotion in lazy circles on a girl's naked back. I'd love Jack to touch me like that, but would he want a stick insect for a girlfriend? Dad says I've got the right build for an athlete if I could be bothered. I can't. Too much exercise gives you burn-out. Dad's proved it by not being here — jogging in this temperature must be exhausting.

"It will be hot," he said, "so travel light." I wore my denim shorts yesterday and just packed a couple of bikinis, a few tops and leggings, this long beach shirt and the white shorts for when I'm tanned. Izzie said if you've got it, flaunt it, but I know she was joking. I'm the tallest in my class and slim as an unused exercise book. My bust is virtually non-existent! It's so unfair, especially when Izzie's is full on. I'm not asking to be a celebrity — bet some of them have implants anyway — but when you're nearly sixteen, don't you have a right to expect more?

You've also got a right to your own space. Before we left home, The Woman bounced into my bedroom and volunteered to help me pack. I guess she was trying to be helpful, but she just doesn't get it: one moment she's treating me like someone her own age and the next, she's in my face like I'm a baby.

Swinging open the café door, I look around, but Dad isn't here yet. I text him and two minutes later he texts back.

Sorry, delayed. Mangroves amazing. c u at café in 20 mins. xx.

I look at my watch. It's 9:46 am.

+++

MARTI

It's impossible: the water has gone out so quickly. The tide is a thin white sheet rolled up in the distance, almost touching the sky. I've never seen so much beach before. Tourist boats are stuck, hulls wedged into the sand. Leaning over the sea wall, I see fish flapping, desperate to be in the water.

As I watch a child pick up a fish, something jumps in my mind. And I'm back on our Kabang with Grandma and she's telling me ancient stories of our people. I remember her eyes expanding in her wrinkled face as she lifted her arms and told me of the Seventh wave:

"The Laboon once swallowed whole villages. When the crabs crawl to the forest and the birds stop singing and the tide disappears into the mist, you must run."

+++

KRISTA

I'm sipping a coke, when my phone beeps. *Running back. c u in 10 mins. Love Dad xx*

A door slams — that can't be him already? A girl is shouting something about a geography lesson. She runs over to her parents, then they jump up and rush outside. Scooping up toddlers and handbags, a flock of tourists follow. I can hear little gasps buzzing outside, ricocheting off each other. Intrigued, I walk out of the café.

It's amazing: the tide's gone way out. How could all that water just vanish? Either I've been stuck in a time-warp, or someone's pulled the plug out of the sea.

Everyone is staring or snapping photos of the weird white crescent on the horizon. Something tickles my leg and I glance down quickly. Then smile. Kneeling, I cradle an orange and white clown fish, one like in the movie *Finding Nemo*.

A shout. I look up. The sea is growing. Fast.

Mountains of white bubbling foam are pouring towards us. The dribble of people turns into a stream. Wide-eyed tourists stumble over deckchairs, running for the sea wall. My toes curl. My heart starts hammering. I grab the locket through a fistful of blouse. Clashing colours race past; a blur of screaming figures. "Get off the beach!" one yells at me.

But I'm frozen, staring at the massive wall of water storming towards me, frothing and clashing like an angry battle of the gods.

Bursting out of the café, the waitress yells, but the thunder of water drowns out her words. She knocks into my arm as she scrambles onto a café table, then I see her leap towards the balcony, clawing at the window ledge. The dark wave is arching up. A scream tears my throat. Leaping onto the table, I slam my body against the building. Pure horror is on the girl's face as I look up. The monster is about to attack. My ribs almost split as I reach for her outstretched hand. Veins bulge in her neck, as she leans over and grabs my wrist.

A single breath later, the ocean explodes. Thunder crashes into me, smashing my body onto the roof. Can't see. Can't breathe. A giant whip is lashing my back, trying to rip me off. I'm going to be shattered like glass. Cut into pieces. The building is trembling with fear – or is it me? I know I am going to die.

10. Devastation

MARTI

"Get down!" I shout, grabbing the girl's podgy arm. Her bikini strap pings and she giggles. She and her friend have tracked me down and they are showing off by standing on the seawall with outstretched palms and straight arms, like they are more powerful than the wind and waves. The spirits won't like that.

I've never seen the ocean so angry. The whole beach has been eaten. What was smooth, yellow sand is a swirling dark mass. Reclining wooden chairs are crushed into matchwood, as the waves pound them.

Coral! The snack shack is so flimsy, there's no way it would have survived. *Nor would she.* My fists clench, trying to crush the thought.

Raging waves pound my ears. The only structure left is a café roof poking out like a drowning boat. Through the spray, I see a figure clinging onto the roof, in the middle of the ocean. The poor guy hasn't got a chance – he'll be sucked under the waves.

+++

KRISTA

I'm free. The pain in my chest has gone and I can breathe. But it feels like a rock is still pounding my head. Don't know how long the waves were attacking the building – felt like hours. I was terrified it was going to collapse, throwing me into the sea. The roaring has stopped, but I'm scared of what's out there.

Bright sunshine shrinks my eyelids. I lift my shoulders, trying to move, but my fingers have gone rigid. Wrenching one hand off the roof, I squint down the tunnel between my thumb and cupped fingers. It's gone! Through a blur of stinging lashes, I see the beach is empty, but the horizon is black. How can the monster shrink like that, it's impossible; the waves were wild.

Relief floods me. Can't believe we're safe. I turn to look at the waitress, but there's an empty space. Staring at the ridge where I last saw the girl, I can still feel the warmth of her hand. It's unreal. People can't just die like that. She was just here. Alive. Now she's been swept away like rubbish.

The sun is burning my back. Need to cover my skin. Reaching behind with one arm, I find the beach shirt is bunched up around my shoulders; the ripped material flaps like butterflies' wings. Must get away. I crawl along the roof, but with each lurch forward, the building shakes. One wrong move and the house of cards will cave in. Peering over the ridge, I see a glint in the dirt. Broken glass. My flip flops have gone and I'm frightened to jump, but I've got no choice. Edging closer, I lower my body over the edge, holding onto the ridge with my fingertips. Then let go.

+++

MARTI

Men lean on motorbikes, staring. Tourists with bright eyes and wide mouths are taking photos. But out there, people are dying. I can see a woman clawing onto a palm tree, clinging onto life, as water tries to rip her body.

As a large man wearing a checked jacket lifts his arm to point, sweat wafts into my face and my nose wrinkles. He looks briefly in my direction, but doesn't make eye contact. "Wowee, isn't this just awesome!" I don't answer. When the ocean roars, you have to listen. It isn't awesome, it's deadly. It is ripping palm trees, hurling branches into its jaws. And people.

Waves are lashing against the sloping sea wall and jets shoot up, arching over our heads. The girls squeal with laughter.

"Get away from the wall!" I shout again, and the smaller girl turns, dark eyes in a white face. She drops her arms and bends her knees, ready to jump to safety. The taller one steadies her friend's shoulder, eyes sparkling, red cheeks lifted by a wide smile. Shaking her head, she takes the girl's hand, pulling her back to her feet. They are standing together an inch from death. One wave too strong and they will be torn off the wall.

People like them were on the beach just minutes ago, sunning themselves, loving life. I try not to think of the beautiful English girl, but when I squeeze my eyes shut, all I see is her golden hair. If she was on the beach, she had no chance. No-one did.

I know the ocean. It's in me and I'm part of it. The Laboon has energy like I've never seen, power from inside: its spirit is greater than any monsoon when the skies darken and lightning tears the sky. If the Laboon decides to flood over the wall, we will all be eaten. Running is not a coward's way out, it's the only way to survive.

+++

KRISTA

A sharp pain shoots up my arm as I scrape against the door frame, falling onto thick mud. Breathing heavily, I stare at the red line sprouting below my left elbow. Raw flesh. Looks deep. Cradling my arm to my chest, I sink my right hand into the mud, trying to regain my balance. I bend my knees and lever myself upright. Pain shoots up my arm and blood soaks into my shirt. I watch it turn red. My teeth start to chatter, knocking against each other.

Beside me is a gaping hole. The door has been ripped off and the sea has raided the café. Tables, chairs, even the heavy till have all gone. Knives and forks are sticking out of the wall like the sea has performed an execution. Then I see the victim. I've never seen a body, but know instantly he's dead. His eyes are open, but they are looking into nothing.

My stomach contracts and my head starts spinning. I retch and watch the sick drip down my legs. *Got to get out of here!* I pull my bare feet out of the mud. *What if I cut my feet on glass?* Have to risk it. The firing squad has shot back into the distance, but it could be planning another attack. I turn my back on the horizon, but the man is still looking at me with those dead eyes. I clench my fists and swallow the sick feeling in my throat. *Come on Krista, run!*

+++

MARTI

"You're safe here." I've brought the girl and her friend back to the hotel lounge, but I have to find my sister. It's chaos outside: a jumble of broken umbrellas and upturned tables. People are streaming past the windows, screaming. A spongy hand grabs mine, then the girl starts shrieking about losing her ring. People are dying out there and all she cares about is a stupid bit of jewellery.

I would love to tell her she's a pathetic, spoilt brat, but I need to keep my job. The manager would never believe a sea gypsy, as we have the same rights as rats: none. I stare at the girl's bright red lipstick and feel disgust. I'm getting out of here.

+++

KRISTA

Large hands haul me onto the sea wall. "Gee, this is unreal!" says an American voice. He stands next to me, pointing at the sea. Breathing raggedly, I stare at the red stream dripping down my arm. I'm standing in a pool of blood. The man hasn't noticed as he is taking photos of the disaster scene. I look up. The beach is empty. Apart from the café, everything has been swept away. It's not possible, it couldn't have happened. But it has.

In a daze, I glance across at the resort. It feels like days since I waved goodbye to Dad. He said he was only going to be ten minutes, so where is he? Why did he go for a stupid run? My vision blurs. He's my dad — he can't be dead.

Angrily, I wipe away stinging tears. My face feels hot and sticky. I stare at the purple gash on my forearm, not knowing what to do. I can hear the American gushing excitement and other high-pitched voices, but they merge into white background noise.

Then a woman runs past screaming, her eyes wild with fear: "The water, it's coming back!" It's like she's kicked me in the stomach. A wall of water is sweeping towards us, swirling like a wizard's black cloak. I'm caught up in the flood of people shouting and screaming. The road is alive with hooting vehicles and revving motorbikes, skidding. I sprint across the hotel lawn and

57

around the pool.

As I touch the front door, I hear an explosion. *Don't turn round! Don't look!* But I have to see. Waves have broken over the sea wall. Dark tongues of water are flying into the air and plunging onto the boulevard. Brown frothing energy is pouring across the grass. The American's checked jacket has disappeared. He's gone. Now it's coming for me.

+++

MARTI

An explosion! Somewhere along the beach, deep violent thuds sound like big boats dynamiting fish. The windows are rattling and the wind is wrapping itself around palm trees. Suddenly, an enormous force slams against the concrete walls of the hotel. I fall back, as glass spits into the room.

+++

KRISTA

Following the crowd, I rush into the foyer. The wide-eyed receptionist is hobbling about, waving his hands. "Run!" he shouts in English, pointing at the ceiling. Heart pounding, I push into the crowd. A mass of jumbled screams echoes in my ears. Spotting the ornate curve of the staircase, I push forward.

Suddenly, breath is ripped from my body and I'm flying across the room. The wall looms into my face. Blackness.

11. The Little Boy

MARTI

The girls are screaming, clinging to me, but I shake them
off. Tipping some flowers out of a heavy vase, I punch
out the remaining fins of glass. A huge brown tide is
pouring across the lawn, sucking up deckchairs. The
swimming pool has disappeared, like it was never there.
Everywhere is a boiling sea.

I run to the side window overlooking the street. A
river is storming past the hotel, eating the road. The thick
tide picks up a signpost, hurling it against a wooden shop
front. The pounding waves hurl a car against a palm tree.
I can see people inside, struggling to get out — hope they
survive.

The Laboon is swallowing the resort: motorbikes,
street lamps, shacks, then spitting out half-digested
remains. Broken bits of wood and corrugated iron pour
past. Furniture is sucked out of buildings and thrown into
the tangled mess of broken wood and palm fronds.

A man is being swept along in the tide, helpless,
then he is sucked underwater. Pushing past the girls, I
rush out. Must find Rune. With his bad leg, he won't be
able to run.

Holding the stair-rail, I jump down two at a time.
Turning the corner, I nearly fall into water. The bottom
steps are blocked by a swirling mass of debris. And a

59

body is floating. I gag, clasping my hand over my mouth.

It's not Rune, but some other poor man. My friend must have escaped the Laboon; surely he could have limped up the stairs, dragging his twisted leg. It is not his time to die.

Without thinking, I heave the body onto a higher step, then run back upstairs. The second floor corridor is jammed with people, like a frenzied shoal of fish. Kicking open a bedroom door, I run to the window.

A woman is clinging to a lamppost, gripping a child's waist with her free hand. My stomach clenches, willing her to cling on, as an air-conditioning unit surges towards them. The metal monster is sucked under, but it bobs back up, spinning towards the lamppost. The woman's mouth is open wide in a scream that is eaten by the roar of the tide. Her hand is reaching into nothing. The child has disappeared.

My stomach is falling; I swallow sick in my throat. I stare horrified, willing the child to reappear. The sea can't be doing this; it can't be happening. A whirlpool of rubbish is rushing down the street. The junk tide is thick with splintered wood, bicycles and refrigerators. And people. A youth is clinging onto a bonnet of a car which is swirling towards the hotel.

"Grab onto the balcony!" I yell, but the car spins out of control, throwing him off.

It's horrific. Unreal. But it's happening. Death is all around, screaming.

Bursting into the corridor, I almost trip over a white haired lady who is crouching beside an old man. As I step around them, I gasp. A jagged bit of glass is protruding out of his arm and the shirt sleeve looks like a red sponge. The old lady's lips are trembling; maybe she's praying to her god.

My ribs expand as I take a deep breath. Leaning

forward, I pull out a piece of glass as sharp and pointed as the tip of a spear. The lady tries to cover the wound with her handkerchief, but a red circle is growing through the white material. She clutches my arm and stares. I don't know what to do, what to say; the injury looks bad. "I...I'll try to find help," I stammer, but I'm not sure if they understand.

Ahead, a clump of people cling together. They don't look up, so I barge through, kicking the next door. When it swings open, I fall through, scraping my face. For several seconds, I lie, winded. Clothes are scattered over the chair, like someone has just changed for the beach. Christmas wrapping paper is scrunched in a ball in the corner and children's toys and a brown teddy bear are lying on the bed. But no-one's here.

Crawling over, I pick up the child's teddy. The fur is smooth, with bare patches, like it's been cuddled a lot. It only has one eye. I feel a lump rush into my throat and crush the toy against my chest. Where is the poor kid? I wonder if it was a girl or boy and if they will ever be coming back.

Hearing a loud crash, I drop the bear and stumble over to the cracked window. A minibus has hit a lamppost in half and the vehicle is now being swept towards the hotel. The power of the tide jams it into the gap between our building and Bay View Hotel. It must be crushing anything and anyone below.

Then I notice a child clinging to the balcony of Bay View, so close I can see the whites of his eyes. "Get inside!" I shout, but the roar of water drowns my voice. Why is he out there? The railing could break and he could fall onto the bus or into the deadly tide.

A pick-up truck is powering towards us, swirling like a boat in a storm. The boy disappears in a jumble of movement as the truck smashes into his hotel. The wall has eaten half the truck; its boot is hanging in mid-air, one wheel still spinning. Then I spot him lying on the balcony – he's not fallen! But the railing is swaying. Bricks are crumbling, falling into the river. The horn won't stop, like it's screaming.

Grabbing the curtain, I tug, pulling down the rail with flowery yellow and blue material. I wind it into a thick ball around my hand, knocking out the splintered glass.

The boy is staring at me with huge eyes. When I step onto the balcony, it shudders. There is a gap as wide as a longboat between the buildings, but the truck and bus are almost touching like a bridge. Heart thudding, I lean as far as possible over the railing. His patio door is hanging off. He's stuck on the tiny balcony and the Laboon is still hungry.

Dark shapes are swirling below, making me feel dizzy. The spirits must be very angry, cutting open the belly of the resort and gouging out the entrails. But surely they will let me rescue one little boy. He has grabbed his knees and I can see him rocking.

My legs are shaking and I can't control my rapid breathing. If I judge it just right, I can save him — jump onto the roof of the bus, leap across to the truck's boot and climb onto his balcony. I clutch the rail with white knuckles; short rasping breaths tear my throat. It's too dangerous. On a normal day, in a calm sea, it would be easy to jump that far, or swallow dive, but leaping two metres over an angry tide is different. If I miss the truck, I'll be sucked into the crunching, matted tide.

Sweeping my damp hair from my eyes, I force myself to look at the boy. I can't hear his voice above the roaring river, but his eyes are fixed on me like I'm his only hope. I glance through the broken window, the entrance to safety. To life. And place one foot inside. But the boy's eyes are tugging at my heart: huge, beautiful, so like Petal's. What if another person was looking at my little sister right now and turned away? I'll never forgive myself if I don't try.

Stepping back, I assess the gap. The bus is jammed tight with rubble piling up around it. The pick-up truck is almost touching it now, like a bridge. If I land just right, I can scramble up and grab the boy's hand.

Gripping the railing with both hands, I swing my body over until I'm balancing like a tourist scared to jump off a boat into the sea. There's no going back. My body weight carries me over the railings. For a second, my legs are dangling over the torrent and I'm hanging by my fingertips. Then I feel the hard ridge with my tiptoes and flatten myself against the railing, facing the window. I need to let go with one hand and turn around. My fingers turn to rock.

Heart pounding, I dip my left shoulder, twisting my hips. My hands are trembling; my whole body is shaking. I squeeze my eyes shut, until they are little balls, pushed up by my cheeks. *Relax, pretend this is the side of a boat.*

I've done it. I stare at the Laboon's vomit. My lips are numb. My tongue is stuck to the back of my mouth. My toes curl into the ledge. My hands are slippery with sweat. Taking a deep breath, I jump.

12. Whisper of Hope

KRISTA

A giant whirlpool is sucking me in. Dark waves are towering over my head and invisible hands are pulling me down, brushing my face as I spin faster and faster.

My heart is pounding. My forehead is damp with sweat. As I shift my body, pain shoots down my left arm. It feels thicker, like something is covering it.

I unstick my eyelids. Slowly, the room comes into focus. I'm staring at a bandage wrapped around my forearm. Transfixed by the bloodstain, I reach for the rug with my bare toes. The floor is smooth and hard. Where am I? When I press my feet down, pain cuts into me like sharp nails. With a sinking feeling, I examine the balls of my feet. Red raw; cuts and scratches all over. The room starts spinning.

Tucking up my knees, I clasp both hands behind my neck, pulling my head down. I've felt like this once before, in a biology lesson at school, when we had to cut into a pig's heart.

When the pulse inside my head has stopped trying to knock me out, I slowly sit up. I rub the corner of each eye with the tip of my ring finger, then stare at the tiny grains of black grit.

My stomach falls into a hole as I remember. Dead eyes watching me. And Dad's figure disappearing into the distance.

The door handle turns. I grip the bed, leaning forward. "Dad?" My cheeks fall as Jo rushes over, her scarf flowing over my arm. Thankfully, she didn't seem to notice my disappointment and I'm glad because I didn't mean to hurt her; she makes me feel safer just being here.

"Krista, you're awake at last. I've been so worried. How are you feeling?" I can't help wincing as she touches me, and she backs off. "I'm so sorry, it must still hurt. I should have thought."

"It's fine, thanks." I try to smile. "Where's Dad?"

My step-mum's cheeks start twitching. "You're tired, of course you are. After everything's that's happened. I'll go back downstairs, leave you to sleep." She starts to back away. "Yes, leave you to sleep, that's best."

"Why, what's happened? Please, tell me what's happened?" Jo's whole body is trembling and she won't look at me. She is biting one side of her cheek, so her mouth is squished to one side – I'm getting scared. Now she is backing away and grabbing the door handle.

"Please don't go, I need you!"

Suddenly she bursts into tears. Great long sobs that seem to pull her body in two. This horrible fear grabs me. My step-mum is usually so happy, so something really bad must have happened. Where's Dad? My fingernails are digging into my fists. Panic is swirling around me. Waves, huge waves. I can't breathe.

"Krista…?" I hear a voice in the storm. I force myself to focus, but wonder if I'm dreaming when I see Jo wiping her nose with the scarf. She never does things like that. Then her neck juts forward. "You know don't you, Krista... you remember?"

Before I can answer, suddenly Jo is all over the

place. She jerks backwards, tries to sit down on the bed, then jumps up as if it's on fire. "I didn't see it at first, I was in the boutique on the first floor buying a... well it doesn't matter what I was buying... but suddenly everyone was screaming." She is twisting her fingers over her lips like she's trying to remould them like clay.

She stares over my left shoulder, like a TV presenter talking to the wrong camera. "The waves were unreal, like they were alive, storming past the hotel, a river of black things." She sucks in a sudden breath. "And I didn't know where you were. Or your dad." Jo grips my shoulder, shaking me. "I thought you were out there..." Her voice cracks as she stares at me. "C...caught in the tsunami!"

Beads of sweat are glistening on her forehead and her cheeks are smudged with mascara. Red blotches spot her cheeks and her frizzy hair is like a spider's web gone wrong. It's so tangled, it looks like she's been stressing it for hours. I feel the bed shake as Jo sits down. She is twisting her hands together in her lap. "Krista, I can't find Rob. I haven't heard from him. I don't know what's happened to him... all those bodies. She sniffs and wipes a hand over her mouth. "He was out running. What if he..." Wet eyes stare at me like I'm her last hope.

My lips have dried up; I keep rubbing them together and swallowing. "Dad's a fast runner, he'll be fine."

My step-mum's hands are pressing in her cheeks, fingers splayed wide. "Do you really think so? Why hasn't he phoned? I've been trying his mobile for hours!"

I swallow another mouthful of air. "He texted me, he was only ten minutes away, he has to be alright..."

"He texted? When? What did he say?" The questions shoot at me and I feel like they're hurting me all over again like the waves. I can't answer; this terrible fear is hanging over me. *Dad, where are you?*

"It was awful," she continues. "Some poor people didn't have a chance: cuts and blood everywhere." I don't want to hear, but her voice gets faster and faster, like a whirlpool. She's babbling on about standing on the stairs, looking at people running into the foyer. She suddenly stops. I look up and she's staring into my eyes. "It was then that I saw you."

Now I need to know everything. Jo clutches my arm, then bites her lip at my intake of breath. "Oh, I'm so sorry, I didn't think. Are you alright?" I nod and her lips tremble. "When you rushed into the lobby, I was so relieved. But then this massive surge of water burst in... just poured through the door, like the swimming pool had overflowed." My step-mum is staring at my left eyebrow now, as if she's still locked in the scene. "It was so sudden, there was no time. The power of the water threw people across the room."

Her grip tightens, but I don't care; I have to know what happened. Her eyes are huge and mascara is running in new wrinkles below her them. "You were under the water, Krista. I thought you were gone. I was desperate to get to you, but there were so many people jamming the stairs." She squeezes my arm so tightly it's like a blood pressure test. "I managed to get to the third step and then I saw him. A man was bending over, pulling bodies out of the water. My heart stopped, I can tell you."

I'm trying to wriggle free, when I hear her say the man was cradling a body. Something in the way she says *cradling*, makes my mouth feel dry. Jo's lip is wobbling and her hands are twisting round like she's trying to obsessively dry them. I can see the whites of her eyes as she stares at me.

"Krista, it was you. I didn't know if you were alive — you'd been underwater — I thought you were dead..."

I grab a fistful of scarf. "What happened?

She coughs, then looks at my left eyebrow again. "It was horrible. Debris was everywhere. I saw a Christmas tree floating and chairs, things floating in the frothing water. Dark, everywhere was dark, like it was oil."

"What about me?"

"He was amazing — waded right through the debris to the stairs. And he was crippled, couldn't walk properly. People were screaming, but he was calm. He carried you past me, right up to the first flight, and laid you down in the corridor. It was awful. I couldn't tell if you were breathing, but he bent down and laid his face against your cheek. *She's going to be fine*: these were his only words. He spoke in English, but he was foreign, Thai, I think. I was going to thank him, but he went straight downstairs again. I leant over the bannister and saw him plunge straight back into the water."

"Was he ok?"

She looks at her hands, twisting them together. "I don't know. I didn't see him again. I had to help you, get someone to look at your arm, it was bad."

"So he could have survived?"

She doesn't look at me. "I'm sure he managed to get out."

The bed springs up as Jo stands. She smooths her crumpled dress, pushing both hands over her hips, obsessively. "At least there's a doctor here. He's been working non-stop. He's one of the other guests; he's on holiday. He cleaned the wound and gave you two Paracetamol." Her voice is hurting my ears, she's talking so fast. "Oh, and you're not to get it wet."

Rolling onto my side, I try to remember, but all I can think of is Dad in his red running shorts, waving goodbye.

When I move my arm, the pain kicks in. Biting my lip, I breathe heavily. Then notice an empty space on my wrist — my watch must have been torn off by the force of the water. My ripped beach shirt is lying on the floor and I have a horrible feeling that the brown stains are dried blood. I pull the sheet closer, covering my bikini top.

"How long have I been asleep?"

She shrugs. "I'm not sure, so much has happened. There's no electricity and the telephones are all cut off. No-one knows what to do, where to go. Some people have gone to search for survivors on the beach, but no-one is telling us anything." She stares at me with huge eyes. "I don't know where your dad is, no-one does, no-one knows anything!"

Marker pen veins stand out as I clench my fists. "We've got to look for him. We can't just sit here while he's out there!" My step-mum can't keep still. Her hands flutter over her forehead, then cup her mouth like she's going to be sick. She moans, clasping her shoulders as if she is afraid she'll fall apart. Suddenly I feel cold.

Dad, you have to be alive! I won't let you die like Mum! Please Dad, you have to be alive!

Rolling onto my other side, I try to sit up, but pain explodes in my head. A horrible emptiness is trying to pull me into oblivion.

She's there. Holding my shoulders. Stroking my hair. Telling me to breathe slowly. Saying it will be alright. Her voice is soft, a whisper of hope in the darkness. My head stops throbbing, but my body is trembling like I've been outside in a massive hailstorm without a coat. Pulling the sheet closer, I curl up like a baby. Then feel something digging into my chest.

The locket! It's still here! I sit up, gripping the treasure in my right hand, forcing the dizziness to vanish. If the locket is safe, then Dad is going to be safe, too.

Jo tugs my arm. "You had me worried for a moment — you've got more colour in your cheeks now." My step-mum fetches a bottle of water, but I can't hold it steady and it keeps bashing my teeth. She holds out her hand. "Here, let me." I can't believe I'm letting her drip feed me like a baby. She wipes my mouth and kneels down beside the bed. "Just take things slowly and you'll be fine in no time."

"And Dad...?"

Her eyebrows crease as worry lines reappear on her forehead. She brushes them away with her hand. "He'll be walking into the hotel any minute, just you wait and see."

Suddenly I realise where Dad is. "He must have gone back to the bungalow, he'll be waiting for us!"

Why isn't she answering? Her neck muscles tighten as she swallows. "I'm sorry love, there's nothing left."

My heart races. "There can't be! We're staying there, all my stuff is there!"

"The waves tore right through the buildings, one of the other guests said. He only just escaped in time."

An image flashes into my mind of a massive wave smashing into the wide front window of our bungalow. "Everything's gone, hasn't it?"

My step-mum looks at me, but doesn't speak.

"All our presents?"

She clears her throat and tries to smile. "But we're lucky, really, because we've been offered this room in the hotel."

"For all of us, Dad too?"

She twists her scarf round her finger. "You can have the double bed until Rob is...." She sighs then indicates the single bed in the corner. "I'll sleep there. The manager said we could use anything in the room.

Jo must have noticed me looking at my ruined shirt, for she points to two suitcases propped up by the wardrobe. "He said those are spare, so if we need anything…"

Shaking my head, I sink back onto the bed. It makes a noise like a sigh, or was that my step-mum? Her forehead creases. "I know what you mean, but I'm sure the guests have just left them, just rushed off when the tsunami struck, grabbed a taxi...got the first flight out of here…" She doesn't even sound convincing. We both know why those cases are here and there's no way I'm wearing a dead person's clothes.

She seems suddenly tired: her back is curved and her head is almost touching her chest. I want to reach out and touch my step-mum, tell her it's going to be ok, but I don't know how. Then she sniffs loudly and stands up. "I'm going downstairs. There might be news." Jo holds the door handle, then she swirls around, her eyes shining. "That's it! Rob's lost his mobile, that's why he hasn't been able to phone, he must be looking for us too!"

I catch her excitement. "And he couldn't find us because the bungalows are…"

"Not there!" She rushes back to the bed. "But I'm sure Rob is safe, he'll come back to us."

"Do you really think so?"

My step-mum takes my hands and holds them gently. "I'll go down to the lobby now and as soon as I find out anything…" She squeezes my fingers and nods so her hair jumps up and down. "As soon as I know anything, I'll tell you straight away."

Not wanting to be left behind, I try to sit up, but my head is swirling.

"No, it's best you stay here and rest. I'll be back in no time, don't worry."

As the door clicks, I slide my feet onto the floor, this time moving more slowly. But I'm not staying in here when Dad might be walking into the hotel any moment. I edge off the side of the bed and slowly stand up.

Dizziness attacks again, forcing me to sit down.

The third time, I find I can stand without swaying. Now for my clothes — can't go down in my bikini. My long beach shirt is ruined. I glance at the suitcases sitting on the floor. There's no way I'm wearing any of those clothes. The people might come back...or if they don't, that means... No, I'm not going to think about what it means. Just want my own stuff. Haven't even worn the cool denim jacket Jo bought in Dubai. I've lost everything, my mascara, foundation, plum lipstick, everything.

Feeling lost, I clasp my hands over my face. But I can't hide. My mind is filled with screams and this giant tower of black water. People are running towards me, hands begging me to help, bodies crashing into my stomach. I force my eyes open, but I can still see the girl on the roof. My breath shivers. What do I care about stupid possessions; people have died out there. It was just a normal morning, tourists lounging around or hotel staff working, when life was snatched away from them in seconds. And they'll never be coming back.

13. Torn Apart

MARTI

It's over. Like a deadly cobra, it slithered along the horizon, then uncoiled its giant hood, striking the coast as far as I could see. Sucking in life and spewing out death. Having eaten as much as it wanted, it has sunk under the sea. The spirits have been appeased. And those it has left have to pick up the pieces.

The resort has been ripped apart. Street lamps have been pulled from their anchors and telephone wires are hanging loose, tangled like torn spiders' webs. A line of palm trees next to the sea wall has simply gone. Trees I climbed to pick coconuts to sell to tourists are lying flattened. It is worse than a hotel developer uprooting them with a big digger. It's impossible, it couldn't happen, but it has. The world has been tipped up and shaken.

And a little boy is holding my hand like he never wants to let go.

He doesn't know I'm a sea gypsy, he doesn't care. I am a person, like him. He follows me everywhere. I don't know his name. He's western, European maybe, or American. Except for the wide eyes, you wouldn't know anything is wrong. There are no scratches. Just his silence like the ocean, now the Laboon has disappeared.

He was clutching a toy car when I kicked the door

open and he hasn't let it go. Why would anyone lock a little child in a room? It makes me angry. After we escaped, I tried leaving him with an English couple, but the boy's fingers dug into my hand. The people wandered away with flat white faces, eyes seeing us, but not seeing. So we returned to the boy's room to see if his parents had come back. I sank onto the soft sheet and the boy curled onto my lap like a stray dog. Several people must have slept here, for beside the large bed, there is a mattress on the floor, and two beds squeezed into the corner of the room, one hanging above the other.

When I heard someone shout, "The water's coming back!" I jumped up and the boy gripped his red car. People were running for shelter, but the ocean was peaceful. The Laboon is satisfied; it won't attack again.

The sun was at its height, when I heard sirens and saw an ambulance. I wanted to ask a medic to check my aching back, but the boy glued to me tighter than a crab to its shell. I couldn't leave him, just as I couldn't when I saw him on the balcony. It all happened so fast: a rush of darkness about to swallow me; the jarring pain as I hit the metal bus; then leaping across the chasm and nearly falling off the truck as I reached for the balcony of Bay View Hotel.

He grabbed my legs through the railings; I almost slipped and screamed at him to let go. When I climbed over the railing, the boy clung like a monkey. I lifted him through the open doorway into a bedroom, then collapsed, shaking. He started moaning — must have thought I was dying. That helped: I have to stay strong for him.

The street looks like a pod of sharks have gorged themselves and vomited the remains. The bus is clogging the gap between the four-storey Bay View and The Green Turtle. The pick-up truck is still hanging in the wall and oil and excrement are stinking in the heat. My leather sandals sink into the mud, but most people don't even have shoes; they are wandering around with bare feet and beachwear. One man has been stripped naked by the sea, but nobody stares; normal embarrassment has dissolved. There are worse things to worry about — like staying alive.

The boy is shaking, but he does not cry. Petal would be squawking like a parrot by now, but the boy is a silent shadow. Rune will know what to do; I'm sure he will be back at his post by now. We trudge past the belly of the bus, to The Green Turtle. Puddles of brown water and froth cling to the door frame and the door is hanging off. The marble floor is filthy with footprints in the mud. Sticks of broken furniture are jammed up against the far wall, strewn with seaweed.

Movement on the stairs. A room maid is mopping up. I've seen her before, in the kitchen. She calls to me and I am surprised that she knows my name; most people just call me *Fish Boy*. "I'm so glad to see you, Marti. The other staff... don't know where most of them are... it's horrible..." Her voice floats away.

When I step towards her, the boy tugs me back. He is staring at the mud, terrified, and he has nearly dropped his toy car; it's dangling by one wheel. Staying by his side, I ask the maid if she's seen Rune.

She shakes her head. "The water, it came in, right up to here." She gestures to the third stair. "I was upstairs changing beds. When I heard the noise, I rushed down." She sniffs. "It was black. No-one had a chance. Everyone who was down here, they've all gone." She wrinkles her nose. "Or been taken."

"Taken?"

The room maid points in the direction of the open door. "To the makeshift mortuary, in the Buddhist temple."

I can't believe Rune is just a number, he has to be alive.

The boy's hand has gone limp. His face is white and I'm afraid he's going to faint. Lifting him into my arms, I walk into the sunlight. Mud clings to my sandals, oozing between my toes. For the first time, I see that he is wearing slippers. Why didn't I notice that before? But then there were more important things on my mind — like how to escape the black wall of death.

It is impossible to cross the street. Motorbikes are trying to weave through the rubble like they are swimming against the tide. People are taking anything they can carry, desperate to get out of here. The Laboon has swept through the market stalls, ripping colourful flags and scarves, leaving a grey sludge. Gone are the stallholders and the kiosks selling sweets and cigarettes.

Coral! Please be safe. Please don't have come to the snack shack this morning.

"We will go to the beach," I tell the boy. "We will look for your parents." He doesn't answer, but I feel his fingers curl into a small fist in my hand.

14. Trapped

KRISTA

I'm sick of false alarms. Every time we hear shouting, my heart starts hammering. We're on constant high-alert and it's exhausting. Jo keeps rushing to the window, her voice going off the scale like a siren. We sit down again and wait.

To be told it's safe to go out.

For the water and electricity to come back on.

For Dad to arrive.

My step-mum is being bright and brittle, like a boiled egg — she'll crack in a minute. "How are you feeling? Does your arm hurt? Can I do anything?" *Please just sit here with me; you don't have to say anything.* My arm is throbbing, my feet hurt whenever they touch the sheet and I feel like I'm sinking when I move my head. But I'm not telling her that. Need to get out and find Dad.

We're trapped. The room is like a box with a low ceiling. How will I find the right corridor to get out? What if we get stuck in the lift? No, we can't use the lift, it won't be working. Have to use the stairs. But which is safer: the back or the front? I wish we'd been staying here in the main hotel, not the bungalow, then I would have known the layout. All my stuff would be here. And Dad... maybe Dad would be here, too.

Cramp locks my fingers, so I can't straighten them:

they look like witches' hands — gnarled twigs. Jo says my arm is weeping, so she peels off the bandage. It hurts. Her eyes widen as she takes a deep breath. I squeeze my head into the pillow and close my eyes. A bottle is being unscrewed. Cold liquid numbs my arm, then it's burning, stinging like nettles. Arching my back, I try not to scream, but I can't help it.

The bandage curves around my arm and a voice murmurs. A pill is pressed into my hand and my fingers curl around it. When I open my eyes, my step-mum's forehead has more wrinkles than I remember. She shakes the Paracetamol box. "Is one enough, or do you need two?" A waft of perfume hits me as she takes off her sparkly scarf and folds it in a triangle. "Here, this should help to take the pressure off your arm."

When you're in pain, you think it's never going to stop. Feels like hours before I can sit up. But I can't bear to put any weight on my feet. Wish I had some comfy slippers — although there are so many little cuts that another layer of cushioning might not help. Jo was right about one thing: my arm doesn't feel so heavy now I'm wearing the sling, and the pain is less intense.

She sweeps my hair away from my face. "Is that better?"

"Yes, thanks."

She smiles and for the first time, I feel we're on the same side. For a minute, we sit in silence. Then someone screams outside in the street. A towering wall of black waves rushes into my mind and I watch my step-mum sliding across to the window.

"Is it...?" I ask.

"No, thank God. I can see a woman... a woman and a child..." I look away. I don't want to hear that someone's dead, especially a child.

"I'm going down to see if I can help." Her shoulders

rise as she takes a deep breath. "There might be news of your dad."

+++

It seems only moments later that she's here again, but she apologises for being so long. I must have fallen asleep. Bubbling, that's the only word I can use to describe her. Bubbling with words. I'm glad Jo's back; feel safer with her around. Just wish she'd stop talking, it's exhausting. I'm staring out of the window, hoping she'll get the hint. She doesn't.

I don't want to know that hundreds of people have died in Thailand and thousands more all around the Indian Ocean. I don't want to know that the hospitals are bursting, full of bodies, and doctors are operating in the corridors. I don't want to know that crews are pumping out water and looking for bodies. Dad is somewhere out there.

Jo says she's phoned my grandparents, but I was asleep and she didn't want to disturb me. "They said they'll book a flight if Rob is... I mean, if he isn't..." Her voice cracks and she breathes heavily. "But they can't come over for several days."

"Why can't I talk to Granny and Grandad?"

"You can. They said they'll phone tonight."

I feel my whole life is wrapped in bandages and I'm stuck, unable to make my own decisions. She says she's trying her best, but there's been no news yet. "People keep asking to use my phone to contact their relatives and I can't really say no, can I?"

"Can I phone Izzie?"

She clutches her phone like it's a winning Lottery ticket. "Sorry. I need to save it in case..."

"That's shocking! Izzie could tell everyone I'm ok..."

"I'm sorry, love, but I need to save my credit for important calls."

"Friends are important!" I glare at The Woman. "You've just let some random people use your phone..."

"The young man was worried his parents might think he hadn't made it... It was only for a couple of minutes..."

"What about Dad? Haven't you ever thought that he might be dying for us to call?"

Her voice cracks. "Don't you think I've tried? I keep phoning and texting, but his mobile is still dead."

Like him. No, I won't let my dad be dead.

The Woman buries her face in a wad of tissues and makes a trumpeting noise like an elephant, then sniffs loudly and stuffs the tissue in her sleeve. She's being so unfair. I wish I hadn't lost my phone – the force of the water must have torn it out of my pocket. The last time I saw it was when Dad texted.

Why did you have to go for a run? If only you hadn't gone to the stupid mangroves.

"Stop letting random people steal our airtime!" I shout. "Dad needs it! He doesn't even know we're alive." I hate the tears that are in my voice. "I can't even look for him — haven't got any clothes."

The Woman is glancing at the large suitcase. "Haven't you opened it yet? I'm using the other one." I stare at the smart black case. It isn't even scuffed — no-one would leave it. I know why the people haven't come back.

She crosses the room and lifts a pink gift bag off the dressing table. "Here, this is for you." She lifts out a dark blue box with a silver rim around the edges. "I bought it in the boutique this morning, before the... well, I thought you might still like it."

"You mean you carried it past all the dead bodies?"

She goes quiet, but I don't care. Gifts won't bring back Dad. A sick feeling clogs my throat, as I have a vision of our Christmas presents floating around the wrecked bungalow. Feel like screaming that I don't care about presents. There are more important things, such as how to stand up without falling over and how to plan my route out of here.

15. Sea of Junk

MARTI

The sea is lapping at the shoreline, like nothing has happened. A plastic bucket is drifting in and out on the waves. I look to where the ocean meets the sky, turning my head to follow the faint line. All is blue apart from streaks of black oil on the water.

The sun is shining and everything is calm. Until you look inland. The beautiful smooth beach has gone. Jet skis and yachts have been flung into the scrap heap of concrete blocks, plastic and tangled wood. The Laboon threw up cars as if they were soft toys, but they need strong tractors to drag them away. It's impossible, but it has happened. The waves have left a sea of junk. Street lamps are leaning like trees in the wind, tilting towards the road.

I am alive, standing in death. Everywhere, there is thick brown mud. Right now I should be working, picking up sweet wrappers and empty cans, but instead I'll be clearing away rubble for the rest of my life. The Laboon opened its mouth like a giant whale, swallowing hundreds of red umbrellas and deck chairs. It sucked in mouthful after mouthful, then spat out buckets and spades like crumbs. I wish it hadn't happened, but the spirits have spoken.

I lift the boy onto the sea wall, holding onto his legs

for safety. His head is level with my chest, and beyond us, rubbish stretches into the distance. I try not to think about our lagoon, but the Laboon was so strong, it may have bitten the entire coast and swallowed Surin and Myanmar.

It feels like several tides have flowed since the two girls were standing here, defying the spirits, but it can't be, for the sun is still high in the sky. I hoist myself up, trying to see the waterfront bungalows. The skyline looks different, empty. The roofs have been torn off and only skeletons of the buildings remain. *Rune!*

When I lead the boy towards the bungalows, we are faced with a mountain of crushed plastic, planks and blocks of concrete. He is clinging to my leg, so I swing him onto my shoulders like I remember Papa doing when I was little.

Papa, where are you and Grandad? Please look after Mama and Petal. Coral, please don't let the ocean have given you enough treasure to sell; please be safe at home.

Even as the thoughts rush through my mind, I know the Laboon was hungry enough to eat our huts. And if Grandad went fishing after I left, he would have been caught on the wings of the waves and swept inland. His Kabang would have been crushed.

The boy feels heavier every step. His legs are bumping my chest as my feet slip and slide; we nearly fall into an open freezer which is lying like an empty coffin.

Then I see Rune's bungalow. My body tenses and my hands tighten around the boy's ankles. The ocean has ripped right through the house. Two walls lean inwards, like open jaws of a giant clam. The door is half buried in the sand, sticking out at an angle.

The balcony where I stood when I made my decision to tell Papa. Gone. The stomach of the house is exposed to the sky. I feel a sudden chill. Rune was the first person on land who treated me like I'm human, not a street rat. I look at the empty space, remembering Rune's hand on my shoulder. Was that the last time I will ever see him?

The boy is squirming like an eel on my shoulders, so I swing him over my head onto a dirty patch of sand. Then he whines because his feet are sinking in sludge and his slippers have disappeared. I kneel down. "We'll find them." His lip starts trembling and his mouth droops. I know he is thinking of his parents, not his slippers.

"Do you want me to carry you again?" He nods, so I hoist him back onto my shoulders. Small arms wrap around my neck and I feel a tear dripping onto my cheek. The boy is crying silently, but still he doesn't speak. I don't know what to do; I have to find help. Figures are combing the beach, climbing over splintered wood, looking for survivors. Bodies are lying in the hot sun. I've seen death before: glassy eyes of fish, gaping open mouths; breath snatched in seconds. But these are people with families, loved ones. I know that the Laboon was hungry, but why couldn't it just eat the buildings and leave the people alone?

A man wades through the wreckage towards us, holding a whimpering child in his arms. As he passes, I make eye contact. "We need help!" I call. The man lifts one palm and gestures to his child, then continues walking. I shake my head. "You don't understand, this boy isn't mine, he's got his own family..." The man doesn't turn round.

I feel the boy's hand in my hair, touching me. He accepts me just as I am. The waves have flooded over all of us: brown or white, Islander or Land lover. The wind kisses our cheeks whether we are born on a boat and have no possessions and no education; or a rich western girl with knowledge and beauty and golden hair that flies in the wind.

How many tides will it be before all the bodies wash up, how many sunrises, how many new moons before we can start to live again? I thought I wanted the bright lights, but now I just want my family. Grandad, Mama, Coral, Petal.

And Papa, yes, I want Papa to be safe. I meant the things I said, but I want to see him again. But we can't search around the headland; there is too much rubble and the boy would fall. I raise my arms, lifting him off my shoulders. "We will walk along the shoreline," I tell him. "Other people are searching, so maybe they have found your Mum and Dad." The boy is clinging to my leg, so I take his small hand in mine. It feels warm, although the boy's face looks cold and as white as fog.

A body blocks our way, battered and bloody, so I cover the boy's eyes and pull him away quickly. As I look up, I see a wooden fishing boat speared into the thick layer of tangled rubbish. I catch my breath as I recognise it.

The Kabang is lying head first on the shore, as if it can't bear to look. Waves are tapping against the wooden sides, warning me of something. But the flotilla won't have sailed today. The elders would have read the signs and heard the silence of the birds.

Edging forward, I see a body trapped under the hull. This was a person who had been laughing and joking, now just a body, face down in the water. My stomach clenches and my heart starts thumping my chest. *He is Moken. Who is it?* Letting go of the boy's hand, I clamber over debris on my hands and knees.

The shape of his head looks familiar. Sick shoots into my throat. But he wouldn't come here, near the resort — no, it must be another poor man. My mouth feels dry. My neck starts to prickle. It can't be him; it can't be.

Surely he didn't chose today of all days to go fishing? Last night's argument slices through my mind. *You're a waste of space...you don't even go fishing anymore.* I'll never be mean again, please just let him be alive.

Finding strength from deep within, I heave the shoulders onto the broken boat. Sunshine glints on water, so I crouch to avoid the glare. The body is lifeless and grey. I feel a terrible chill. Holding my breath, I turn the head. And look into Papa's dead eyes.

16. Rumours

KRISTA

My stomach rumbles. What a silly thing food is when death is all around, when lives are being torn apart. Yet I am hungry. I wonder if the guests left any food in the room. The blue case has moved to the side of the single bed, so my step-mum must have been inside it again. She is in the en-suite, using bottled water to clean her face, but you can't wash everything away as if it hadn't happened.

I perch on the bed, tucking my body in, like a child on the first day at school. The black case is sitting there, daring me to open it. Edging forward, I bend my knees, flexing my toes. The man would have closed those two brass clasps, excited to catch the flight and enjoy his dream holiday. I look at the smaller blue case. Did it belong to his girlfriend or wife? I can almost see her smiling as she packed the last clothes inside, then zipped it.

Trying not to think of what's happened to her, I limp across the parquet flooring, grateful that it is clean. When I open the wardrobe, a flimsy dress floats over my hands. Midnight blue, turning to purple at the hem. There's also a long sequinned black evening gown and a short strappy white dress. I'm tempted, but it feels wrong to wear a pretty dress if death is still out there.

Perhaps the man has something I could fit into. I glance at the black suitcase out of the corner of my eye, then cross my arms. *Come on Krista, it's only an object.* Feeling braver, I edge towards it. But what if the dead people are watching, they might haunt me or something if I take their stuff? *Now you're going crazy!*

I feel like a thief as I touch the handle. My hand hovers over the zip. Squeezing my eyelids and blotting out my eyes, I try to imagine the people fleeing the tsunami and speeding out of the resort; saving their lives rather than their luggage. Taking a deep breath, I look inside.

It's packed neatly, but it feels like stealing, even looking at the clothes. A sun hat and two pairs of shoes are tucked at the sides of the case. The guy must have had small feet, for when I slip on the trainers, they are only a bit loose. I can't do up the laces with only one free hand, but anything is better than walking in bare feet — especially with cuts all over like train tracks. The long-sleeved stripy shirt could act as a mini-dress, but looks like a sack. A black leather belt makes the shirt less baggy, but the material gathers up so my bikini is visible. Ditching the outfit, I pick a T shirt instead.

My step-mum's head protrudes like a tortoise's, as she peers out of the bathroom. "Wow, that's bright!" I hate blushing in front of her. It's not like I am wearing the neon orange T shirt with palm leaves, just modelling it. I throw it away, embarrassed.

When I look up, Jo is holding out an embroidered white Gypsy blouse and a pair of shorts. "These are from the other case, they'll fit you better." She gently levers off the scarf-sling and motions for me to lift up my hands like a little kid. I feel like crying — the last person who did that was Mum. Before I know it, Jo has popped the blouse over my head. Then she holds out some black shorts and I step into them. "They fit well. And those trainers seem fine too, but would you like some socks? Let me see…"

She rummages in the suitcase, like it's a jumble sale. I don't think the man would be too pleased, but is he even alive? I sigh when I see my step-mum holding up some sports socks like a trophy. "Your feet will rub, surely you want…" I shake my head. His socks feel too personal.

"Do you need any help with the laces?"

"No thanks." But I had no idea how difficult it was to tie laces with one hand. I smell a waft of perfume as she kneels in front of me. Choking up, I tell Jo not to fuss. But inside my head, I'm saying *"Please don't leave me, I need you!"*

I am about to thank her, when she gets up and slips the sling back over my shoulder. I hear the wardrobe door banging, then see my step-mum trying to squeeze into the white sun dress that is at least two sizes too small and far too short for her. She raises her eyebrows. "My other dress needed a wash; do you think this is ok?" She looks like a fairy on a Christmas tree gone wrong. I nod and she smiles. "Oh good. I thought perhaps it was a bit…well, too young for me. But if you say it's fine, we'll go down to the lounge."

My toes are curling as I arch my feet. My soles don't hurt so much this way, but it's tiring hobbling and I'm glad to sit down when we reach the dining room. An old man is silent as a ghost, staring out of the window. A young couple is tangled together on the sofa. A thin stick of a lady is biting her lip. I'm one of the silent ones, while my step-mum is a talker. She finds a table for us, then barges into a conversation with some random people. "Has anyone seen a tall man wearing red running shorts?"

No-one answers. When the stick lady shakes her head, my step-mum leans towards her, grabbing her bony fingers. "You'd easily notice him — my husband is six foot three. Please, tell me if you've seen him." Blank eyes stare back.

A bald man adjusts his glasses. He takes them off, then puts them on again repeatedly. "I stood on the balcony and called for him, but he wasn't there," he tells everyone. "He was right there, then he was gone. My son, I have to find my son!" He rips off his glasses and covers his face with tattooed hands. My step-mum murmurs something, but the man isn't listening. "One second he was there and then he was gone — just like that. Sam, my little Sammy! I couldn't hold on… his hand slipped away like butter. But I should have, I should have... he's got his whole life to live."

I've never heard a man cry before, not even Dad. If he cried his tears for Mum, he did it when he was alone. I'm starting to feel dizzy. I find a strand of hair near my ear and twiddle it around my finger. If I force myself not to think, I won't see the wave coming, won't feel the building shaking beneath me and won't feel the biting lash of the monster. I'll be free. If only I could, but I can't. What if the girl hadn't grabbed my wrist? And what if I'd climbed up more quickly; maybe we could have clung together and both have been saved. Or maybe we would have both been torn off the roof? I can't stop thinking of *what if's* and *if only's*.

Everybody has gone quiet, when a voice splits the room: "Run!" The ghost by the window has come to life, his eyes like torches. "The water's coming back!"

A man shouts something in French, then yells at his wife. Screams have no language: they all sound the same. I'm caught up in the tide of people streaming through the lobby, heading for the stairs. They are pushing me, shoving my backside as I'm carried along in the wave.

We wait in a huddle on the second floor, like

penguins — there is hardly any room to breathe. Silence. More screams. Then silence again. What's happening?

The stick lady starts chattering, her words spilling into the crowd. "Did you hear that? I'm sure it was another explosion. We're all going to die!" Terror is contagious; I can feel it spreading, infecting all of us.

"Someone shut her up!" growls the old man. "We're safe up here, it's that lot down there you need to worry about."

"I've got no-one left — why was I was spared while he was taken?" she moans. Suddenly, she grabs a handful of my blouse and her eyes bore into mine. "Why did it happen: why?"

The material is hurting my neck as her words flow faster and faster. "...our villa has a pool overlooking the sea... we arrived yesterday... jet-lagged... he must have slept in..."

Stop it! My Dad is still out there!

"I saw this wave; it was huge. Thought Arthur would want to see it, you know, but he was still asleep, snoring." She stares through me. "He was snoring when it happened. It's the last sound I ever heard him make." Then she makes a low hollow sound.

I tug free, but there's such a crush that I can't escape. And the lady won't stop babbling. "I'd opened the window to get a good snap, but the wave was getting too big and I thought his camera might get wet." She turns to me. "Arthur loves his camera, you see: he'd do anything for a good photo. There was this roaring, then I saw water pouring under the door of our villa." She closes her eyes and her eyelids look like dark rings. "It was horrible, coming for me, moving like a wild animal." She stops abruptly, her eyes staring into nothing.

A shiver goes right through me, but she hasn't finished. "It smashed... the window smashed and this monster wave crashed in."

"But you're safe now," says a young guy with blond hair scraped back into a ponytail.

The stick lady ignores him; her eyes are huge as she opens her mouth. "I was catapulted across the room. I couldn't breathe."

"But you're here now."

"I was being tossed round like a spin dryer, things cutting into me, I couldn't move my arms or legs. Then I hit something hard. My back, it's red raw," she explains.

No, please don't show us!

"But at least you are alive."

The whisper of the young guy affects me more than the manic words of the stick lady; I feel a lump in my throat.

The lady is staring into the crowd. "But where's Arthur?" Her voice is whirling round us like a twister. "Where's Arthur?"

Another shrill voice competes for attention. "My daughter is ill, let me through!"

I've never been so pleased to see anyone! I smile gratefully at my step-mum. She may only be just over five foot, but she's solid enough to shield me by barging through the crowd.

We reach the second-floor corridor and hide in our room. She turns on the light, but nothing happens. I hear her breathing fast and ragged. "Krista, if the waves come back, I just want you to know…" Her voice breaks and I can tell she's trying not to cry. "Krista, I do care for you, my dear."

Tears sting my eyes and I feel like hugging her. She squeezes my hand. "I know I'm not your mum, but I think of you as a daughter, honestly I do."

My hand freezes. I can feel her warmth but I am suddenly cold. *Don't mention Mum, please don't mention*

Mum.

When I let go of her hand, she leans forward and holds both my shoulders. "Please don't shut yourself off from me, Krista! I'm not trying to replace your Mum, I know I could never do that. Rob's told me how wonderful she was, how you were such a tight unit, how Sarah loved you so much…I'm not expecting things to be the same..."

I'm falling. A dirty garden glove is ripping off yellow rose petals and a large boot is stamping on the flowers, crushing them. I want to press my fingers in my ears and block her out. *How dare you talk about Mum as if you knew her!*

I hear a sob and hands start shaking me. "Krista, you have to listen! Any minute we might die! You have to believe me – your dad and I, we love each other very much…" She chokes and I feel spit on my cheek. "Krista, please! I don't want things to be like this. I love you!"

The knot tightens in my stomach until it's about to cut me in two. "Go away and leave me alone!" I shout before I can stop myself.

Her hands drop. There's no reply, no sound. I glance at her face and it's white. She won't look at me. And I feel really horrible, tangled up. I don't want her to go. I don't want to be alone. I want to say sorry, but my legs won't move, my mouth won't speak.

She's standing by the door. Waiting. My jaw clenches. It's too late to pretend she loves me. The Woman is only saying all this because she thinks we're going to die. Why can't she stop telling me what to do and work on her own life? Dad doesn't seem to notice, but she needs a serious make-over. Her hair looks like it's been electrocuted, it's so frizzy. Sharp scissors appear in my mind and I imagine slicing off the thin wispy bits. And those flowery dresses, they do nothing for her. *"Lose the strapless dresses, darling,"* I can almost hear a fashion guru say. She needs a year's gym membership and a subscription to Slimmers World. How can she possibly make Dad happy; she's nothing like Mum.

This all whizzes through my mind in seconds.

The door opens. She's gone.

And I feel alone. And bad. Really bad.

I wish I hadn't said it. Jo didn't steal Mum away from Dad. Cancer did. Ate into her until she faded away. I hate it. It ate into all of us. Dad couldn't smile for a long time, not really. Of course he had a right to marry again. And it's mean to criticise The Woman's weight, even in my mind. Who cares anyway? It's just that Mum was slim like me and I miss her so much.

Especially now.

17. Guilt

MARTI

"The ocean is my universe; I was born with the sound of the waves in my ears and the smell of the sea filling my body. And the ocean is still inside me."

Papa cannot see or talk or breathe, but his words are still crashing around my head. They were inside me as I knelt beside his body, begging the spirits to breathe life, to see the rise and fall of his chest. But I knew it wouldn't happen. Just as I know I should have died, not him. I wish I could dive back into my angry words and hook them, but it is too late. I shouldn't have accused him, shouldn't have argued. Why was he here? He thinks the resort is evil with the nightclubs and bars. I don't understand. It must be my fault.

He is no longer lying in the water, but hidden in the back of a truck, covered with a white sheet. The soldiers said they are waiting for more bodies to be retrieved before taking them to the Temple. Papa will soon be stuffed into a body bag tied up with string, lying next to hundreds of other body bags tied up with string.

The sun is hot on my neck, but I feel cold. Then a little hand slips into mine. I have to be strong for the boy. He needs to find his family, even though I have lost mine. We cannot follow the truck, for vehicles fly like the wind. My people have no word for sorry, but I wish I could say it. It's too late. Too late for Papa, but maybe we will find the boy's family alive.

We walk back down the steps to the beach and stand under the shade of a palm tree. Its leaves have been shredded like a gutted fish. I stand looking at the devastation and the boy sinks onto the ground and drives his toy car over a plastic Coca Cola bottle. The red plastic car with fat yellow wheels is the only clean thing around. It looks like all the rubbish in the world has been tipped here; the beauty of the beach hidden under a tumbled mass of trash. Perhaps we will never see clean golden sand again. Here and there, I see dots moving: people looking for survivors.

Suddenly, I hear a shout, "This one's still alive!" A young Thai man is waving his arms by a pile of rubbish heaped around another palm tree. An older, thicker set man is bending down over a body. I don't want the boy to see this, so leave him playing with his toy and walk towards them.

The long body is naked, scratched and bloated like a jellyfish – must have swallowed a lot of water. His face is pale, but his leg is a mess; a piece of skin is hanging off. I watch the older Thai man pull a metal object out of the victim's leg and blood shoots out in a fountain, spraying his face. He yells and wipes it off quickly. Then sees me. "What are you looking at? It's your fault, Dirty Islander!" He does a rude gesture, then drags the younger guy away. He would rather leave the tall man to die than touch a sea gypsy.

Blood is oozing out of his leg, but he is still breathing. I need something to clean the wound. *The Coca Cola bottle!* The boy has fallen asleep, so I pick up the empty bottle and wade through the splintered wood to the shoreline.

When I return, I am surprised to see the younger

Thai guy holding a dirty cloth over the victim's leg. As I approach, he backs away like a scared dog. Tipping up the bottle, I dribble seawater over the wound. My body starts to retch. The victim has a hole gouged out of his thigh with exposed bone and skin and muscle. I stumble backwards and I am sick on the rubble.

"Told you he was disgusting," shouts a rough voice. Looking up, I notice the older man standing about five metres away. He points at me, then speaks in a loud voice. "Let's go. We don't want Moken scum infecting us, do we?" The younger guy glances at his friend, then at me, caught in the middle.

Having wiped off the sick, I place my feet wide. "Do you want him to die?" Hesitation is in the young man's eyes, but he doesn't move.

I clasp the victim's shoulders and heave the tall man onto his side. He starts moaning and shaking, then it is his turn to be violently sick. Blood and sand and thick brown mucus are spouting out of his mouth. The young guy scrambles away from the smell and joins his friend. I'm left to cope alone.

The injured man has stopped emptying his stomach; I am trying not to empty mine again. He is breathing like a fish out of water, gasping for air. I feel a tug at my shirt and look down. I hadn't even noticed the little boy was awake.

"Oy! What are you doing with that tourist kid?"

Ignoring the loud abuse, I pull the boy towards me. He wraps himself around my thigh and stares at the victim's naked body. I wish we had something to cover the man, but treating his leg is more important. Pulling my shirt over my head, I tear it down the middle, creating long strips. "Here," I say to the boy, "let's make a bandage."

Trying to get the material to stay on the wound is

difficult. Eventually, the blood flow is stemmed and I relax. A little. I hear voices. Footsteps crunch towards me, then two pairs of dirty boots halt beside the victim. Looking up, I see the Thai men balancing a broken door between them. The older man won't look at me, but at least he's helping.

We don't speak. The injured man is so tall, it will be difficult to lift him onto the stretcher. The men hoist the wide shoulders while I slide my arms under his legs. Then, as one, we lift him onto the door. The victim cries out and tries to clutch his leg. My shirt is growing red. The young guy strips off his shirt and places it on top of my torn one. He keeps his gaze on the injured man and doesn't talk to me, but I know he's saying more by helping than he could have with words.

We bend our knees and lift the stretcher, then carry the man up the beach, the little boy trotting next to me. Every step we take, the man grows paler and I fear we will be too late. We hear the sound of a chopper. The boy shouts at the sky and waves his arms, but I don't expect they will see us. We stop for a rest at the wall before climbing the steps. The man is whiter than the whitest clouds and, when I bend my head to see if he is still breathing, I cannot feel his breath on my cheek.

A soldier is leaning over the wall and he calls for backup. Soon, two medics appear and cover the victim's naked body with a sheet. The young guy who gave his shirt, nods to me as he walks away.

When I glance at the boy, he is grasping his toy and staring at the yellow liquid which a medic is dripping onto the wound. As it touches the victim, he screams like a gull being attacked.

"This casualty won't last long if we don't take him to the chopper zone," I hear a medic say.

"You know the chopper has priority head wounds,"

says his colleague.

"Up to you. Let's get him in the truck. By the time we get across town to the basketball court, they may have taken off again."

The victim's lips are moving. His breath is shaky, like he is afraid to take the last deep dive into death. I kneel on the sand and try to see his eyes through the swollen skin around his cheeks.

"My w...wife," he mouths, "and d...daughter..."

The soldiers are getting impatient. "Get off, scum! Do you want him to die?" I feel the stretcher move.

The man is looking at the boy beside me and his eyelids are flickering; he is trying to tell me something. I lean closer and his fingers touch mine. "Your... brother? My... daughter... find her... please."

I can't believe a western man would talk to me, let alone touch me. I nod; what can I do, he's dying. His breathing is getting shallower; I think this is it. His skin is so bloated that I can't tell if he's swallowing or choking. I lean as close as I dare, but I'm being hit and arms are trying to pull me away. The soldier is swearing, but I'm staring at the victim's lips; they're moving. He says one last word before his head falls back: "Kriss...sta."

Rough arms pull me away and I stumble; it's too late to avoid the kick. The boy runs over to me, crying. The soldiers look through me, like I'm seaweed to be trodden on. One is glancing at the little boy and beckoning him over, but he shrinks closer to my chest.

I put my arms around him. "He's with me."

+++

Papa will never again sail on a Kabang or dive through the coral reefs. His spirit is travelling to the west to be with our ancestors. Is he sailing in the clouds, looking down on the broken world, or is he far beyond us? Am I

99

lost from his thoughts, or does he still see me? Does he see Coral; does he even know if she's still alive? If my sister has gone to be with Papa, I will feel like flying there too.

I force my mind down to the earth, to the boy. He needs me. I take his hand and we walk back to The Green Turtle Hotel. Soldiers are guarding the entrance to Bay View, saying it is unsafe. If Rune were here, he'd know what to do. The boy is hungry and needs to rest. Usually at this time, Chef would be preparing dinner for the guests: delicious fruit arranged in colourful fans on clean white plates. I hope that the Laboon has not swept all the food into its jaws.

When I peer through the window, there is no-one in the lobby, just some tourists. As I'm not supposed to use the front door, I take the boy round to the kitchen entrance. The generator is humming, but no heat is coming from the electric oven and there are no red lights on the fridge.

We sludge through the muddy floor trying to avoid broken crockery. A man is cowering in the corner. Virote. Bloodshot eyes; no longer balls of fire. He slides across the mud and grabs my arm. I can feel him trembling. Suddenly he crumbles in front of me, babbling on about water and terror and blood. And Chaow.

"He was there, then he was gone. The water smashed through the windows and I ran." He shakes my arm. "I was serving breakfast. Fried prawns. I can still smell them. Now they've been sucked back into the sea." He lurches forward and grabs my shirt. "Fish Boy! You must know what to do, you live in the sea, don't you?"

Ignoring his words, I breathe deeply, like before a dive. Imagine gliding silently along the ocean floor touching soft fronds of trailing green weed. When I look up, Virote has collapsed into a chair. I always knew he was weak.

Free diving was all I ever wanted, until I met people like him and discovered how Moken are treated. Until I saw my Mama's cheek flaming like fire. I was young, playing on the beach. She had been selling shell necklaces in the snack shack, and I hoped we could buy some rice as I was hungry. But her hands were empty. She'd been told not to come back, as one of her necklaces had broken. I remember Mama telling Papa that she had seen this woman fiddling with it, then all the shells had slipped off the plaited twine. The woman turned into a viper and stung Mama, accusing her of destroying it. I've never forgotten and I never will.

I feel like spitting in his face like he did to me, but I take the boy outside. Need some fresh air.

A girl is standing in the shade of a surviving palm tree, glued to her cell phone. "I've already tried; no-one's telling us anything," she says. "Yes, she's here, but she's hurt... No, I feel so useless, all she wants is her dad, and what if he... Oh God..."

As she looks up, I see she's much older than I first thought.

"Can you help me; do you work here?" Her voice sounds like she's in a hurry, but she doesn't let me answer.

"My husband was out running; he was wearing a white top and red shorts...and he is six foot three, so you couldn't miss him." She waves her hands as she talks, trying to demonstrate his height. Then her hands clasp her face as she stares at me. "But it's been over eight hours and he hasn't come back."

An image of the injured man on the beach flashes into my mind. I screw up my eyes trying to recall if he was wearing red shorts, but if he had been, they had been stripped off by the power of the waves.

I hear the woman suck in a deep breath. "We've only been married four months!" She bites her lip, then exhales like a rush of wind. "What if something's happened to him? I have to find him!"

I don't know what to say. White people don't usually talk to me. I live on the edge of their world. Most people only notice me, to order me around. But the Laboon has loosened their tongues: this English woman is talking to me, as did the sick man on the beach.

Her floaty scarf is touching my bare chest. When I flinch, it brushes off like a fly. "I have to go," I say, taking the boy's hand. The woman suddenly cries out. Dropping his hand, I spin around. "What's wrong?"

She is staring at me. "Your back, it looks so painful. You should put something on that or it will get infected."

I shake my head. "It's fine. The boy needs help, not me. He's lost his family."

Her hand flutters to her chest. "He looks exhausted." She kneels, so her eyes are level with him. "What's your name?" He doesn't answer, but his fingers tighten around his toy car.

"My name is Jo," she says. Then she asks if he is hungry. The boy shrinks closer to me. Jo's hair falls around her face as she sighs. Then she pushes her shoulders back. "Never mind, I was just going to get some food." She smiles at the boy and looks at me. "Shall I find your brother something to eat?"

"He's not my brother," I explain for the second time that day. The boy is sticking to me like a limpet to a rock, but he accepts the sweets she takes out of her handbag. Then she offers me sweets. I can't believe it: a white woman is talking to me and I am being listened to like I am a real person with thoughts and ideas, not a blank palm leaf. She has asked my name, like I am important.

She leads us to the entrance, but the hotel is for

guests, not the likes of me. Plus, I am bare-chested and the manager would explode if he saw me. But the little boy won't go in without me. Jo tells us to wait, and the sun has hardly moved in the sky when she returns with a striped shirt, a pair of black trousers and a black tie. I know how to knot rope, but tying this is much more difficult. Jo stands behind me, then before I take another breath, it's done.

"Very smart." She stands back, looking up at me. Smoothing the tie down the centre of the shirt with my palm, I push back my shoulders. I feel like a different person, that Sky has been swept away. With Papa. Has the ocean torn away everyone I love? Everything I've ever known? I let the woman pull me into the future. I just hope it doesn't turn into a Laboon and destroy me.

We pass the dining room with white napkins and silver cutlery on the tables. When I notice a thin lady staring at my feet, I try to tuck my shoes under the hem of the trousers. Hope she won't tell the manager, or he'll grab my new shirt and drag me away. I'm floating in a new world, just keeping my head above the water. I hover behind Jo as she sits on a comfortable chair in the lounge. Pictures of dazzling beaches and fiery sunsets stare at me from the walls. The boy is holding my hand, but when Jo pats her chair, I lift him onto her lap.

The woman is round like a little puffer fish, but I don't think she has poison. She is letting the boy play with her bracelet, a shiny coil of silver. Her face is smiling, but her eyes are sad. I wonder what she's thinking. Maybe her dreams have died with the waves, because she has lost her husband. Perhaps she is swimming through the deep caves, unable to find her way back to the light? I know how she must be feeling.

When Virote enters the room, I shrink behind the armchair. He is holding a tray and doesn't notice me; the new clothes must be working. Suddenly, his eyes expand as if he's seen a ghost. His fins are up, but he can't kick me out, because Jo has invited me in here and I'm wearing a tie. He dumps the tray hard on the coffee table so the cups dance. He's still Stonefish, waiting to give a painful sting.

The drink is tasteless, but there are nice biscuits. Jo invites us to stay for dinner and says the boy and I can *"freshen up"* while we wait. I think she means wash, or use the toilet. I am bruised and filthy underneath the clothes, but she doesn't seem to mind. I should tell her I'm a garbage collector and go back to my chores, but the little boy is looking at me and I know I can't leave him. So I stay.

Her room is on the second floor. She suggests I use the bathroom in the corridor while she and the boy take turns in using her 'en-suite.' How can a bedroom have its own toilet? These people must be rich. The bathroom is shiny and I don't like to touch it. I step onto the cold white marble floor. There is a tap by the sink, so I twist it. Nothing. Pressing with my palm, I manage to get a dribble of water, so I twist my head, trying to put my face under. Instead, my chin hits the tap. "Ouch!"

My reflection stares at me. Brown wavy hair reaches my necklace on its black leather cord. I touch the beads, running my finger along the brown ones to the raised yellow bead, then along to the next one. Coral made it for me many moons ago. I stare into the glass imagining seeing my sister's smooth face instead of mine.

Where are you? I can't feel you any longer. I can't believe you've gone. You could do anything, be anyone. You could marry a foreigner and be rich, but instead you sell souvenirs and live where the mangroves meet the ocean.

Nothing happens when I turn the dial. Rune's

shower used to be a hot monsoon — almost as good as lying back on a hot rock with a waterfall splashing my face, cleansing me of bad spirits and refreshing my body. But this shower is dead; there is no water. My back is stinging and I'd love to rinse it. Twisting my head, I catch a reflection of a big purple bruise. No wonder it hurts.

There is a knock on the door. I hear Jo's voice. "Sorry, the water's still not on, I didn't realise." I pull on my clothes quickly. When Jo enters, she gives me a bottle of water to wash my face, then gently lifts my shirt and spreads some ointment on my back. She doesn't ask and I'm glad because I would have said no; and whatever she used feels cool and soothing.

"The whole place has stopped working," she says. "I don't know if the electricity will ever come on again." She sighs. "And now my step-daughter has disappeared. She's had a rough time, but I thought she might like to help with this little one." She looks at me, hands upturned, fingers apart. "I'm not very good with children, never had one of my own."

I kneel down beside the boy. He is holding the edge of the duvet in his fingers and twiddling the corner round and round his fingers. Grabbing a handful of the material, I tuck it around my face. "How do I look?" I ask, trying to make him smile. The boy's eyelids flicker and his lips curve upwards, then sink back. Then he starts driving his car along the edges of the wooden shapes on the floor like they are roads.

"Probably best to leave him for a while," I say, "he's in his own world right now."

Jo sighs. "I know all about that. I was in my own world for 16 years — and that's lonely, believe me." I murmur politely, hoping she'll stop talking, but I must have encouraged her, because she leans towards me. "I was engaged once before; he was in the forces... Tim was only 23 when he was killed by a landmine." I look at my hands, wishing I was somewhere else, but Jo grabs my arm. "We were getting married in two months. Instead we held his funeral."

I want the woman to stop talking, it's embarrassing. She is twisting a silver ring around her finger as she tells me that for a long time she felt numb. When she eventually met the man who would become her husband, he was still grieving for his dead wife. They bonded as she could understand his grief. She longed to make him smile again and when he did, she knew they could build a life together. But his daughter makes it difficult.

Jo grips her ring and sighs. "I don't think she likes me. Whatever I say, it's never right; I can never replace her mother and doesn't she make that clear! I try, but how do I know how to talk to a teenager, let alone one who doesn't want me there?"

I back away. "I should go."

She nods. "Sorry, I shouldn't have gone on like that, I don't normally do that. It's just..." Shaking her head, she follows me to the door. She writes a message for the boy's parents and asks me to leave it at reception. I am walking into the corridor when I hear little feet behind me and a hand reaches into mine.

"You want to come with me?" I ask. "Let's see if Rune is at reception, shall we?" I feel stronger holding the boy's hand. The young guy who carried the make-shift stretcher gives me a knowing nod as we pass in the lobby. As I place the note on the desk, I run my hand over the smooth wood; it's damp. We are still standing there, when the manager appears in his white jacket. When he shouts at me, the boy starts moaning. I'm told that I have no right to be touching one of the guests or upsetting them. I'm told to get outside where I belong. Then the manager pulls the limpet off me.

"Not go Marti, not go!" the little boy screams, stamping his foot. I can't believe it: he knows my name.

I take a pace towards him, but the manager steps in between us. The boy flings himself at the red faced man and kicks his shins. Now it's the manager's turn to scream.

An elderly man peers over the landing. "Is anything the matter?"

The manager's face stretches, but I know inside he's not smiling. "Nothing sir, everything's under control."

As the man leans forward, his glasses almost slip off his nose. "Well. if you're sure…I thought, perhaps, the little lad was…"

"Upset? Yes, his family are…" The manager's shoulders rise as he opens his hands to the ceiling. Taking his opportunity to be off the hook, the boy runs towards me.

Feeling protective, I kneel down so my head is level with his. "It's ok. This man will find Jo for you. She will look after you, as I'm not allowed."

The boy's lower lip sticks out. He glares at the manager through his eyelashes. "Nasty man!"

The manager turns as red as a lobster and he's breathing so hard I think he'll burst. "Who is this Jo and how do you know him?" he whispers through his teeth.

I shake my head. "She's a woman." His face turns purple — now I'll lose my job for sure. I quickly tell him that the lady is in Room 12 upstairs.

"I didn't think it was on the ground floor. I *do* know my hotel," he snaps. I keep my eyes level, although I feel like sliding to the floor. "Find her!" he snaps. I take a step forwards, but the boy is clinging onto my leg. The manager raises his eyes to the ceiling and growls: "Take that… kid with you. He's upsetting the guests — what's left of them." As we pass, he raises a sweaty armpit.

"You'd better be quick," he hisses. "Leave the kid with this *Jo*, then get outside in the muck where you belong."

The elderly man is walking down the stairs, so the manager's arms drop. He pretends to smile as he looks at me. "If you don't want to go home, you're welcome to stay here tonight." His mouth stretches, lifting his cheeks, but his eyes are hard. "You know where to sleep, I've offered you the place before." He leans towards me and whispers, "Got it?"

Under pressure, I agree. The boy's blue eyes start to water. "You'll be fine," I whisper. "Your parents will see the note and find you." As little hot fingers touch mine, a flashback hits me of Papa holding my hand when I was young. Sucking in my pain, I smile at the boy. "Jo will look after you tonight. I don't sleep in the hotel."

"Why?" I hear the boy's question, but he doesn't need to know. I explain I have a special place to sleep in as I work outside.

"Can I go there?"

"Not now. I'll take you back to Jo, then see you when new light touches the sky."

When the boy is safe in Room 12, I hurry outside. Car lights expose the thick mud blocking the shed door. I push it open and gasp at the mess. The mower has been thrown against the tools and a spade is sticking out of the wall. And everywhere is thick sticky mud. I crouch down and hug my chest, trying to protect the stripy shirt.

Need to blot out the pain. Mustn't think of Papa's body in the water, but his dead eyes keep staring into my mind. If only I hadn't argued. If only I hadn't told Coral I'd meet her in the snack shack. Can't stop seeing the huge black wave towering above the beach.

I go round and round, like a dog trying to catch his tail, wondering what happened to Coral. Wondering if the boy's family are still alive. If he will ever find them? The

Laboon has hurt so many, not just in this resort, but all along the coast, maybe the whole world.

18. Survival

KRISTA

Running back. c u in 10 mins. Love Dad xx. The text message keeps flashing around my mind — why hasn't he come back? I'm trying to visualise Dad sheltering in the hills, but he's running faster and faster along the beach with this massive wave about to swallow him. *No!* Forcing the image from my thoughts, I walk downstairs. Every minute I waste, is a minute further away from finding him.

I've stepped into chaos. How is it possible the waves could get that big and pour over the seawall? I still can't believe it. Was Christmas just yesterday? People were having fun, enjoying their holidays. The hotel grounds were immaculate with perfect smooth grass. No rubbish. The sea was calm and as blue as it is now — like a giant hand has smoothed it over after a battle of the Greek gods. Poseidon unleashed his fury, then sank under the waves, leaving the resort in chaos. Debris is strewn over the lawn; where's the pool? Thinking about water makes me feel dizzy, so I grab the cracked door frame for support.

I'm trying to walk to our bungalow, but a mass of rubble is blocking the way. My arm is aching when I get back to the hotel room, and my body feels like I've been forced to do a whole day of star-jumps and sit-ups. I've got a splitting headache; all I want to do is crash out, but there's this little kid sitting on the bed running a toy car up and down the pillow. I mean, come on, it's not a crèche!

The en-suite door creaks open and my step-mum walks into the room. When her face lights up, guilt hits me in the stomach. My tongue suddenly feels in the way and there's a lump in my throat. I feel so bad about the things I said and want to apologise. *I'm sorry, Jo, I'm really sorry!* But it's like I'm trying to swallow a pill and just can't do it. Whenever I try to say something, the words swirl around my mind and don't come out.

So we don't talk about it. I glance at the little boy, then back at my step-mum.

"I'm taking care of him..." —Jo nods at the toddler — "...just for now." The boy's eyes are blue like mine. He's cute, but I hope he doesn't need a nappy, because I haven't got a clue.

My step-mum sits in the only armchair, so I perch next to the little boy. I hear her clearing her throat. "Where have you been?"

"Outside."

"I was worried. How is your arm? Your head? Are you feeling any better?

"Fine." We're like strangers talking in a dentist's waiting room. There's nothing to tell: all I did was wander around for a bit. I couldn't even see our bungalow.

"Are you sure? You seemed so stressed before. Can I fetch you a bottle of water?"

She's not blaming me; she seems really concerned. I can feel my face flushing and know that my breathing is getting faster. I'm choking up. Finally I manage to speak, but in a whisper. "I'm sorry."

Jo holds up her hand to stop me. "There's no need to

say anything. You were worried about your dad – I am too." When she smiles, I feel like bursting into tears.

Perhaps Jo knows how I'm feeling, for she stands up and reaches for her mobile. "I'll try to get a connection downstairs," she tells me in a whisper. "I want to contact the police about the boy." Her eyebrows crease together. "You can entertain him for a few minutes, can't you?" I nod, but I don't know anything about kids; I'm nearly sixteen with my arm in a sparkly sling.

My head starts spinning as I lean over too quickly. There I was, thinking the boy might pee on the bed and instead, I'm going to puke all over it. Breathing heavily, I tuck my knees up until the feeling goes away.

The boy is now sitting cross legged on the floor, like we used to do as infants in school. I wonder what's happened to his parents, poor kid. He is tracing the edges of the wooden blocks which fit together like a jigsaw puzzle, then staring at his hands. His breathing is getting faster and ragged, like he is going to cry.

"Sorry about that." I pat the bed. "Do you want to sit back up here?" His lip stops trembling and he climbs onto the bed, so close that I can feel the warmth of his body. He leans against me and for a second, I tense. Then I remember cuddling up to Mum when I was four or five, asking if I could have a brother or sister for my birthday. She laughed and said you couldn't order a child like a parcel from a department store

A little hand reaches up and touches my hair. Perhaps I remind him of someone. I put my good arm around him. "What's your name?"

"Harry."

"Right, Harry, you can help me. I need to write a note so Dad knows where I am. My step-mum has written, but he'll want to hear from me too, won't he?" Harry starts pulling a corner of the duvet and I smile. "We

112

can't write on that!"

I look around the room. In the welcome pack, I find a pencil with writing around the side that I don't understand, and lots of leaflets. I choose one advertising turtles hatching, hundreds of tiny shapes running down the beach. When the pen doesn't work on the shiny paper, I pick up a paper napkin and rest it on a drinks tray. "Let's write a note for your parents as well."

Harry jumps onto the floor, leaving his toy on the bed. "Me not write."

"Sorry, of course you can't."

He holds out his hand. "Me draw." I tear the napkin in half and give Harry the pencil. He draws a half moon shape, then scribbles so hard that the paper is tearing.

"Is that the wave?" I ask. The pencil stops digging into the napkin, but the boy doesn't look at me.

"Harry, is that water? Were you in the water?" The pencil starts moving again. Four stick men with circles for hands and long spiky fingers.

"Are they your family?" He touches the stick men and a tear falls onto the drawing. The tears flow faster, blotting out the people. What's he seen? Suddenly, Harry scrunches the drawing and throws the pencil across the room. We both watch it spinning. When it stops, I lift him into my arms, and we snuggle in the armchair. "Shush, it will be alright, I'm sure we'll find them," I say, hoping that it is true.

When Harry has stopped crying, I wriggle out of the chair. He watches while I press the creases out of his drawing. "There, you can hardly tell. We'll take it downstairs and as soon as your parents see it, they will know it's from you." I write Harry's name on the napkin, then compose a message to Dad.

Hi Dad,

I know you said you'd only be 10 min's, and timing isn't your thing, but all day is a bit extreme! I bet you ran into the mangroves to escape the tsunami and you're getting lots of research for your lectures! You'll be having a BBQ up in the hills with some villagers, if I know you, getting to know the local customs.

Please come back soon.
Lots of love, Kris xxx

In the lobby, I grab a postcard and write a large sign on the back: *Professor Robert Tunstall.* There's no sign of the little guy with the bad leg. He was nice — I hope he survived. I approach a lady and ask where I should leave the messages, but she is obsessively scratching a fingernail and doesn't look up. I exchange a glance with a lad who is chewing gum, then my stomach makes a loud grumble.

"Let's find something to eat," I say to Harry, trying not to show any embarrassment. I prop up our letters on the reception desk and we're walking towards the tables when I hear a familiar voice and see Jo running towards us. "There you are! I was so worried. I thought you'd run off again." Her hair is worse than usual — she must be really stressed. I try to calm her down by asking if she's hungry.

My step-mum insists on choosing the table right in the middle of the room, when I wanted a quiet place in the corner. The stick lady is sitting opposite the young guy with a scruffy beard and a blonde ponytail. I recognise the couple sitting by the window; the man is clutching a wad of banknotes, scrunching them in his fist. If he doesn't want them, I'll have them. I ask Jo to pass the menu, then wish I hadn't, because she keeps stressing

114

about the rising number of deaths.

I'm trying to slide noodles down my throat, only to be told that Banda Aceh has been obliterated like an atomic bomb has exploded. It's too big to get my head around. I know each death is a tragedy, but right now, all I can think of is Dad lying in the darkness needing help. *No, he's not dead, I won't let him be.*

Suddenly, the young couple unstick their faces from the window, grab their cases and race to the door. Outside, a car horn is hooting. Wish I was going with them.

Harry and I grab the couple's spot by the window and we watch them throwing their bags into the car boot. Car lights look like red eyes glaring in the darkness. There are no street lamps and no signs lit up along the road. It's dark except for twinkling lights from hotels on higher ground and the occasional torch bobbing along.

Jo joins us and we eat by candlelight. Usually I like candles, but the flickering light casts spooky shadows like waves. If the water comes back, which way is the best way out of here? There are two windows and two doors. What if I choose the wrong one and water bursts in on us? We'd have no chance. It's like supermarket queues: I always choose the wrong one.

Excited voices outside. Harry's face lights up. A few minutes later, a group bursts into the room. There are five of them: a middle aged couple and their children and granny, maybe. The dad sweeps his gaze around the room. "What on earth's happened to the resort? What was it: a hurricane?"

"Don't you know, where have you been all day?" asks my step-mum.

The man skims his cap onto a table. "Out sailing." I hear these gasps go round the room and people lean towards him. The man rests his hands on the back of a chair, while his wife gathers her children around her like chicks.

Everybody is staring at the family now, including me. "You mean you were out in it?" I ask. "It's not possible…"

"We didn't get any snorkelling in," says the dad, ruffling his son's hair. "And now…" he points out of the dark window, "we never will. It looks like the whole place has been decimated."

We lean towards him like he's a magnet. Jo is the first to speak. "Thailand has just experienced the biggest earthquake in history: 9.1 on the Richter scale!"

"9.3!" the long-haired guy shouts through a mouthful of gum.

"It triggered a huge tsunami," my step-mum continues as if he hadn't spoken. "It hit all around the Indian Ocean. The News has reported massive devastation in over ten countries and reports keep coming in. I don't see how you survived?"

The man nods. "That explains it. We were driven back out to sea for hours. Tossed around like toys."

"But the waves were massive, surely you would have been swallowed up?"

"We were lucky. Another fishing boat shot out of the mist and we heard shouting, 'Go out to sea, big wave coming!' Then we saw the white crest of this giant wave."

"I thought it was a ship," says the teenage lad. "We headed straight for it, went way up, then down this scary drop. I thought we were going to Davy Jones' locker!"

"Yes and you were nearly sick." says the man, smiling.

"Your dad *was* sick afterwards!" says the granny. "Very sick!" They laugh, which seems weird when so many people have died out there.

"Not quite the trip we planned! When we left early

this morning, the water was smooth, like water in a tank, but then it got rougher and looked dark and sandy through the glass viewing deck."

"Don't forget the fish, Dad!" The boy turns to us. "It was weird; all these fish were jumping on the surface. The captain said they were deep sea fish and he'd never seen anything like it."

"And dolphins," says the mum, speaking for the first time. "Hundreds of them, heading for deeper water."

"Did you catch any of it on camera?"

The dad presses his chin on his chest as he looks at his son. "Someone dropped the camera overboard."

"It wasn't my fault. We were in a tsunami!"

He rests one hand on his son's shoulder, then sweeps his other hand to indicate the rest of us. "So what happened to you lot?"

"This mighty wind hit our chalet…"

"Rattling the windows and shaking the palm trees. The overhead lights went out, then all this water roared at us…"

"Can't they put the lights back on?" The stick lady's voice cuts into the crowd. She is clutching her shiny handbag on her lap and her pointed shoes are touching at the toes. "If we're trapped here all night in the dark, I won't be able to stand it!"

"I'm sure we'll be given candles." The ponytail guy is trying to make her feel better.

"What use are candles?" The stick lady shakes him off and pushes her chair back. "I need proper light and I need a phone. This trip was supposed to be celebrating my Ruby Wedding!" Her body is gearing up like she's going to sneeze. "We came here on our honeymoon and again on our Silver Wedding, but if I can't find my husband, this might be my last trip to Thailand!" Then she's sobbing, huge breaths draining her lungs. It's embarrassing and frightening; grown-ups don't do that.

"Some people will never come back." The words hang over us and people start to drift away. I realise I'm so tired I can hardly stand. A chair scrapes and Jo offers to help me back to my room.

"I'm fine," I tell her, then stumble against the table leg. I let my step-mum put her arm around me until I regain my balance.

But my mind won't stay still. I lie back on the bed, trying to assess the escape route. I work out hundreds of different scenarios, but it's impossible to escape, even in my imagination. My body is so tense that I flinch whenever a door slams, or someone talks in the corridor. I wish we had never come. I wish Dad was here. I wish I could rewind the day and tell him not to go out running. We could catch a plane tomorrow and get out of here and go back to normal. Except there is no normal anymore.

PART 3 – AFTERMATH

The waves have flooded over all of us:
brown or white, Islander or Land lover.
The wind kisses our cheeks,
whether we are born on a boat and have no
possessions or education;
or a rich western girl with knowledge and
beauty and golden hair that flies in the wind.

– Marti

19. Dead People Walking

27th December 2004

MARTI

When light creeps through the shed door, I wake. I ache all over and smell bad. Dried mud is sticking to my clothes as if I've been wallowing like an elephant.

Pushing open the door, I blink. An aeroplane line shoots into the sky, with a coiled smoke trail behind it like a giant eel. It grows into clouds that expand and are touched with white gold. They are glinting in the sun, while down here bodies are stinking in the heat and flies are everywhere.

Jo told me there is a Missing Person's Board at the temple where people have left messages. If the spirits are with me, the manager won't notice if I sneak out. But he'll smell me coming if I don't find somewhere to wash.

The air is hot when I get back from the ocean. It was difficult wading through the rubble. My back was stinging from the salty water, but when I ducked my head under, it felt so refreshing and wonderful to be clean again. The sun dried my body — it didn't take long.

The coast road is busy. People escaping. But there is

no music. No laughter. The Laboon has stolen most of the shop signs, and any canopies that survive hang like shrouds for the dead. When I reach the crossroads, an old woman stands as if she is lost. We all are. A man is wading through the sludge holding a woman in his arms, her head flopping. His face is like stone, eyes straight ahead as if he is sleepwalking. I follow him up the hill, and we merge into the flow of people. Some people are silent, but others are wailing, questioning, screaming.

A gong echoes on and on. Tall white pillars stretch like great tree trunks holding up the temple roof. Monks in sunset coloured robes are chanting a mantra. I follow the group inside, then wish I hadn't. There are bodies, many bodies. They are covered in white sheets, some with fixed expressions and twisted limbs. Or no limbs. It is very hot and many of the people wandering around are holding cloths over their mouths. Flies are buzzing, drawn by the smell of death. I gag and clamp my hand over my mouth.

The smell is overpowering. Sick jumps into my throat and I spit into the dust. It lies here for a moment, like the people are lying there. There are so many, shrouded in white, tied up like hostages...except they're dead. They may be rich or poor, but they are the same in death.

And one could be Coral. If I see her, death will be final. *No!* Coral didn't come to the snack shack, I would have felt it, I would have known. When my sister threw the pebble, it didn't reach the waves, so that means the spirits are keeping her safe and the dark water didn't sweep over her. But... if the pebble was lying on the sand, maybe this means Coral was still on the beach when the Laboon roared towards us?

Not Coral, please!

My sister wants to be with Cloud; I have seen the

way they look at each other. She has everything to live for. She may only live in a bamboo hut, but that doesn't mean she hasn't got dreams. I won't let myself believe Coral is just a body. She is light and laughter; she is beauty and freedom. She cannot die.

I try to tell myself the bodies are like fish, once flapping in the sea, now caught in a net; that death is normal, it happens to all of us. But I can see a little white bundle lying on its side, knees bent. No-one deserves to end their life like that. Kids should be playing on the beach, not tied in body bags, just a number, no name.

Wiping stray dribbles of sick off my chin, I lean against a pillar trying to breathe fresh air. Other people are wandering along the rows — if they can do it, so can I. So why are my toes anchored to the ground?

Feet trample past: muddy boots, dusty sandals, colourful flip flops, even some high heels. Each one is alive — near so many dead. Black, brown, sandy coloured, orange, black, sandy... I keep seeing the same sand coloured pointed shoes. My gaze follows the figure; the man is wearing a checked blue shirt over grey trousers and a cap the colour of a storm cloud. He stops at the edge of the temple, then turns and walks back. He keeps turning his head to look at people. He must be searching for someone.

He follows a mother and child to a long chart: numbers of the dead and injured and those who have disappeared, are listed under different columns. What does it matter if they are Thai or foreign, they are all people. Another board has bits of paper flapping in the breeze: messages from people to their loved ones. The mother reaches into her bag, pulls out a photo and pins it onto the board. The family stand there, welded together like one person and I know they have lost someone. When they walk away, I see the man's finger touching the same picture. Perhaps he knows the person.

He is standing there watching people. And I stand there watching him. Wave after wave of people walk up to the board, some crying and some hugging each other. Others cover their faces and walk up the steps and step between the pillars. I can't wait any longer; I have to face the bodies.

+++

KRISTA

"They are taking the bodies to the Buddhist Temple." My step-mum speaks as if she is a newsreader: no expression, just facts. But by the way she is clenching her hands, it's obvious that she's trying to stop herself from breaking into pieces. Her dress swishes as she sits next to me. She moves the cutlery and places her hands on the table, then keeps twisting her wedding ring and giving me little glances. "How are you feeling? Did you get much sleep? I don't mind admitting I was worried sick. I kept thinking what if the waves come back and we're all in the dark and we can't see..."

I don't want to make her feel worse. She doesn't need to know that my arm throbs when I move my shoulder and I'm shattered because I couldn't sleep for ages. When I finally nodded off, Poseidon rose out of the frothing black waves and kept attacking me with his trident.

"I'm so pleased you're feeling better." Jo is trying to smile, but her lips are trembling; I can tell she's close to tears. "Could you look after the boy for a couple of hours while I check the Missing Person's board?" Her knuckles stand out as she clenches her fist. "I'm sure he's not there, but ..." Her voice trails off and I don't answer.

"Krista?" She touches my hand. "You have heard

me, haven't you? Will you look after the child?"

"His name is Harry."

She stares at me. "How do you know?"

"He told me."

My step-mum kneels down next to the boy, but he's in a different world, driving his car around a napkin. She holds his hand still, forcing him to look at her. "Is Harry really your name?" When he nods, I can't help feeling kind of special that he told me first. Jo shakes her head as if she can't understand why he told me, not her.

"Right...well, do you want to stay here or come with me?" She makes it sound like one of those package holiday trips. Harry looks at Jo then back at me. Her lips turn up at the corners. "I think he wants both of us, don't you, Harry. How about we write another note for your family, then we'll pin it on the board." She's trying to be cheerful, but hope is running out. I've spent hours waiting for Dad to show up and it's the worst feeling ever. He only went for a run, he said he'd be back in ten minutes, he promised.

Harry crashes his car into a spoon, again and again like he's trying to run it over. He's so young, he must be lost and frightened. I push my chair back and stand up. "Let's go, then." I whisper the next part to Jo, so Harry can't hear. "But I'm not going to look at bodies."

A rubbish dump has been tipped all around the hotel. We walk slowly:

1. because there is so much debris,

2. because my feet are hurting,

3. because Harry stops every time we see another western man or woman. When he looks at their faces, his little lip trembles Poor kid.

A woman approaches us in a torn dress, dragging her bare right leg behind, then pulling it stiffly forward with her right hand. Dark bruises cover it like black paint. I glance at my arm and feel a bit embarrassed that I have a nice clean bandage and a sling. The bleeding has stopped, although it throbs if I move it too quickly.

Zombies are wandering the streets, dead people walking. Both lanes are full with taxis and motorbikes and cars and pick-up trucks: a mass exodus. The air is full of sirens and whistles and horns blaring. My music teacher would love this cacophony of noise, he's really alternative. Last term, we had a project creating music out of recycled stuff like bottles and tin cans.

We're walking up a hill and I'm sweating — we all are. Heat is blasting me on my neck and the backs of my legs. Harry is clutching my hand and my step-mum is encouraging him we'll find his family really soon, but she sounds too cheerful, like she's really trying to convince herself. We don't even know what Harry's family look like — he won't tell us anything.

When we reach a large, imposing building, Jo falls silent. I've seen scenes like this, earthquakes in China or famines in Africa, but you can always turn off the TV. This disaster is right here and I can't believe I'm living in one. Every step I take, it gets worse. The smell is horrible. Flies are settling on the white sheets and flying out of the edges.

If I step inside the temple, I will see real-live dead people. They are lying in neat rows, lining the walls. Some are covered in sheets and some are in body bags tied up with string. I see a monk lighting candles and placing them next to bowls in front of a statue of the Buddha. What good will that do: these are people who had breakfast, who got dressed for the beach, who were looking forward to another day in paradise. That never came.

I cuddle Harry close to my chest, trying to hide his face. The plastic car is digging into my ribs – I wish he'd left it at the hotel. Suddenly Jo clutches my arm and when I peep over Harry's head, I see her eyes darting from side to side. "Look, there's a TV crew. I'm going over to see if they know what's happening." A reporter is snooping around asking questions like we're some kind of side-show. It's alright for the media: they just fly down on a helicopter, then back to safety. Leaving us stranded.

My step-mum marches over to the camera, jostling a man with a long black beard. "Excuse me, I have a little boy here who needs to find his family." The man blocks her, so she waves me over with Harry. "Can't anyone help? I've found this little English boy, we need to get him to the British Embassy!"

The bearded man looks at her as if she is mad. "Do you think a diplomat is going to fall out of thin air? We all need help, not just you."

"But the child isn't mine..."

"Look, I'm sorry, lady, but I'm the one being interviewed here, not you." He glares at my step-mum.

The reporter adjusts her glasses and looks at the camera. "There are extra flights laid on, but some people are too traumatized to escape the chaos." She directs the microphone at the man. "Are you waiting to fly out, or have you decided to complete your holiday?"

He rolls his eyes. "My wife may be dead and you're talking about completing my holiday?"

"I'm so sorry for your loss. Perhaps you'd rather not be interviewed?"

"No, the world needs to hear this. We need help out here."

The reporter leans forward. "So, you were caught in the tsunami?"

"We were in our bungalow," the man answers. "I woke late, we'd been drinking till the early hours, you see." The reporter nods and motions for him to continue.

"The room was shaking violently. I saw a dark wall of water exploding around the side of the bungalow in front of ours."

"How high would you estimate the wave was?"

The man points half-way up the stone pillar. "It was huge and speeding towards us." He stops and I can see white all around his eyes.

"And?"

He stares straight into the camera. "I looked at the woman I loved. That was the last time I saw her."

The reporter is talking to the viewers now, saying how devastating the tsunami was and how the number of dead is steadily rising. "It could take a long time to identify some of the victims, and the risk of disease increases in temperatures of over 35% degrees with flies everywhere." She shakes her hair, as if flies are attacking her personally. I see the cameraman give the thumbs up sign and the man drifts into the crowd.

Jo nudges me. "Let's go."

I've always dreamed of being on TV, but that was in a different life. I follow my step-mum to the noticeboard stretching along the side of the building. So many photos. Names and addresses. Messages. Begging their relatives to be alive. A little girl stares at me from a photo; she only looks about ten. She's smiling, sitting in a paddling pool. I hope so much that she's still alive.

Perhaps Dad has left a message for us. He might be looking for us, so he'll find my note when he returns. I move along the board, but I'm still holding Harry. He's getting twisty and holding his tummy — bet he's desperate for a pee. I put him down quickly and he toddles off after Jo somewhere. I keep scanning the bits of paper, hoping to see a message from Dad, but when I get to the end of the board, I have this horrible feeling that I'll never see him again.

A man coughs. He's standing a few feet away and he's got shades on — but I'm sure he's staring at me. My gaze falls to his tan pointed shoes, tapping in the dust. He takes a step towards me, then stops and taps his foot again. Then he slowly lifts off his shades, watching me the whole time. *Freaky.* He raises his navy blue cap, then squashes it down on his cropped hair. I'm getting out of here.

Heavy breathing. My heart starts hammering, but it's not him. Jo is running towards me, red in the face. "Krista, there you are! Where's Harry?"

"He was following you… I thought you were taking him to the loo."

Her neck stretches and her chin juts forward. "What? No! Where is he?"

"It's not my fault!" I shout, feeling scared.

"You were looking after him!"

I haven't seen The Woman really angry before; I know she's worried, but I am too; there's no need to take it out on me. I glance to my right and left, but I can't see the Harry. Or that man.

She starts flapping, calling Harry's name. Then a child screams. We look at each other, shouting at the same time: "Harry!" We run around the other side of the board. To see the creepy man holding Harry in his arms.

Jo rushes forward. "Oh thank you, thank you, we didn't know where he'd gone. I thought my step-daughter had him, but…"

The man smiles. "You have a lively son and a very pretty stepdaughter," he says in English, with the faint trace of an accent. He lifts Harry into Jo's arms, but his eyes are fixed on me.

"Let's go," I say, striding ahead. Why is she still talking to him? I risk a glance behind me and notice he is taking a little card out of his jacket pocket. My step-mum is clasping it in both hands and nodding like a toy dog in a car window. Weird.

"Harry needs the toilet; we have to go now!" I shout. The man looks at me and winks. Jo says something to him, then walks towards me cuddling Harry.

As I clutch her arm, her eyes grow moist. "What's brought this on?"

I feel like bursting in tears. "Can we go now?"

She smiles, then looks at Harry. "After we've found a toilet for this young man." Harry is wriggling so much he looks like a break dancer. I agree to meet them by the main entrance. Need to stay where there are lots of people. I can't see the man, but I have a feeling that he is still watching.

+++

MARTI

I've done it. I've lifted the sheets and looked at the faces. Some looked peaceful like they were asleep; others like a giant shark was about to swallow them alive. That was the worst thing I have ever done.

But I didn't see Coral or Rune. My sister must have decided not to sell her necklaces this morning because the ocean didn't give enough shells. Of course: that's it. She will be safe with Cloud. And my friend will be somewhere helping people. Rune is a survivor. He has coped with a twisted leg all his life — polio I think he calls it — so he must have survived the Laboon. I try to convince myself, but I can still smell the stench of bodies.

Resting my back against the temple wall, I tell myself I'm not sinking. I am swimming with angelfish, they are beautiful. I take a deep breath and open my eyes.

Then I see her — the girl from the hotel. I know it's her straight away, even though her hair is tangled like

129

knotted seaweed. She keeps looking over her shoulder and her eyes are wide, like she's scared. I wonder if she is looking for someone. I'd love to smooth her hair down her back and make her smile. I want to talk to her, but I what can I say? *I am so glad you weren't swept up in the waves? Are you alone? Can I help?* She would think I was dangling a hook, trying to catch her.

As I'm watching, a short plump woman walks towards the girl, carrying a child with light coloured hair. It's Jo and the little boy I rescued. The English girl must be Jo's step-daughter! But why is the girl running to hug her; Jo said her step-daughter was like a dark cloud when she was around?

The little boy wriggles in Jo's arms: he's seen me! I smile and lift my arm to wave, but Jo bends her neck and starts stroking the boy's hair so I can't see his face. The girl says something to her and they walk down the path. My hand falls like a sail with no wind. I'm so stupid! I wanted to see the little lad smile at me, to know he's alright. But he's with English people who can look after him now. And the girl would never look at a sea gypsy, I need to forget her.

I will go to our village and make sure my family are safe. I have to tell them about Papa. But how can I? Mama would shrink into herself like a dry sponge. A dead sponge. Moken don't drown, we learn to swim before we can walk. The ocean is our playground.

A deep breath lifts my chest. The manager expects me to clean up the grounds; it will take many tides before the sea of rubbish has gone. But I can't stay. If the manager doesn't like it, I'll quit. Life is more than work; life is family and I'm going to find mine.

20. Searching

28th December 2004

KRISTA

I'm going insane! Can't stay cooped up in the hotel while my step-mum trawls round the hospitals. She said someone has offered to help her search, so she wants me to be here in case Dad comes back.

I was awake half the night. The moon was shining through one end of the thin curtains, and when I next noticed, it had sailed to the far side. I considered tiptoeing over to the window, but I didn't want to wake Harry. Then I tried to imagine the moon shining on Dad, but it started to roll faster and faster until it reached the other side of the world. When I tried to force the moon to come back, it just rolled out of the sky.

She's standing right in my face. "I'm not waiting any longer, Krista. I can't get through on the phone, so I'm hiring a taxi and going straight there." She slides a picture out of her purse. "I'm taking this photo of Rob to put up in the hospital. When the medical staff see it, they'll recognise him and let me know where he is."

"You can't!" I stare at the photo. Dad is smiling at me. Dad in his scuba gear wading onto a beach in Cornwall, his hair blowing in the breeze, his face alive with laughter. He had just caught a crab in his boots and it was so funny.

I'm not letting The Woman pin Dad onto a board with dead people. I won't let him be another one of their statistics, one of the bodies pulled out of the sea. But she isn't listening; she is sliding Dad's photo back in her bag. "I'm sorry, Krista, really I am, but it's only a photo. If it brings him back, it's worth it. We can get another photo, but you can't get another father."

"So why are you trying to be my mother?"

As soon as I say it, I know I shouldn't have, but it's too late. It's like pressing Send, when I should have hit Delete. The Woman's face snaps shut and I feel Dad slipping away from me as she walks across the room. She takes Harry's hand and opens the door. She doesn't slam it; I almost wish she would.

If Dad's smiling face was pinned on a board, that would make him dead. What's the point in consulting me? People often say teenagers are rebellious and do their own thing, but it's adults who always do what they want, and kids have no rights. Well, if The Woman won't listen, I'm going to the beach to find Dad. He might be hurt. I can't just stay here and do nothing.

I look at the suitcase. It looks at me. I swallow nervously. *Be prepared!* Dad's motto comes into my head — he used to be a scout. Sighing, I pick up the sports socks. I wish I'd taken my step-mum's advice. My heels kept sliding in the man's trainers on the way to the temple and now I've got blisters as well as cuts. Holding the sock with my right hand, I wriggle my foot inside, lodging it against my other leg. Then I slide off the scarf-sling, but by the time I've managed to tie the laces, my arm is throbbing again. I'd rather not wear the sparkly sling, but I guess I'll have to. It was really embarrassing at the Temple when that freaky man stared at it. And me.

After a long drink, I stuff three packets of jelly beans into the green rucksack I find at the bottom of the case. The guy sure does likes kids' sweets. I chew some pink ones for an energy boost, pick up a fresh bottle of water and slide it into the side compartment of the bag. For a moment, I think of Harry. Maybe I should have gone with him and Jo. She's worried sick about Dad, so why did I have to be so mean?

Since we've been sharing the same room, it's like we've become a sort of family. My step-mum may have kept me awake half the night, tossing and turning in the single bed, but I know it's because she's terrified that Dad must have drowned. So am I. But I'm not going to let myself believe that – I'd crack up if I did. First Jo said she was too hot and threw off the sheet, wafting sweat in my direction; then when she eventually fell asleep, she started snoring so loudly I thought she'd wake up the whole hotel.

This morning, she looked stressed, but she still took time to play an imaginary game with Harry. Once, when he wasn't watching, I saw her looking at him with a sad expression and I think she knows his family are never coming back. Or perhaps she's thinking of herself — maybe she's always wanted her own child.

Slipping the rucksack over my good shoulder, I look at the room one last time. Soon I am walking across the foyer into bright sunlight. Diggers are clearing the paths, so walking is getting a little easier. I hear a siren. As the ambulance rushes past, I think of my step-mum searching hospital wards with Harry and know I should have told her where I'm going. Then I think of Dad running to the mangroves, so that's where I'm heading.

Telephone poles lie tangled together like a game when you twist the sticks and they fall at random angles. Except these aren't matchsticks, they are massive. It's hard to avoid getting splinters from all the wood. I climb over twisted metal, half eaten chairs and shredded bags. Then stop, because a kid's koala bear is peeping out of the mud. The material feels hard and stiff and it looks sad lying in my hands. I wipe off the mud on the smooth edge of a fridge randomly sitting on the pavement, then sit the koala on top. It is only a toy, but a child must have loved it once.

There is enough wood here to last a lifetime of bonfires. Like a giant has scooped up the whole resort then dumped it from the sky, landing in a jumbled heap stretching right along the shore. By the time I reach the beachfront, the trainers are scuffed and clogged with stinking sludge, but I'm glad of the socks as they keep out most of the grit. Everything is a total mess. The pretty pink and red bushes have been stripped, only grey stalks remaining.

Then I see the holiday bungalows: roofs torn off, no windows or doors, just empty shells. How could the waves get that big, that manic? Why? Somewhere in this chaos, I hung up mini decorations and we wished each other a Merry Christmas. The lounge, with its panoramic view of the sea, has caved in. The plastic reindeer that I strung up over the blind must have been tossed into the waves.

And Dad's Christmas present. If only he'd worn it... It was neon yellow, one of those visibility ones he likes. I spent three weeks' pocket money on the running jacket and he looked really pleased when he unwrapped it. *Why didn't you wear it? I'll never ask for pocket money again if only you're alive; if only I can find you.*

We'd only just arrived, hardly unpacked. After looking around the market and eating, we had a fun evening playing charades. Dad did this crazy impersonation of an elephant and Jo and I guessed in a millisecond, but he was trumpeting so loudly that we kept him acting for ages! Then my step-mum tried to do an impression of a turtle. Dad guessed at once, then dived onto the floor and did this flipper thing like a street dancer gone wrong. It was hilarious.

Running back. c u in ten mins. Love Dad xx.

My hands turn into fists, happy memories crushed. *Where are you?* I lean over the sea wall. Total devastation. Crushed. Twisted. Torn. Smashed. The café is the only structure left standing. My heart pounds. Roaring monster waves smash into me. I dig my toes into the front of the trainers until my mind stops swaying. Mustn't think about the water. Mustn't think about the waitress. Mustn't think of the dead man's eyes.

Instead, I focus on a crowd of people kneeling near the shore. They've found something. Or someone. Two men lift a body, one clasping the legs and the other, the shoulders. Its head tips back. I bite my lip and look away, to where the coast road starts to climb the hill.

It's hard work, forging a path through the debris. When the sun hits a piece of metal it almost blinds me. Why didn't I think of bringing the man's sun hat? I'm using my good arm to help me balance while I clamber over rubble. It's hard to find a foothold and I keep misjudging; I've got several more scratches on my legs. For the first time ever, I wish I was wearing longer shorts. The pretty white blouse is already filthy, no chance of staying clean. It reminds me of the dirt clinging to houses built next to railway lines, but at least it shields my body from the sun and hides my bikini top.

The buildings look small now, and the coast road has disappeared into the forest. When I hear voices, I let them float into the wind. I'll walk as far as the headland and if Dad isn't on the beach, I'll find him in the mangroves. I try not to think of the creepy branches rising out of the water. I'll find him, I know I will.

My arm is heavy, aching with every step. I tripped on a rock and now the front of one trainer is flapping and sand is gritting up my toes — so much for bringing the socks! My feet sting like needles are jabbing into me, but I refuse to stop.

It's so hot. There was a whole stack of bottles in the room — why didn't I take more? I wish the sea was fresh water that you could drink. So much water, yet people are dying of thirst. And how can it be so calm? It's impossible it was rearing up and destroying everything, just yesterday. Or was it the day before? I can't remember.

Can't go on. My feet are killing me. Burning. Nothing to drink. Need fresh water. Mangroves? So far away. Trees keep disappearing. Where is the beach? Can't see anything. Just white. And grey. And white.

21. Wisdom

MARTI

The sun is high in the sky. Splinters of light hit me through the trees. Far below, mangroves dig into the ocean between the bays. I'm following the path around the headland where undergrowth has been pressed down.

As I head towards the lagoon, it is clear that the Laboon has not spared us. One of the huts still has walls and waves are lapping around the stilts, but the others lie like felled trees. We don't own much, but even that has been sucked away. Gone are the clothes drying on the wooden railings. Gone is the palm mat Mama wove for us to lie on and the coconut shell I hollowed out to hold rice. Gone are the fishing hooks and spears Papa once used and the model Kabang that Grandad is crafting. Petal's shell collection has also been stolen by the sea. She loves stringing little shells together, copying Mama and Coral.

Where are you all? It feels like a rope is tightening around my ribs, crushing me. I take a bottle from my bag and liquid floods my chest. Wiping the sweat off my face, I slot the bottle back on top of the food Jo gave me this morning. I think she felt sad that I had slept in the shed.

The posh stripy shirt was a dirty mess, but she wasn't angry at me – just at the manager. The boy didn't mind either: he ran towards me, dropping his toy car, and I held out my arms to catch him. He squealed as I swung him on top of my shoulders. A moment without pain. A moment to treasure. Jo told me his name is Harry and she is making enquiries about his parents. When I told her I was returning to my family, so we could honour the dead, she said *"I'll be two seconds!"* She came back with some fruit, a bag of rice, some cooking oil and several bottles of water. Very kind.

A shout from the shoreline alerts me, but no-one's there. The voice calls again, then I spot a dark head bobbing above the waterline. A figure swims towards the shore and wades out. He scoops the water off his face. I wave and he climbs over the debris. We meet on a bare patch of sand, an island in the rubble.

Grandad stabs his spear upright in the sand like a totem pole, then clutches my shoulders. "The spirits have spoken, you're alive!" His eyes are running with tears and mine are too. Happy and sad mixed together like grains of sand. But have the spirits told him about Papa? I touch his spear and ask if he has caught any fish, but he unties the string bag from his waist; it's empty.

My stomach clenches, my whole body holds its breath. Now is the time. Words spring up but die. Instead, I ask where the rest of the family is.

He looks out to sea and his eyes crinkle at the edges. "We knew, didn't we? Our forefathers gave us the knowledge to escape the seventh wave."

"Where are they?"

"The elders read the signs in the wind and the waves. They held up their hands, asking the spirits to spare us." Grandad lifts his arms to the sky. "No sea birds were flying. We started to drag our Kabangs to the safety of the mangroves before the giant seventh wave came to eat the huts."

"Is everyone safe?"

"We ran to the hills. We took what we could."

"All of our family?"

"Your Mama and Petal were collecting seaweed. I don't remember seeing Coral." He jerks his head, indicating the direction they took. "We all went, even the old, like me."

I look at Grandad. "You're not old." His body is thin and wrinkled, but he is strong. Not like Papa, whose stomach is flabby from lack of work. *Papa!* My stomach falls into a cavern deep in the ocean, too far to reach. I pick up a stone rock, trying to draw strength from its solid shape and its age.

His voice sinks into me. "But Papa went to warn you."

My heart races as I stare at Grandad.

"Sky, you are his only son, he couldn't rest while you were in danger.

"Papa came to warn me?" I repeat slowly.

"Sailed his Kabang against the elders' advice. Said he would find your hotel, bring you to our people." Grandad smiles. "And you are here, so he found you!"

The sharp rock digs into my flesh. *Papa came to warn me. If I hadn't defied him, he'd still be alive.*

Grandad's cheeks are flat and his eyes lost in wrinkles. He knows, I'm sure he knows. I run towards the ocean and hurl the rock into the waves. They spit on my face. Through the mist, I see him walking slowly towards me.

"The Laboon took Papa," I whisper, but words aren't necessary. Grandad's legs have stopped moving; he is frozen.

Rain is flattening our hair, soaking our clothes, washing away the tears. He stands with his back to me, staring at the ocean. "Where did you find him?"

I swallow a mouthful of air. "Papa was lying on the beach near the Kabang."

Grandad doesn't turn but I hear his voice: "We are part of the ocean; she is always there, in us and around us."

And she kills us, I think, gritting my teeth.

As the rain dies, Grandad faces me: "You were his treasure, Sky, his only son." Grandad's shoulders shake as he sheds silent tears. Papa was his first-born. I grab a handful of gritty sand and uncurl my fist, throwing the particles into the air. The wind blows it back into my eyes like it's saying I'm useless. I am.

His body droops as he climbs over the splintered remains of my home. At the edge of the beach, a Kabang is trapped between long black roots. The mast and sail have been torn off by the Laboon, but the roof canopy with its arching bamboo is intact. We don't talk as we drag the ancient boat out of the mangroves, edging it onto the beach. The shell of the boat is strong, dug out from a single tree; it has not broken like the tourists' fancy yachts.

"Help me cut some palm leaves," Grandad asks me, as if I've not just told him about Papa.

"What's the point? Most of them have been torn off. And the oars and the motor have gone." Grandad gestures to another boat lying on its back like a beached whale. When I reach the battered hull, I notice some objects resting on top: two oars, an empty engine oil container, a little stove, a saucepan, an old kettle, the string bag we always use in the Kabang and a plastic fertiliser bag.

"I brought back what I could," says Grandad, resting his arms on the hull. "The Laboon has spoken. Now we need to live again." I see his jaw clench. "My son is lost to us, but our way of life will go on. The elders will stay in the hills until the sun has risen and set again, but I asked to return." He looks up at the palm tree. "Cut down those leaves, Sky. We will make a new sail."

Lowering my arm around his shoulders, I nod. Tremors run through my fingers as the old man quivers. For the first time in my life, Grandad seems frail. I'm not sure I can shin up the tree, as my leg and arm muscles are now only used for sweeping rubbish, but I can't fail him. Gripping the trunk with my knees, I concentrate on moving each hand, each foot until I reach the branch.

When I pull off the remaining palm fronds, Grandad weaves twine through, and the sail begins to form. His fingers are wrinkled, but they move fast. I remember him crouching like this and repairing part of the woven side of the boat, when I sat on the Kabang and let my hand drift through the water. Grandad can read the waves and he taught me their language and exactly when we would see a shoal of fish. Grandma would sit next to me, her eyes sparkling like stars as she told me ancient stories of our forefathers.

We work until the sun starts dipping in the sky. "Go find our people, Sky. The spirits will not like it if darkness covers the forest and you are alone." Grandad does not say much, but what he says is always right. I leave him with the gifts of food from Jo and follow the direction in which he is pointing. When I stop at the edge of the beach, he doesn't look up. He is hugging his knees and rubbing mud off the hull of the Kabang with his bare hands.

22. Mangroves

KRISTA

My head is killing me and every second, a giant pulse jabs into my arm. When I swallow, a jagged pain tears down my throat. I rub my eyes and the world slowly comes into focus. The bag is lying beside me, so I feel inside until I touch the bottle of water. Half empty. I watch the water turn into bubbles as I swill it around. No, I am not going to drink it — I'll keep it for emergencies. *I must be losing the plot... this is an emergency!* Unscrewing the lid, I take a sip. And another. My lips feel like they aren't mine and they have been pumped up like a wannabe celebrity. I want to drink the lot, but I force myself not to. If I have a few drops left, there's still hope.

This is unreal. I am an ordinary English girl on a standard package holiday in a well-known tourist destination. This shouldn't be happening. All I see is sand and debris and sea and sky. And more sand and debris and sea and sky. My skin feels rough and my eyes are dry like the moisture has all been sucked out. I stink of sweat. I long for a shower or to soak in a bubble bath, but I'm scared to dip my head in the sea — the waves might come back and I'd be sucked under.

Must get out of the sun, find shelter. I've always wanted a decent tan, but my legs are bright red. It's far too hot on the beach — and I've seen things I'd rather forget. Cupping a hand over my forehead, I squint back along the way I have come. The beach has shrunk like a triangle. Somewhere out there are my footprints and somewhere out there is the hotel. And somewhere out here is my dad.

As I walk towards the headland, a forest of black roots twists out of the sand, invading the beach. Thin, spindly tree trunks are sticking out of the water like stilts. I shiver: I've reached the mangroves. A bird cries and I stumble, as large wings flap above me. I wish I could fly above the green canopy. Dad must have walked into the mangroves and found a way up to higher ground. He'll be waiting until it's safe to return to the resort.

The first step isn't too bad; the water just comes up to my ankles. Then my knees...then my thighs. *Don't think about it, just keep going.* But how deep does this stream go? There is a gap between the trees, almost like a tunnel, inviting me in. Trees are on either side. I wade through, hoping it will lead me onto the bank, but there is a maze of channels and the water is deeper. What if the waves come back; I'll be trapped by an army of stilts. Ghostly arms are reaching out like they are trying to strangle me.

What was that? A screeching noise. I hope there aren't any dangerous animals that come out at dusk. Long shadows slant through the trees. I'm suddenly not just afraid for Dad, I'm afraid for me. This is crazy. Haven't even got a survival kit, just a few sweets in the rucksack. I'm hungry and thirsty and I need the toilet.

Sliding the trainers along the riverbed, I push further into the unknown, wading through the leafy waterway. Finally, I feel the ground rising. Sighing in relief, I climb onto leafy undergrowth. I lean against a tree and try to wriggle my shorts down, but it takes a while as they cling to my legs.

143

Relieved, I rinse my hands, hoping there aren't leeches in the water. Something touches my hand and I shriek. Then a night bird flaps its wings, crashing above me. I'm screaming and so is the bird — I don't know who is more frightened. Yes, I do. I'm lost in a swamp in the dark and no-one knows I'm here. Don't even have a torch. Tiny lights are all around: animals or insects watching, waiting to bite or sting or suck me dry.

I've never felt so alone. I could get bitten or drown and no-one would know. Pressing the sling closer to my chest, I feel the locket hard against my rib cage. *Stay calm. Stay awake. Don't move. Don't fall in.* I repeat the phrase over and over.

Tucking up my legs, I wrap my good arm around them, but my body is tense and tight. How can I relax when all around me are creepy crawlies, maybe snakes? It's like being in central London with a maze of roads and not knowing which one to take. But instead of taxi headlights, everywhere there are eyes glinting. I'm terrified of being bitten alive.

Use the scarf!

Where did that thought come from? Bending my neck, I slide the scarf-sling off, but it takes a long time until I can untie the knot. When it's freed, I drape the scarf over my head to protect my neck and face.

Wind rustles the branches giving glimpses of the moon. If Dad was here, he'd focus on the sky and plot his direction, but I've never been into astronomy. I only know Orion has the sword and the belt; and Pleiades is the cluster with lots of sisters. I think the North Star is the shiniest, but there are more stars here than I've ever seen and they're all so bright.

My stomach muscles suddenly dig in. *Are you really alive? Are you looking up at the same stars, thinking of me?*

Why does life have to change? When Mum died, I felt so numb, lost, empty. Then one day, Dad brought home this woman from his department called Jo, who wanted to be my friend. Dad started to smile again; not with his head tipped back like he used to, but his cheeks lifted. He brought The Woman home many more times, until one day, came the announcement I was dreading. I was told I was getting a new Mum.

I was forced to attend the wedding. Everyone was trying to make me feel happy. It didn't work. When The Woman swayed down the aisle, all I could think of was my petite, gorgeous Mum who always laughed. When I was little, she used to push me on the swing, and every swoosh forwards, Mum's face would grow larger, her smile expanding until it covered her whole face. Then the whole world was smiling. But when Dad married again, I felt as cold as the marble floor. When The Woman said *"I do,"* I was shouting *"I don't!"* so loudly in my head I'll never know why the whole church didn't hear me.

No-one can hear me now, whatever I do. I'm trapped in this stinking mangrove. No-one will come and look for me. No-one even knows I'm here. Not even my step-mum. Why did I have to run off — I should have waited for her.

"Krista, if the waves are too big, I just want you to know…" I can almost feel her arms around me as the words swirl around my mind: *"I do care for you."*

I wish I'd told her.

I wish I'd been nicer to her.

I wish she was here.

23. Beyond the Western Seas

MARTI

Darkness has stolen the daylight when I reach the top of the hill. Following Grandad's directions, I walk towards the rocky outcrop where the Moken are staying. The moon shines a path for me and soon I smell smoke and see flames.

Mama crushes me to her chest. "My son, I thought the Laboon had taken you!" Then I hear her muffled voice in my ear, telling me that Petal is safe.

"And Coral?" I pull away from Mama's embrace to look into her eyes.

"She's with Cloud. The elders warned her not to go to the snack shack when they read the signs in the sea and sky."

Coral's still alive! Both my sisters are alive!

I wrap my arms around Mama. Now is not the time to tell her. She thinks Papa is safe, but he is travelling beyond the western seas like Grandma. She went back to the spirits many, many tides ago, before Petal was born.

When I feel a tug at my shoulder, I spin around. Mama laughs as my little sister jumps into my arms and can't stop talking. She tells me that Lucky, the stray dog, ran into the hills before the giant wave came, like he'd known. He's thin and scruffy, so perhaps the spirits warned him, thinking he deserved a second chance. Petal says she ran after the dog and Mama followed, so the dog saved all their lives — but I know the elders raised the alarm and ordered everyone to run.

Petal chats like everything is fine, so maybe being young helps. I smooth her wavy dark hair, then think of Harry. He's about the same age, but he is silent most of the time.

Mama waits for a gap in the stream of words, then wades in. "Is Papa helping Grandad repair the Kabang?"

This is it. But my tongue is stuck to the roof of my mouth. I feel a soft hand on my shoulder. "He warned you about the Laboon, didn't he?" Mama's head is nodding as if she is telling herself Papa is safe. "He left as soon as the elders picked up the totem poles and told us to run to the hills."

I don't answer. Mama must have felt my sigh, for she grasps my shoulders, looking into my eyes. Then her head starts shaking from side to side. Her eyes are moist. I don't answer, just let Mama cling to me; I don't know what else to do. Pain and hopelessness flow between us. And love.

Suddenly, she pulls away and cups my face in her hands. "He's hurt, isn't he; tell me he's just hurt?" I can't speak. Her lips part and her mouth falls open as she looks up at me. "Does he live?" I slowly shake my head. My chest drops and she slips to the ground. She's rocking her body and I wonder if she will ever stop.

The elders question me about Papa, then they are silent and stare at the totem pole. When they start chanting, I sit in the darkness and stare at the full moon. Is Papa's spirit looking down on me, or far away in the western seas? The moon sees everything: love and death.

She must have watched beyond the edge of the ocean, as the giant waves rushed towards the land. Watched as people fled for their lives; some finding safety, others swept away. Watched as the Kabang was swept into the jaws of the Laboon.

Mama has not blamed me, but we both know that if I had not been working at the hotel, Papa would still be alive. But if he wouldn't fish, how else could we buy the fuel and rice and curry paste Mama needs? Coral's shell necklaces are pretty, but tourists do not pay much. Without my job, our family would be stagnant as mangrove backwater. I'm not like a squawking sea bird circling a boat, greedy for scraps of fish; I want to catch my own. Papa did not understand and now he never will.

My stomach clenches with pain, as my last words echo in my mind: I wish I hadn't argued; he was sick. I knew that really. The last time I sailed with Papa on our Kabang, his chest was strong, his shoulders level, not bowed inwards with coughing. He was holding the rudder, bare feet planted on the edge of the boat, his hair blowing in the breeze. I wanted to impress him, so I concentrated on breathing deeply, then dived into the ocean. I swam down to the coral reef, my spear leading the way, ready to strike.

A shoal of little fish scattered when I moved my hands, following the star-shaped, purple coral bushes. I saw a manta ray and stalked it, slowly inching along the rock, my arm outstretched. Its wings were like a giant bird and its long thin tail longer than my body. Then *bam!* I speared it, but it flapped and twisted away. I was disappointed that I would have nothing to show Papa: a manta ray would have been a great prize. Grasping the spear, I kicked away from the ocean floor. I was still holding my breath, when I saw the sparkle of the shell. Flipping sideways, I plucked it off the coral. Then I pulled a bag from my waist, pushed the shell inside and swam up and up into the light.

Papa was proud of me. "I'll keep this," he said, tracing the smooth pink inside of the shell. It was like an ear, but the outside was grey and crinkled like mountain ridges. He put it on the shelf under the roof of the Kabang and smiled at me. I wish I'd checked with Grandad if my shell was still there. I hope the Laboon didn't suck it back under the ocean. Like Papa.

24. Lost

29th December 2004

KRISTA

Damp and twitching and terrified, somehow sleep must have taken over my mind. And I'm glad, for that was the worst night of my life. Worse even than when Mum died. I wasn't haunted with fear then, just empty.

Mist is rising from the water, forming little clouds. Hundreds of tiny insects are dancing just above the surface. I seem to be on the bank of a small river running through the trees. Spindly dark trunks stick out of the water shadowed by a green canopy.

Arching my back, I lift my head to face the morning; then hunch my shoulders, rolling them in circles to ease the stiffness from lying scrunched in a ball. A long yawn stretches my mouth and I suck in morning air.

I feel like a contestant on one of these reality TV shows, stuck on an island in a jungle, when the guys run out of water and get red blotches all over their faces. But this is for real. There is no hidden support crew to rescue me. I'm all on my own with no phone and no backup. If only I had told Jo where I was going.

Anything could be down there, lurking in the green sludge. Things that bite and things that sting and things that suck your blood. Black stalks crawl out of the water like a thousand spider legs blocking the way back to the sea.

Trying to conquer my fear, I tie the scarf around my neck, and put on the rucksack. Then I slide my legs into the water until I feel the riverbed. Fear is not the right word; I'm breathing so much that you'd think I was having a heart attack. What if I fall in? I push one foot into the thick heavy sludge, then force my hands to act as oars, dragging the water past me on either side.

Don't stop! Don't think about the danger or the swamp or the mangrove forest. Just keep going!

The water has risen to my waist. My hands are scooping leaves and silky fronds behind me in a mini wake, but I am getting slower. The water seems to be fighting me and all I can see is more swamp.

What if it gets too deep? What if I have to swim? My heart starts speeding and I can hear myself panting like a dog. But I've got to go on, there's no choice. Instinctively, I touch the locket for strength — it helps just knowing it's there.

What if the photo gets wet? Digging my heels into the mud, I tense my body. Slide off the rucksack. Clutch it against my chest. Dangle the locket above a deep pocket. If I mess up, it will sink into deep green sludge. Forever. Placing my feet wide, I hold the locket, not wanting to let go. Not wanting to let Mum go. But I have to.

Once the locket is safely zipped up and the rucksack is on my back again, I breathe deeply and look for a way out. Nothing: just hundreds of roots arching up with water swirling around them. A stick flows towards me and I pick it up, then smash it against the surface of the water. A fountain of salty dirty water splashes my face. Yuck! It's probably full of disease. I wipe my face quickly, then see a green bug clinging to my hand. Screaming, I flick it into the air. There aren't any red marks, but my hand feels hot. Great, now I've got two bad arms. I'm dying to cool it, but dare not put it back in the water.

It feels like tiny spiders are crawling over my flesh, building a web on my hand. I bite my lip, clenching my fists, then give into temptation, scratching as hard as I can. It helps for a second, then the stinging is unbearable. "Bugs, come and get me if you want to, I don't care — I have to get rid of this stinging!" I plunge my arm into the swamp.

The pain is slowly drifting away. I focus on a shrivelled leaf, feeling a growing excitement. It's moving past me...and the water is salty... so if I wade upstream, I'll get to the sea!

Fighting against the tide is hard work. But now I know the right direction, the mangrove forest feels less scary. Dappled colours dance on the water, making it seem like a magical kingdom. The water is shimmering with green and turquoise. Pink light is creeping through the trees. I can hear birds. I can smell the sea! I've never been so glad of anything in my whole life. Checking that the bag is securely on my back, I kick up my feet and swim towards the blue light shining through the arching tree line. Freedom!

A vast expanse of blue stretches in front of me, with stray tree roots arching up. I thrash around in the water for a foothold. Worry digs in when I can't touch the bottom. Then my ankle hits something sharp, but I don't mind the pain, if it means I can stand.

My shoulders are above the water level now and I wade, heading for a strip of sand. When my toes hit land, relief isn't the right word. It's like I've been strapped into a plane in bad weather, my stomach dropping every time it lurches, then it skids onto the tarmac, juddering so much you're scared it won't stop. As I step out of the water, I can almost hear the pilot telling us we've landed.

I tear open the rucksack – have to see Mum. My plan worked: the picture is still dry! No-one's here, so I strip off and lie on the ground, naked. Sunshine is warming me and giving me hope. I'm alive!

Long rulers of colour are streaking across the sky when my clothes are dry. I dress, then lie watching the salmon pink clouds touching the baby blue, stretching out as if the sky is a Lycra garment. It is dabbed with orange, then the colours merge, blurring the pattern out of shape.

As I look over my left shoulder, I can see the sun; a winking golden ball. I'm confused – I saw the sun setting, so the beach must have faced west. Then I remember that the resort is at the southernmost tip of the island – I must have climbed right around the headland.

The sun is red gold between my fingers as I squint, trying to see other islands. Now I can't look or I will see a million suns in my mind and go blind. I should be scared, alone in the middle of nowhere, yet as the sun pushes out of the water, it feels like the whole world has come alive. Two gulls skim across the waves, their white wings tinged with gold. A flock of birds rises and circles above the water. I always wonder if their flight is random, or if there is a leader? Does one say, *"Come on guys, let's go?"*

Rays of sunshine are touching the beach and pools of water are tinged with pink. Shadowy trees rise out of the morning mist, like pencil sketches, unfinished until the sun burns away the mist and the full picture is revealed. Beams of light shine on the tree trunks like a torch has turned on.

The sun is gazing down on earth. The pinks and red gold and amber have gone; just faint wisps remain. I'm alone, totally alone on the beach. Free of the darkness, the water, the bugs. The horrible mangroves are behind me.

Nothing to do but look at sea. Oceans of it. I scan the horizon for boats. Just one dark dot on the horizon. A faint sound of an engine reaches my ears. I jump up and down, yelling; then rip off the blouse and wave it wildly, but the boat disappears.

My head is swirling. Need water. I fumble in the sodden bag, then tip it up, so the bottle falls on the sand. One last drop dribbles into my mouth. Anger spurts through me and I hurl the useless bit of plastic. There is no answer, just the wind whistling through the empty bottle. Can't even throw that properly. It lies a few feet away, mocking me. Stamping over, I fling it into the sea.

The bottle is pulled back by the waves. Forward and back it bobs up and down, gradually being dragged further away from me. Like Mum and Dad. I couldn't save Mum and now I can't even save Dad.

The sun is scorching my shoulders and neck. I touch my swollen lips, then try to swill saliva around my mouth with my tongue, but my throat is a dried up river bed.

Images flash through my head as I remember the coca cola bottle Izzie once shook for a laugh. Her Mum hadn't been too pleased at the brown stains on the ceiling when she returned, but it was wild at the time. We took turns, placing a thumb over the spout, then spraying the dregs. It was one of those times when you just had to be there. Epic.

I long to be back home, giggling over the latest celebrity fashion mistakes with my friend. She's obsessed with Hello magazine. But all I'm obsessed with right now is water. There is so much out there, but I'm drowning with thirst.

The bottle is floating further away. Suddenly, I want to save it. If I wade in, I could just reach it, I'm sure I can…there is still time.

Got it! I feel ecstatic. It is only a plastic bottle, one

of millions of plastic bottles, but somehow it gives me hope. I'll think of happy things: that's what people do when they are lost.

Home. My duvet wrapped around me. Watching movies.

Drinking hot chocolate with squirty cream and little marshmallows on top.

Pretending to be pop stars with Izzie and dancing around her room. We were probably way out of tune, but it was fun. A snatch of a song touches the edge of my mind, then dives under the radar. I reach for it with all my strength, then start to sing.

A tapping sound. Is that me? Blinking through tired, crusted eyes, I try to focus on the seashore, but the glare of the sun is too bright. I rub my eyes. Is something moving on the shoreline? A bird? I shade my eyes from the sun and see a figure crouching by a boat. I must be hallucinating.

My cry is a whisper in the wind. I flap one hand like a dry piece of cloth. He stands up. Has he noticed me? I kneel, one hand pressed into the sand. Why is the sky swirling round in circles? Why is the beach rushing towards me? I topple over, then everything goes white.

The sea arches up in a massive wave and hundreds of black spiders crawl out with long legs. I can see their hairs tensing, as they out shoot strong wires. I'm stuck in a tangled web. Can't cry out, can't see, can't breathe.

My eyelids burst open; the web dissolves.

And an old man is staring at me.

25. Hero

MARTI

Mama's silence was too painful, so I've come back to the hotel. The paths are clear now, but the walls are splintered with heaps of rubble. The manager was furious that I went missing and ordered me to clear all the rubbish trapped in the swimming pool. You can't even see the bottom: it's piled high with broken plastic pool beds and furniture sucked out of the bungalows. Palm fronds are sticking out of a small fridge. Anything could lie under the stinking brown liquid. What am I supposed to do, jump in?

Throughout the morning, I hook small objects, but there's no way I can reach the heavier items, they'd suck me under. This is far more dangerous than facing any of the sea creatures in the ocean, even the mighty shark.

Nobody thanks me; I'm just Marti who works in the background. Invisible. But work stops me thinking of Papa and all those people taken by the Laboon. It is crazy to pretend nothing has happened, but it helps.

When I take a break, the water is back on at last. Splashing my face takes away some of the smell. Wandering out of the staff wash room, I lean against a palm tree. The Green Turtle is still open, as only the ground floor got ruined. Some aid workers have arrived in a white truck with a red cross on the side. There aren't many tourists left, only those waiting for news of relatives or visiting the injured in hospital — like the woman, Jo.

She is sitting in the corner by the window where I can see her; lifting a spoon to the boy's mouth. Half the kitchen staff are missing, so I hope Virote didn't help prepare the food, or Harry might get sick.

He doesn't seem to eat much, just stares outside and drives his car along the glass and back again. His eyes light up when he sees me and he places his fingers wide like a starfish. Looking around to see if anyone is watching, I tiptoe across the path. I stretch out my fingers on the other side of the window, covering Harry's. He smiles and moves his hand. I place my hand over his and he moves it again. Then I place mine higher and he lifts his hand to touch mine through the glass.

It's a fun game until Jo pulls him back, eyes wide with worry. She relaxes when she recognises me. Then she takes Harry's hand and they disappear. I don't know why I'm disappointed; they are guests and I am just the garbage boy.

Trudging back to the pool, I stare at the disgusting mess. Then I hear shouting. *What have I done now?* Turning around, I see Jo waving at me. Harry is running towards me. The manager may be spying on us, but if I don't hold out my arms, the boy will fall into the pool. I give him a flying hug and he clings onto me like a monkey. Suddenly, my chest is heaving in great breaths. It's like all the tears for **Papa** are pouring out, the tears for the bodies in the temple and the tears for Rune, still missing.

A soft hand touches my face. "Not cry."

Soaking into my pain, the little boy's innocence and concern bring comfort. I lift the lad down and kneel on his level. "You remembered my name!"

"Marti not cry," sings the little boy. His expression is so serious that I want to please him. I wipe my hand across my face like a cloth.

Jo is smiling, cheek bones high in her face. "They are the first words he's spoken all day! He must really like you." Tears threaten my eyes again, but I don't let them spring out. Harry wants to play the window game again, this time, outside the hotel. I move my hand around so fast, that he slaps the glass, trying to catch me. When it's Harry's turn, I pretend to be too slow, unable to catch his hand before he moves it. He loves it. For those few minutes, the waves are forgotten and he is a little kid again. His laughter is like a stone you throw in the sea and it ripples out touching everything.

Then Jo's phone rings. Her face goes white and she clutches my arm for support. "Yes, yes it is…" I can see a muscle twitching as she clenches her jaw. Then she gasps and her cheeks turn pink. "Oh, I'm so pleased you saw it...yes, he's right here with me, he's been playing a game...yes of course you can." Jo bends down and holds Harry's shoulders. "Your Dad wants to speak to you!"

Harry's face changes like the wind: his eyebrows crease and his mouth starts to wobble. Jo puts her arm around him and holds the phone to his ear. When the phone call has finished, Jo turns to me, flapping her arms as she talks. "This young man," she says, smiling like an arrow of sunshine shooing through the clouds, "is about to meet his family!"

"Mummy and Daddy!" shouts Harry. Jo turns her face away and her expression changes; the sunlight is clouded. "Not long now. Your Dad said the taxi will be here in less than fifteen minutes. Isn't it exciting!"

Harry tugs my hand. "They saw my drawing?"

Jo nods. "Your sister spotted it, then your Dad read my message."

"And Mummy," says the little boy, his face beaming. I look at Jo and she blinks several times.

No! Please let his mother be alive.

I've got no right to be there for the reunion, but I want to. Living without a nationality, my only right is to forage from the sea. The boy is like family and I need to know that he's safe. The manager will sack me if I enter the hotel, so I wait outside. Jo has taken Harry into the lounge; I can see him leaning on his elbows, staring at the road.

I'm watching through the window. Harry is swept up in a shoal of arms, as his Dad and sister hug him. Everyone is crying and laughing and crying again. Then I see Harry's lips move as he says something and his sister starts to cry, big sobs that make me want to cry too. The man is kneeling in front of Harry and telling him something that makes the little boy crumble. He is like a lost dog needing to find a home. I know his Mummy has gone and she is never coming back.

Why does happiness have to have a sting? I walk to the pool and stare into the mess. A yellow bucket has reached the surface. A child must have been playing with that, digging happily in the sand...until the waves came. I pick up a long broom, then lean over the pool, sliding the bucket onto the handle. *Got it!* The bucket is hanging in the air, slopping out brown water as I reel it in. But is that child safe now, or lying in a body bag at the temple? Anger causes me to swing the broom, flinging the bucket across the lawn, splatting water against a palm tree. Why did the Laboon have to take so many lives?

"I feel like that too!" I spin around to see Jo walking towards me. "Don't get me wrong," she says, "I'm so pleased for Harry, but my husband is still out there somewhere and now my stepdaughter has gone missing again..." Jo sighs and her hands twist together. Then she looks at me and her cheeks lift. "But that's not your problem." Crinkles appear around her eyes as she smiles. "Marti, they want you inside, Harry's Dad wants to thank you."

"What for?"

"Saving his life!"

Jo tells me to be prepared, because Harry's Mummy is missing and his older sister is in hospital. As we cross the lobby, I glance at the reception desk and sigh. Then we are entering the lounge and Jo is pulling me forward, introducing me to Harry's dad. "This is Marti who saved your son, Mr Skelton."

The man in a suit lifts Harry onto the carpet and strides across with his arms out. "How can I ever thank you?" His hand closes over mine and he holds it so tightly it feels like I'm part of him. I don't like to think that I blushed, but I probably did.

"I'm forever in your debt, Marti. However can I thank you?" he says. I can't speak.

Jo gestures to me with her palm outstretched. "Marti, I'm sure Mr Skel…"

"Please call me George." The man releases my hand as he smiles at Jo.

Pink colour rises up her cheeks. "Yes of course, Mr… er… George." He laughs and Jo looks up at him, her eyes shining. "Marti was so brave. Your son was standing on the balcony and…"

Harry's dad looks into my eyes. "I'd like to hear it first-hand." I gulp, as he offers me the armchair. He and the girl and Jo are sitting beside me like I'm important.

"So," he says, bouncing Harry on his knee, "you are the hero who saved my son's life!" I nod, but don't say anything, I'm not sure I'm expected to. When he asks me to tell him what happened, I try to answer, but he keeps interrupting, needing to know every detail. His eyes

160

widen when I mentioned there was a gap between the truck and the bus. "You jumped?" Harry's dad and his sister are gazing at me like I am a massive whale.

"Yes, right over the tsunami," Jo says, nodding her head. The man's bushy eyebrows wrinkle and by the way his lips quiver, I think he is trying not to cry.

"I had to leave Harry in the room," he says, nodding as if he's trying to convince himself. He stares at the red car lying on the floor. "I had to warn my wife and the girls." He tucks his other arm around his daughter. "Lucy was out there and Olivia," he sucks in a deep breath. "They were all at the pool." The girl tucks her head into his chest and I see her body shaking.

I know what's coming, but he won't stop. "It was massive, much larger than the first wave." He strokes his daughter's hair as he talks. "You remember, don't you? Mummy phoned me saying I should see this, it was awesome. The waves were coming back and she hadn't seen anything like it." He stares at his daughter, then turns to me. "I told her to get the girls inside, it looked dangerous. The swell was wild, boats were being sucked under, people could be drowning. I thought it might breach the sea wall. I told her to come in, but she said this was a once in a lifetime opportunity for the kids."

He doesn't seem to notice the saliva caught on his lower lip. He sighs like the wind whistling down a tunnel of trees. "Those were the last words I heard her say. Once in a lifetime."

Tears are streaming down his cheeks as he looks at me. "I had to leave him, you see, I wanted my little man to be safe...but they were out there and the water was coming back."

The girl places a hand on his chest. "But Dad, if you hadn't helped, I wouldn't have survived." Her dad doesn't answer; I don't think he can talk right now. The girl turns to me. "I saw Dad running, but I couldn't hear what he was shouting, as there was this massive explosion. Mum was screaming, I knew we wouldn't make it, we couldn't get to the hotel in time. Then I felt Dad grab me and push me up this palm tree."

Mr Skelton is staring at the corner of the room. "*Hang on!* I told her to hang on for dear life." He turns to his daughter. "And Mummy wrapped herself around a tree, didn't she, holding Olivia as high as she could."

Lucy nods. "Then the water came. The last thing I saw was Mummy covering Olivia with her body."

"This powerful current was trying to tear us off," explains her dad. "I couldn't breathe. All I could do was cling onto the tree with my arms and legs and hold you." He touches Lucy's face. "When it stopped lashing into us and we could breathe and I looked...Olivia was still hugging the tree, but Mummy had gone..." His voice breaks into bits. "She wasn't there..."

The room is full of pain. It's like I am their totem pole and they are telling me stuff that is too personal, too special, too awful. Jo is biting her lip and her gaze keeps darting from the man to the girl. "And your other daughter is?"

The man's chest expands, then he sighs. "In hospital, but she's going to be alright, isn't she Lucy?"

The girl's lower lip trembles. She picks up Harry's toy car and hugs it. "We looked and looked, but we couldn't find Mummy."

Mr Skelton pulls her back into his arms and smiles at Harry. "But we've found you, little man." He takes out a large white tissue and blows his nose. "I'm so sorry, but I'd locked the door, so I thought you were safe." He pauses, looking at me. "But when we came back, Harry had gone."

"And Daddy lost his key in the water," says Lucy.

"But I didn't need it," Mr Skelton says, his lips trembling. He looks at his son. "The door was open; someone had broken the lock. But the room was empty; I thought you'd fallen off the balcony." He buries his face in Harry's hair. "My little man, we thought we'd lost you, too..."

Jo tells me the rest of the story, because the family can't speak. "They went everywhere to look: the beach, the town, the morgue..." Her voice drops to a whisper and she shudders. "Then they saw the note I left at the missing person's board with my phone number..."

"And my drawing!" says Harry.

Jo smiles at him with wet eyes. "Yes, you found them, you brought them home." She is happy, but I can see sadness in her eyes, like she's thinking of her husband.

Mr Skelton lifts his head. "How can I ever thank you for looking after my son?"

"It's the least I could do. Harry's a very special young man, I've loved looking after him for you." She kisses Harry on the cheek. The last bit is whispered so the family don't hear, but I do: "And being a Mum for a short time."

26. The Old Fisherman

KRISTA

When I open my eyes, the old man is crouching, a cap shadowing his face. His chest is bare, taut for his age, with just a few wrinkles. Lines are etched across his face, like he's seen a lot of struggles — or death. I lean away from him, feeling exposed, then notice my blouse is wrapped around my shoulders. Did the man do that? He stands to his feet in one fluid motion. As he reaches out a brown, wiry arm, my stomach clenches and my shoulders lock with fear. Then he points towards the sea and I exhale, not realising I'd been holding my breath.

Following the direction of his finger, I notice a thin path snaking through the tangled branches and crushed bamboo. What good is one little bit of cleaning up in a world of chaos? Somewhere beyond the mangroves is a resort full of plastic, metal and junk and a woman who is waiting for me. Why didn't I go to the hospital? Jo was going to pin Dad's picture onto the board and someone might have seen it; if he's there, she might find him.

He said he'd only be ten minutes; he promised. I sigh and touch my locket. Mum said she wanted to stay, but she just slipped away one night. In the morning, she looked so peaceful, no stress lines. She still looked like Mum, except she wasn't there anymore.

The man is still staring at the sea. He looks sad. Has he lost family too? I thread the chain through my fingers and the locket glints in the sunshine. As he turns his head, his eyes linger on the golden locket, so I quickly slip it back in my blouse.

The old man gestures towards a wooden boat at the shoreline. "Kabang." His voice is higher than I had expected, but I recognise the word Dad used to describe the model in the market. As the man holds out his hand, I remember Dad's warning about traffickers. Is this a trap? But I've got no choice: the mangroves are blocking the headland. I'll have to trust this man, he's my only hope.

Pressing one hand on the sand, I bend my knees. They buckle. My head whirls, and this horrible sensation is draining my energy.

The next thing I know, I'm with Jack. We are alone on a desert island, the sand is dazzling like jewels and the sky is the bluest blue. I am wearing my new, white shorts and Jack is smiling. A new smile, not the one he gives the other girls, but a genuine smile that holds secret messages. I can't believe it: the most dreamy boy in school is smiling at me.

He speaks softly, his voice like the voice of a child. Not deep or sexy, but high pitched, growing softer as he drifts away. *Come back!* I try to imagine his face, but as his eyes twinkle and fade, there's nothing but the memory of a smile.

My eyelids flutter open. They feel sore, so I lick my finger, then use the moisture to dab the dry skin. Stretching my arm, I feel for the glass of water I always keep in my bedroom. It isn't there. Strange. I sit up, but my shoulder hits something hard. A wave of nausea hits me so I quickly tuck my head between my knees. Where am I?

The old man is crouching with his back to me. He's wearing a sarong around his waist and his bare feet are flat on the floor. A water bottle is lying beside him. I sneak a glance at him, then dribble the bottle towards me with my foot. Cold liquid slides down my throat, sinking into my chest. Each gulp feels like an explosion in my head. I'm terrified the man will turn around and attack me. I want to drink it all, but I can't risk it.

He looks at me and a shiver ripples down my back. Inside his mouth, there is a dark gap where he's lost a tooth. I stare back — I'm not going to let him see I'm afraid, even though my whole body is trembling and I feel so cold. The old man thrusts the bottle of water at me and I flinch. Then he mimes lifting it to my lips, but when I try to drink, I can see two bottles, then it turns into three. The world is swaying. I drop the bottle, then I feel warm hands pressing my shoulders onto my knees.

Once the dizziness has passed, I lift my head. I'm in some kind of peaked tent, but there are no doors. What is this place? I turn onto my side, leaning on one elbow; Tiny slithers of light shine through the woven walls. I'm lying on rounded ribs that look like bamboo.

Feeling braver, I shuffle to the edge of the canopy and narrow my eyes against the glare of the sun. The narrow boat is perched on the beach at the edge of the sea; if I spit I could touch the waves. The man moves outside, sheltered by bamboo windbreaks each side of the boat; he's twisting twine into a rope. As he looks at me, the cave appears in his mouth again — perhaps he is smiling. Then he says something in a sing song voice, but I shrug my shoulders, not understanding. He reaches for the water bottle, sits on the edge of the boat, then disappears.

He has few possessions: a wooden dish, a string bag

hanging from the slatted sides and a little stove. My stomach contracts as I notice the spear lying along the length of the cabin. My heart starts beating faster and my head starts swimming.

I am still staring at the spear when the boat rocks and the old man climbs on board. I swallow nervously as he crouches down, then he offers me a fresh bottle of water. I unscrew the lid and taste it. Yuck – it's salty! The old man laughs and mimes rubbing his face. Oh, he wants me to wash, I must look awful. I can't even push my fingers through my hair, it's so tangled. Wish I had a mirror... no, perhaps not.

Water splashes on my face, trickling down the side of my nose into my mouth. My dry lips are crusted with salt. I tip more water over my head and although my hair still feels rough, my face feels fresher.

The old man holds out his hand for the bottle, then jumps down to fetch some more. He's surprisingly agile — he must be nearly 80 by the amount of wrinkles on his face. He's dipping the bottle into the waves along the shoreline. Suddenly, he tips his head to one side like a bird sensing movement in the ground. His fingers scrabble in the sand and moments later, he is holding a crab. I'm fascinated by the pincers trying to jab the man's hands. One bash with a rock and the crab is lifeless — he must have done this lots of times. He throws the crab on the sand and starts digging with the rock.

Suddenly I hear wild barking. A blur of brown nearly sweeps him off his feet. A small dog jumps into the water, splashing the old man who shouts and raises his arm. The animal ducks down onto its belly; I hope it won't get hit. Ignoring it, the old man walks back to the boat. The dog follows, wagging the tip of its tail. Then the man says something and the dog is all over him.

Why can't I have a dog? The words flash into my

mind. Izzie has a black Labrador and Loren has a whippet. It isn't fair that I'm not allowed a pet. But it's far worse that cancer is so cruel. And the tsunami destroyed so many lives. Now I'm stuck in the middle of nowhere with no-one to talk to, just an old man who doesn't speak my language.

The dog barks in my ear, splitting my thoughts. His nose peeps over the side of the boat, a paw either side. The man's cheeks widen and I see the gap in his teeth. Then he gives a sharp command. Instantly, the dog flattens itself on the sand; head resting on paws, eyes fixed on the old man's wrinkled face. He only strokes the dog once and the dog is his slave. The dog's eyebrows shift following the man's movements as he traces the smooth side of the boat with his finger. He could be a fisherman by his weathered face. Perhaps the little boat was spat out of the sea by the massive waves?

I can feel my eyelids drooping, so I watch the dog as he curls up on the deck. I close my eyes for a moment.

A wonderful smell is curving into my nostrils. I stretch my arms, grazing my fingertips — I'd forgotten I was lying at the side of the boat. The old man is cooking over a small stove. Smoke is drifting out of the canopy into the blue sky like a signal. I hope someone sees and I get rescued.

A crack: the man is twisting off crab legs. He pulls open the shell, then gestures to me to scoop out the flesh. Saliva is forming in my mouth and I can hear the poor dog whining.

Seafood has never tasted so good. I am sitting cross legged and the man is crouching, waiting for me to finish. When I hold out my palm with the empty crab shell, he stands up and flings his shell into the sea. I copy his action, then the dog jumps down and bounces into the waves, dunking his muzzle. Seconds later, he is running around with a crab shell in his mouth. Birds are squawking, then it's a fight between the birds and the dog. He wins.

The man has tipped back his cap and he's staring at the sea. What's he thinking? Who's he looking for? Someone he's lost? Or are his children packed far away in his memories? I scan the horizon for boats, longing for someone to talk to. I need to know if he's seen Dad.

"Where am I?" I speak the words out loud.

"Farang!" The man says something with high pitched musical tones, but I don't know the language, so I just smile — I guess a smile fits into any language. He lifts the string bag off the wooden strut and tips out the contents. A green, oval fruit I don't recognise rocks from side to side then rolls on the floor. The old man smiles. I know it's rude to stare, but my eyes keep drifting to the black hole. If he was my grandad, he would have gone to the dentist and had it fixed. I wonder why he hasn't; perhaps he hasn't got much money; or perhaps some things are more important than a missing tooth.

"Can I help?" The fruit feels rough and surprisingly heavy nestling in my hand, but smells delicious, like lemons. I bend my head and breathe in the delicious scent.

And I am back. Lying on the hammock in my garden, swinging in the midday sun. Watching the swallows darting, swooping, diving. A book is propped on my jeans unopened and Mum is bringing out a tray of drinks. I can see her blue dress flowing in the light breeze and tendrils of hair escaping from her messy bun. I smell the scent of home-made lemonade. As I drink, delicious nectar flows into my body, rolling around my mind.

The scene blurs. I reach for Mum, but she fades until only the scent of lemons is left. I open my eyes to see the old man looking at me with wrinkles creasing the top of his nose. He looks worried, so I offer him the fruit. He shakes his head, pushing my hand back, but I'm scared to take a bite, as it feels so leathery. He wipes it with a weathered hand, then slices it in two with a small knife. The flesh looks juicy and pink.

"What is it?" My voice rises, ending in a question. The black hole appears again as the old man says a word I don't understand. When I bite into the soft fruit, it's delicious. Soon nothing is left but the skin. The old man raises his eyebrows, then gestures for me to pass it. Amazing! He's swallowed the lot! His cheeks crease into deeper wrinkles as he notices my surprise.

Now he's reaching into a thick plastic bag and rolling out a watermelon. Soon sweet melon juice is running down my chin, dripping onto the long shirt. I'm embarrassed, but the old man doesn't seem to notice. He is biting off huge chunks, and drips are raining down his chest. Brushing his hand across his face, he sits cross legged on the bamboo slats and bows his head. He is mumbling, chanting. Perhaps he is praying. I've never heard the sounds before; they are hauntingly beautiful. I close my eyes.

And I'm with my best friend, listening to music. Izzie's bedroom wall is plastered with posters and she is talking about her favourite boy band. "Levi is so dreamy, his dimple is so cute, isn't it?"

I shake my head. "You're obsessed."

"Don't you just love his tattoos?"

"No way! Jack is far cuter."

Izzie throws a cushion at me, but I duck and it sails straight at a picture. The band on are tour, showing off their latest tattoos on the beach. The poster rips, splitting the guys into scraps of paper, which fly around the room. I catch Levi, but when I open my hand to look at the torn paper, his eyes turn deep brown and his nose and mouth

170

grow wider. He looks familiar, but I can't place him. Throwing the scrap into the paper trail swirling around the room, I am being swept into swirling water. Deep dark water.

I wake up drenched with sweat. I'm lying on the deck with my arm resting on a large smooth shell. My bandage has gone. The old man is chanting as he presses green leaves onto the open wound. It hurts. He mutters and lifts the leaves off one by one. I see the red hole and feel sick. Very sick.

27. Rune

MARTI

"Concentrate on one thing," Papa used to say when he was training me to spear fish. *"Focus your energy. Hold your spear in front of you and glide silently towards your prey. If you don't succeed, there will always be another fish: the ocean is full of life."* Nowadays, big boats sweep the sea with their nets and put dynamite down. You hear a loud explosion and water shoots into the air, then fish lie on the surface.

Virote and Chaow used to dynamite me with words, making me feel useless. But I've been given a room in the hotel — me, a sea gypsy! It's got a soft bed and a wardrobe and it's all for me. Not that I've got anything to put in it, but it still feels good to have it. I don't expect Virote will be very happy when he finds out.

Before Harry's Dad left, he asked what job I do and where I live. When I pointed to the shed, he shook his head: "Not any longer!" I was covered in muck from cleaning the pool, but Mr Skelton took my hand: "Come with me." He arranged everything. The manager came out of his office with a smile stretching his cheeks and said that yes, all his staff had the option of sleeping at the back of the hotel and no, he had no idea why I hadn't asked. He agreed with Harry's dad that of course I should sleep in the hotel, and I could have an upgrade as there were spare rooms at present. I wonder how long 'at present' means; perhaps just until Harry's family fly back home.

Mr Skelton is a big man in England: the boss of a company that makes cars. He is booked into The Golden Lotus Hotel near the hospital while Olivia recovers. Harry's mother still hasn't been found, but bodies keep being washed up. Each time I hear a truck go past, I'm afraid it will be my friend Rune, but it must be worse for Harry's family having lost their mum. What if they don't find her: will they wait here forever?

It feels strange without Harry in the hotel. I miss him and I think the English lady does too. Jo is wandering around the grounds like a porpoise separated from its pod.

The resort is dying. The only people left are tourists, waiting for news of loved ones, and those who have poured in to help. Flooding in and out like the tide. Reporters are here: people who tell the world about us and take pictures for their newspapers or television. They get good photos of bad views, nod at each other, then pack away their gear and move out. And we're left with the dirty mess and broken lives.

Aid workers are here, bringing medicines and tents and bottled water. They can help the living, but they can't bring back the dead.

Soldiers are here: people who follow orders. But some of them watch the women and I worry about Coral. I hope Cloud stays close to her.

And I am here, removing junk. Bit by bit. Since Mr Skelton talked to the manager, diggers have come to scoop huge handfuls of rubble out of the pool with their teeth, while I clear the rubbish banked along the hotel walls. Today I shifted an air conditioning unit lying on top of sharp pieces of metal, broken umbrellas and sun loungers.

My nails are broken and the layer of grime is hard to

scrape off, even in the shower. I always had clean hands when I was free diving, even when gutting fish, as the ocean is the best cleaner. Maybe one day, I will wash the memories from my mind, but I still see the white body bags whenever I try to rest, and Papa's dead eyes as I close mine. Sleep should be easy to find; I've never slept on a mattress. It's like lying on soft grass with blue skies and the golden sun shining down on my body. But the comfortable bed doesn't stop the night haunting me with shadows.

When I stumbled out of bed this morning, my eyes flickered like a dying light bulb. After breakfast, I scraped my hand against a rusty nail. I was lucky; I could have sliced it on a jagged piece of wire. There is so much to do and I must work until the sun disappears behind the horizon.

Before heat built up and the metal handle of the spade grew too hot to touch, Mr Skelton and Harry arrived. Not in a taxi, this time, but in a big black car — maybe it belongs to his company. Harry jumped out, followed by Mr Skelton and a thin woman wearing a uniform. He nodded as they passed, but didn't stop. Harry tugged his dad's hand, looking back at me, but he was pulled into the hotel. Perhaps that's how it should be; I need to remember who I am.

It's amazing how one person can change my life! Mr Skelton has just told me that I've been chosen to tell the aid workers what the Thai doctors are saying and tell the Thai people what the English words mean. I hope I can do it — I'm sure there must be people who know a lot more English and Thai than I do. But Harry's dad said that I'm *"the man for the job"* and the manager is happy to let me go. I bet he's pleased to get rid of me. The *'street rat'* will still be sleeping inside the hotel, but he will be working in a place where he is called an interpreter.

When Mr Skelton introduces me to the aid worker, he says I am a brave young man who has shown initiative and resourcefulness. That sounds good, but I wish Rune was here so I could ask him what it means. We are going to the temple. The woman with a red cross on her dress gestures towards the truck door. "Get in, we haven't got all day." I can't step inside. I want to, but I can't. I've seen vehicles flying down the street, but I've never been inside a metal machine before. When trucks come alive, they snort and roar and might throw me out. I'm sure they have spirits of their own.

Car lights look like red eyes watching me. I grit my teeth and touch the door handle, but it stings. Jumping backwards, I bang into Mr Skelton.

"What on earth is the matter?" I can't answer, I can't even look at him, I know I've ruined everything.

"He's got a shock!" laughs the aid worker. I rub my burning fingers and look down at the ground. They must think I'm so stupid. I can't get into a car, so how can I ever be part of their electric world? It's like I'm fading away into the depths of the ocean.

"Marti sit next to Harry!" He is sitting in the back of the machine, but an invisible hand is pulling me away. When I shake my head, Mr Skelton's eyebrows join in a thick line. The aid worker whispers, then the eyebrows relax and he agrees that I can meet them at the temple. "But don't be late and don't waste this chance...you never know where it might lead." He nods, but I see the driver rolling his eyes.

Before the car drives off, I start jogging. Lorry loads of twisted metal pass me. The Toyota truck is lying at the foot of the hotel. I step past it quickly, remembering the fear as I leaped over the jaws of the Laboon. Gone are the colourful signs and the flags and material hanging like sails above the shop fronts. Everything has been stripped away, and what is left is grey. There are no souvenirs — lost under a tangled mess of wood and metal and plastic. Shop owners are trying to clean up, but what is left has been taken by looters. I don't blame them; their homes may be destroyed, their possessions lying at the bottom of the ocean.

When I reach the temple, the aid worker with the red cross is there, but not Harry and his dad. "There has been a development," she tells me. "A body has been found..."

There is no time to think, because a news reporter thrusts a metal ball into my face. He asks me what I think is the greatest need right now. Before I can answer, he tells the camera that viewers' money is going to be used wisely, and the government is giving millions of pounds, but the need is so vast that they need to give more. The west is giving money, lots of it. England and the States and Denmark and France and places I've never heard of, are all giving money to help us.

"And your name is...?" the reporter asks me at last. I'm a fish without water: my mouth is gasping for words. My stomach curls as he stares and I swallow nervously. Finally, I manage to speak and tell them I'm Marti. Sky died with the tsunami. He's never coming back.

I try to steady my voice, but as I translate "f...food and w...water," it's like I'm gargling water. When my mouth touches the microphone, it booms like waves crashing against a rock face. Then I have to listen to horrible stories over and over again. *Don't think, just translate.* But I can't help the horror infecting my voice.

I know I am lucky, but why was I saved when their lives were taken? I know now that the Laboon didn't just eat this island, or even this country, but all along the Indian Ocean. The sea bed cracked, spreading massive waves: the biggest magnitude ever recorded. I have no idea what this means, but it doesn't matter now. Nothing does, except survival.

When the interview is over, I am taken to the temple. People are crowded around: some silent, some talking and some wailing. Men and women wearing see-through plastic and long, yellow gloves are walking around with notebooks, making notes on the dead.

"All I want you to do," says the aid worker, "is translate what the doctor is saying. You do not need to look at anything. In fact, I'd advise you not to." She passes me a stretchy cloth. "Put this on, you'll need it." Copying her actions, I tie the string behind my head, then place the cover over my mouth. It's softer than the masks tourists put on before they dive, but this isn't a fun activity; we're facing death.

We stand in front of a long row of body bags. I try not to think about the people inside, but I can't help it because the first one is lying on its side and the material is bunched up like its knees are bent.

The aid worker is walking over to a doctor. "Excuse me, I'm from The Red Cross. How long have these bodies been here? When will you move them?" I hear the words 'disease' and 'epidemic' and the mask cannot hide the doctor's worry. His eyes speak to me and say that he is scared that many more people will die.

Have to get out. Flies are buzzing and the whole place stinks. I don't want to catch a disease and be the next one to die. When I glance at the aid worker, she's fiddling with her mask. She backs away from the doctor and walks out of the temple. I follow her, grateful to breathe fresh air.

I'm her shadow. She has joined some more people with a red cross on their uniforms, like hers. They are trying to find someone to guide them to remote bays and check if there are any survivors. I volunteer. The ocean was once my playground and the islands were my friends. We walk down to the beach, where I point out the mangroves. "I know a path that leads over the hill, so I can take you down to the lagoon."

She shakes her head. "We can't waste time; we're going by boat." I notice a tourist yacht, one of the few that didn't get smashed up in the Laboon. It must have been out on the ocean when the waves struck.

A path has been cleared through the rubbish, so it is easy to reach the shore. A smaller boat is waiting to take us out to the yacht. It is blue and shiny and looks new. I feel smelly and dirty and scared. I can't do it. I'm used to traditional Kabangs, not fast vessels with high sides and windows and instruments.

Why am I so weak? I remember my last conversation with Papa and his words go round and round my mind: *My son is dishonouring his ancestors and the spirits.* The aid worker is annoyed and chooses someone else to guide them and soon the boat is speeding away, water flying behind it like spit. I would have loved the ride, I know I would. I'm not frightened of water, so why couldn't I step into the boat? Am I rooted to the earth now? Will I ever be able to sail on the ocean and feel the flow of the waves skidding beneath me again?

I am standing between two worlds, like the stray dog that sniffs around Grandad's Kabang: on the edge of the family, not part of it. If I had a totem pole, I could ask the spirits for help — but they didn't help these people, did they? These were real people with hopes and dreams; now they are bodies tied up with string, packed tightly together. Why did the Laboon have to take away their breath? They didn't deserve to die. I'm not sure if the spirits are real any longer. Perhaps they are just like clouds, dissolving when it rains.

The aid workers have gone, flying across the ocean.

And I am here, standing on the shore. I pick up a stone and throw it like a spear. It hits the waves and sinks. I try again with a flatter stone, leaning low to the water and flicking my wrist. The stone bounces on the water, racing along in little jumps. I want to be like that, but I'm not sure where I fit in now: helping my people, working at the hotel, or being an interpreter?

If I go back to the hills, Mama may not be there. The elders may have decided it is safe to return. To what? Our houses are just stilts and most of our boats have been ruined. Grandad's is the best boat left, but you cannot fit a whole tribe on one Kabang. Even if we had a longboat, it could only carry a few families.

If I go back to the hotel, the manager will show his real face once Mr Skelton has gone. I will sleep in the shed, 'garbage boy' again. Or he will kick me out and I will be a real street rat.

If I go to the temple, I will have to face the bodies, the stink and the flies. But I need to know what has happened to Rune, I have to find out if he's alive.

A cloud of flies attacks as I walk up the hill. There is the usual crowd of anxious people standing by the missing person's board. A chart showing names and dates and times is propped up at one side. Someone tugs my arm, then I'm pulled me into the temple. "Aren't you the translator?" It is the doctor, the one whom I saw with the aid worker. "Well," he says, "are you, or aren't you?"

I nod. "No problem."

He wriggles down one of his yellow gloves to check his watch. "They are late."

"Who?"

"The British media: The BBC."

The TV crew arrive in three Jeeps. Small cameras, large cameras, a stick with a furry ball looking like a puffer fish...the equipment keeps pouring out. I am so

179

nervous when they are finally ready that I mess up translating the doctor's first answer and the reporter has to repeat the question.

When they have finished, the crew will fly to safety. The reporter said that life goes on, and it does for some, but it can never be the same. People are walking around like they have lost a part of themselves: friends they will never speak to again, smiles they will never see, arms they will never feel around them and hands they will never touch.

I wish I could pull back the tide. But you can't stop the sun from shining and the moon from crowning the night. Papa is gone, but I will keep searching for my friend. *"A crowd is sometimes the loneliest place to be."* Rune's words echo in my mind as I walk along a row of bodies, their torsos and faces covered with white sheets.

As soon as I see the withered leg, I know. When I lift the sheet, the face isn't his — he was in the water too long — but I know it is Rune. The Laboon's strength must have pulled him away from the hotel, trapped in its deadly jaws. It's unfair that Virote was spared, yet Rune, who never did any harm, who was always generous and kind, was taken.

"I wouldn't charge much, you know, just for food. It would be nice to have someone around"

My palms are clammy and sweat beads are dropping off my forehead, running down the sides of the mask, so I rip it off. *I was going to say yes, I wanted to be your lodger.* I reach out and touch him and my tears fall onto his body.

I feel hands pulling me away. "Do you know this man? Can you identify him?"

I look up and sigh. As the doctor pulls me away to sign a form, I see Rune's scarred face for the last time.

"Goodbye my friend."

28. The Kabang

KRISTA

He has made a decision; I can feel it. Bare feet perched on the edge of the boat, neck stretched. The old man jumps and gestures for me to follow. When I crawl out of the canopy, the dog barks, but he's silenced by one word, his eyes fixed on the old man's face. The man holds out his arms. And I let go. For a second, I relax against his chest, then my feet touch the beach.

We're at the back of the boat and the old man is attempting to push it into the sea, legs braced, muscles bulging. Inch by inch, the boat slides down the beach. There is no point in me helping — as soon as I tense my body, my arm starts throbbing. A few more pushes and the boat is floating, then the old man hoists himself on board. The dog bounces around in circles, then dashes into the water. The man is leaning over the side of the boat, holding out his hand, but my legs are frozen on the sand. In my mind I see a huge black wave pounding towards me, rearing up over the boat.

I hear the scream, but I don't know it's me, until I notice the shocked expression on the old man's face. "I'm s...sorry," I stammer, "it's not your fault."

The dog starts whining and nosing my arm. I don't want to be left alone, but I can still feel the water lashing across my face and hear the thunder in my mind.

The arched roof looks like the wings of an eagle covering the boat – but if it sails away, I'll be stuck in the middle of nowhere with no water and no food and no hope of rescue. The man is standing with his back to me, holding the wooden rudder. My fingernails dig into the centre of my palms, as the oars dip into the waves.

Paws dig into the sand as the dog whimpers, sensing my fear. I am twisting a clump of hair around my finger so tightly I feel the roots pulling. He barks a rough command, again. Finally, the old man turns his head.

"Please take me with you!" I shout, but he doesn't move. Another wave sucks the boat further out and I bite my lip. Perhaps he can't forgive me for screaming. I see him digging an oar in the water. The boat is turning sideways. He shouts and points to the wave. Surely he doesn't expect me to swim?

He is waiting, I know he is, but after being in the mangroves, I can't do it. Swimming isn't my thing; the only water I step into voluntarily is a bath or a shower. I stand on the beach, memories flooding me.

I was nine when it happened and Mum's face got so white I thought she'd turned into a ghost. I remember the exact date, because Izzy had booked a splash birthday party at the leisure centre and I had begged Mum to go. I didn't know then that Mum was scared of water. Dad used to take me to lessons, to give her a break on Saturday mornings. The party was fun at the start: we were all bouncing on the floaty castle, but then some of the boys started going wild and daring each other to jump in the furthest. I didn't fancy it, then this lad pushed me.

I sank straight under the water, and there were all these legs and arms kicking and splashing. My head bumped the hard plastic. I couldn't get out. I was panicking, lashing out, desperate to find a way up. My lungs were screaming at me to breathe, but I knew I had to hold on. Just as I was about to give in, someone grabbed my legs and pulled me up to the surface. I was gulping great mouthfuls of air. I could hear someone screaming, and saw Mum totally panicking on the side. Izzy told me afterwards that my arms were still thrashing; I looked terrified.

Water! The man is standing in front of me dripping water. He doesn't say anything, just takes my hand. I can't do this! Then the dog paddles toward me. I don't know why it helps, but when I see him swimming, I feel calmer. The water slides up to my waist, and all the time, the old man is walking backwards, his arms holding me.

Suddenly, I remember the locket and dig my toes in the sand. I'll never forgive myself if Mum's photo got wet. I am swaying in the water, trying to pull the locket out of my blouse. Then I feel a hand on mine. Swirling round, I splash the man in the face. He is saying something and holding out his hand. *For the locket!*

But what if he wants to keep it; what if he's not going to give it back? Then I hear his voice and remember his gentleness. He's not a thief.

He swims with one hand in the air like he's answering a question at school Except he's holding the locket and taking it to safety on the boat. And expecting me to follow.

My legs have drifted up and the sky is leaning down on me. *I'm going to drown!* I struggle, then suddenly, he's cupping my chin. His voice is a soft comfort blanket. My body goes limp as he guides me backwards. I look up at the intense blue sky and it's like I'm floating on clouds.

When we reach the boat, I grasp the side, while he steps on the wooden end that juts out, and hoists himself up. I have a flashback of Dad holding the model Kabang in the market when I was laughing at the bite mark at the end of the boat. So that's what it's for!

Imitating him, I hold onto the step, placing one foot in the gap. He takes my hand and pulls me over the side. It feels so good to be lying on a firm base. I sweep long strands of wet hair away from my eyes. Leaking from my clothes and oozing from the heavy trainers, is a stream of water. Feeling embarrassed, I watch it drip onto the deck.

The old man covers his face with two hands like he is praying, then shakes his head like a wet dog. *The dog!* It's trying to scramble up the smooth sides of the boat, but can't find a foothold. Not sure the old man wants an animal on board, but we can't leave it. Seeing my expression, he leans over and scoops it out of the water.

The dog shakes his hind quarters, his chest, his head and his ears all in a millisecond, spraying water everywhere. I don't mind, because he's safe. I untie the laces of the trainers, hoping that is the last time they'll get wet. But I'm not taking my clothes off, not with the old man here — I'll have to drip dry.

I am perched on a flat wooden boat that looks like a raft with a tent pitched on it. It rocks when waves splash, but there's no going back now. I watch as the old man wipes his face with both hands, then he bends down and picks something off a hook. *My locket!* Thanking him, I open the catch. I have to see Mum. She hasn't changed: the same smile, the same love reaching me.

The man is lifting a large bundle off the deck. It resembles a rolled up rush bathmat, but when he stretches it out, I see that it is a sail. Looks hand-made, laced together with twine. He uncoils some rope, then gestures to me to hold the material at the base while he unravels it, holding it aloft. As the sail billows out, it reminds me of Viking sails I've seen in schoolbooks: brownish beige and curved. I can't stop gazing; it's beautiful.

Arching his back, the dog yawns. He turns round and round, curling into a tiny ball. My hand drifts onto his back and I stroke his short hairy coat. We are speeding through the waves now and I can feel my body beginning to relax with the smoother motion. I watch the loose end of a rope skimming through the water, creating a continuous shimmering ripple, then dip in my hand, causing a mini fingertip shower.

The shoreline shrinks behind us as we approach an island. The man says something to me and picks up a coil of thick rope with a large stone attached. He throws it over the side and the rope spirals around a wooden block until only a twist is left. He slides a long thin pole from the side of the boat. My stomach contracts as I stare at the bamboo spear: it reaches way past his head and looks very sharp.

The old man's face creases as he throws me his cap. Holding the weapon, he edges forward, his toes curled over the side of the boat. He stands tall, opening his shoulders and takes several deep breaths, then he jumps forwards, splashing into the water.

He doesn't surface. I look again, then scramble across the flat decking. Where is he?

A minute goes by, two, three. The dog is running to the edge and sniffing. I'm afraid he will fall in. What will I do if the old man doesn't come back? I'm alone in the middle of the ocean, perched on a narrow boat with only a tent for shelter. Crawling under the canopy, I tuck up my knees and hold my head in my hands. My eyes are squeezed shut, but I can't avoid seeing the hooded wave of the tsunami rearing up, hovering like a thundercloud, waiting to destroy me.

The dog whines, then noses my elbow and curls into my lap. I've heard the saying 'a dog is a man's best friend' and it's true: this scruffy dog is my only friend right now.

The deck suddenly rocks and my heart races. *The*

water's coming back! Clutching the dog for support, I open my eyes a crack. But it's just the old man: he is shaking his hair, droplets flying everywhere. He grins, the gap in his mouth looking even darker in his glistening white teeth. My mouth must be hanging open like a fish, for he points at me, then at the yellow fish he has speared. He grins, then slides it off the pole. I smile, not because we have food, but because the old man is here: he's alive.

Grasping a knife, he slices off the fins and tail, throwing them overboard — I hope a shark isn't waiting to grab them. The old man's knuckles glow white as he grips his knife, expertly slicing down the belly of a fish. He crouches under the canopy and I sit opposite, watching him prepare the food. On the floor is a small cooker, with folding legs. He pulls out a pan and, with his other hand, feels along a shelving unit for a bottle of oil. It reminds me of our herb and spice cabinet with jars held in place by thin strips of wood – except this shelf is nearly empty except for bottled water and a bag of rice.

It's like being in a caravan: everything useful and in its place. Opposite me is a long, slatted shelf with a thick plastic bag underneath, maybe for storage. A woven basket is hanging on a protruding strut of wood. The man reaches up to a smaller shelf which is held up by a wooden bracket. He lifts down a string bag containing what look like large garlic cloves.

The man has his back to me now, so I don't see him lighting the cooker, but I smell oil burning. I stare at the blue and yellow flame. I'm relieved that he doesn't ask me to assist. The Woman has taken over the cooking at home and I'm glad, because after Mum died, Dad and I lived off ready meals.

Sizzling jets of fat are jumping off the pan — I hope the boat doesn't catch alight. Three large bamboo poles curve across to form the ceiling, which looks like a Vshape from the outside. Two smooth tree trunks are fixed either side of the boat; I guess they keep the structure together, but I'm no engineer. The flooring is also bamboo, linked together with twine, laced over and under: simple, but effective. The planks on the outside deck felt flat, but they must be safer to stand on in rough weather. There is even a hollowed out kind of bum seat right at the back. *Cool!*

It feels unreal that I am about to eat a meal in a traditional Kabang. It feels like a once-in-a-lifetime moment. As soon as I bite into a chunk of flesh, it's like I've never tasted fish before. My taste buds are working on overdrive. Fish fingers and cod steaks have nothing on freshly speared fish from the ocean! I lick my fingers while the old man kneels down and places a heavy kettle on the cooker. Soon, hot liquid is burning my throat. I close my eyes, feeling heat warming my whole body. When I open them, the flames have died and the old man has placed his cap over his eyes. He deserves a rest after diving for five minutes with a single breath. I can only hold my breath for about twenty seconds.

Crawling past him, I pick up the rope the old man was making. I often braid my hair for school. It's become a bit of a competition between Izzy, Loren and me: looking at different styles in fashion magazines and trying to imitate them. I try weaving the strands into the rope, thinking of how Mum used to plait my hair. I can almost feel her hands smoothing my fringe and hear her saying *"it's not quite perfect, but it will do."*

I have been sitting cross legged so long that my legs are going to sleep. Shuffling back under the canopy, I sit with my knees facing the shelf and my heels butted up beside me. It feels warm, cosy, protected from the wind, with intricate interlaced patterns on the 'walls.' Running my finger up and down the V-shapes, I wonder who made it and how long it took to weave.

Quiet and still the waves are now, so different from the morning of the tsunami. It seems impossible this is the same sea that was so harsh, that took so many people's lives. A sigh escapes my lips as I think of Dad. Where is he? Can he really still be alive?

The sun is lower in the sky, casting orange and red and gold rays across the sea. I could draw a smooth line to the horizon, as there is only a touch of wind drifting my hair onto my cheek. I should be scared, alone with the fisherman on a strange boat skimming the surface of the sea, but I feel calm for the first time in days. We are a tiny speck in a dark landscape, but somehow I feel safe on the old wooden boat; it may be handmade, but it must have weathered many storms.

It is so quiet. The rhythmic breathing of the old man is keeping me company, and I can hear the ripple of the waves brushing up against the boat. Gone is the rush and noise of the resort, the stress and fear and fight to find Dad. All I can do is sit and stare into the last rays of disappearing light. Here I am drifting with no pressure, no expectation, or rush to achieve. Tomorrow, I will search for Dad, do whatever it takes; but tonight, here on the Kabang, I can rest. I am free.

29. No Goodbyes

MARTI

The sky is streaked with bright red and orange as if it doesn't want to go to sleep. It teases us with colour, then yawns and fades into mist. I am like that. On Christmas Day I was full of hope and now there's nothing. I couldn't stay at the temple, not after finding Rune. So I'm back at the hotel, treated like dirt again. As soon as I returned, the manager gave me a spade and ordered me to empty the pool, so it is ready for the next batch of tourists — if they ever come back. The digger has scooped out the larger items, leaving a thick layer of mud. I have been up and down the ladder all afternoon and even though the air is cooling in the dusk, I'm hot enough to fry.

"Marti, is that you?" I see Jo's face looking down at me. "What on earth are you doing? I thought you were acting as an interpreter, not a dogsbody?" I climb up and slop the bucket into a container.

"Ooh, that smells vile!" Jo is holding her nose and taking a pace backwards. "Just as well I've eaten. But if you're hungry, I'm sure they could find something for you." I shake my head. How can I eat when my friend is lying dead in the temple?

"George Skelton told me you had a new job up at the makeshift morgue." I nod and she wrinkles her eyebrows. "So what went wrong: why are you back here?" I don't want to tell her about Rune, so I ask if Mr Skelton found his wife at the field hospital.

Jo sighs like a sail being filled, crumpling when the wind dies. "I don't know if we'll find anyone alive now." Her throat stretches, so I can see the veins standing out like thin plant stalks. "My world has been torn apart. I don't think I'll ever see my husband again, and my beautiful step-daughter is still missing. It must be my fault; I pushed her too hard. I'll never forgive myself if she doesn't come back." Jo says something about feeling a failure, but I can't focus on her words; I am thinking about the girl with golden hair.

After sniffing loudly, she blows her nose. "I'm going to check all the field hospitals, to see if... "She raises her eyes, wet with tears. "I just want to know."

Now I have hurt Jo. She is kind and all I have done is scrape off another layer of pain.

When the sun closes its eyes, I creep to my room, close the blind and curl up in bed. And think of Rune. One moment he was there; the next, death had stolen him. I almost wish it could have been a slow sickness, so I could have said goodbye. Rune taught me, a Moken lad, about a world where people say hello and goodbye. But there had been no goodbyes for my friend. Not now. Not ever. Another tide will cover the beach, and if I am lucky, sleep will cover my mind. When the sun rises, it will burn away the mist, but it cannot burn away the pain.

PART 4 – DESTINY

*You're flying through the water with shoals
of tiny fish scattering at your fingertips.
You can go anywhere, do anything;
there are no rules, no boundaries.*

– Marti

30. The Locket

30th December 2004

KRISTA

For the first time since I came to Thailand, I didn't have a nightmare. It is cosy snuggled up under the canopy. I don't know what time it is, but the sun is bright, so I must have slept a long time. Rolling my shoulders, I arch my neck then stretch my arms. The bandage has gone; in its place is a palm leaf tied with twine. Last night I felt sick when I saw the open wound, but when I touch the padding now, my arm doesn't hurt. Whatever kind of herbal drug the man used, it's working. Looking at my bare feet, the cuts seem less visible, no longer bright red.

The dog is whining. He's tied to the mast and straining towards a bowl of fish. I can't help smiling. "Wait a minute, I need to wash!" It's scary leaning over the boat, but I scoop up water and splash my face. Now the dog is dribbling out of both sides of his mouth. "Go on then, I'll untie you. But don't go nosing around: the old man doesn't like that, does he?"

I've called him Sniff. I know the dog's male, because he lifts his leg. His pee stinks, but the old man has persuaded the dog to do his business at the front of the boat. He does swill the puddle with water, but I'm never sitting there again. Having dried my face on my blouse, I wiggle onto the hollowed-out seat and wait for the old man; he must have dived in to catch more fish for breakfast.

I've started thinking of us as a team, almost a family: the old wrinkled fisherman, the girl from across the seas and the little short haired dog whose eyes are fixed on the fish. "Here you are!" Sniff's paws scrabble on the bamboo, but he can't quite reach it. Flattening his body, he stretches like a marine, but the rope won't let him. When I flick the scrap with my bare toes, it's gone in an instant. "You want more?" He licks his lips. "This is for me too," I laugh.

We share the fish, then I swill the pan by dipping it in the sea like I've seen the old man do. He hasn't resurfaced and I'm beginning to get worried. "Where is he, Sniff?" The dog's ears prick up, but the old man doesn't materialize. "He can't still be diving, can he? Perhaps he's on shore finding some more fruit for us?" I stroke the dog's ears and he nestles in closer. He may be dirty and scrawny and he's probably got fleas, but he's the only company I've got.

We are anchored in a bay close to shore; I could swim there if I wasn't scared of water. I scan the beach, but can only see a young couple embracing. I've never kissed a boy. Jack has never asked and I don't fancy the others. Some boys ask any girl, just so they can boast they've had another girlfriend. I'd never go out with that type of guy; I want someone who is fun, but I have to be able to trust him.

The couple have reached the far end of the beach where I can see buildings. This might be my resort! I put my arms around Sniff. "Dad and my step-mum could be over there. That big building, do you see it…" I hold the dog's head in the right direction. "No, that one over there;

I bet it's my hotel." As I strain to see it, I notice another person walking towards the couple. "Sniff, it's him, the old man! Look, he's wearing a cap, I'm sure it's him." The dog is dancing in a circle, about to trip me up, so I untie him. Immediately, he trots up to the pan and licks it spotless.

I'm more interested in getting the fisherman's attention. I cup my hands around my mouth. "Come back!" My feet almost slip as the boat rocks with a wave. Perhaps he can't hear me, or perhaps he isn't bothered. It's not far to the shore, maybe only two lengths of a pool. "I bet he's just gone to buy us some food, Sniff; he won't he long."

Nails scrape across the deck as the dog turns round and round, following his tail, the end of the rope twirling round him. It would be wonderful to curl up in a tiny ball, then wake up and it would all be over. Dad would be here and we'd be safe and happy. I lift my hand, to touch the locket. It's not there! Bending my neck, I push open my blouse.

It's gone, my locket's gone!

Suddenly I know. "He's taken it!" I shout at Sniff. "I saw him last night, he was looking at it again. He pretended he was bandaging my arm, but he must have drugged me!" The dog ignores me. "You saw him, didn't you, Sniff? He took my Mum's locket, the only thing I've got left and he's going to sell it. We've got to stop him!" I remember seeing the old man's eyes light up when he saw my locket glinting in the sun. He must have been eyeing it up all yesterday. "I don't care how much it's worth, it's got Mum's picture in and we're not going to let him sell it."

We face each other, his head in my hands. I stare into his trusting brown eyes. "You know what we've got to do, don't you?" Sniff wags his tail. "That's right: if I do it, so can you."

Picking up the loose end of the dog's rope, I advance slowly like the childhood game, *Granny's footsteps*. "Don't be frightened..." He backs under the canopy. "Look, I don't want to do this anymore than you..." His little body is trembling now, so I free him, slipping the rope off his neck. "Please Sniff, you've got to come with me, I need you." I coil the rope and put it in my rucksack, then tighten the straps over my shoulders. "Look, I've got it now, so you'll be fine." I climb onto the side of the boat, praying he'll follow.

+++

MARTI

I'm woken by loud banging at my door, so I pull the duvet over my head pretending I'm underwater. The knocking gets louder. Forcing my eyes open, I slouch across the room.

"Slept in, did you? The boss is going mad." Virote is leaning against the doorpost. "Now, what was it the boss said...something about Moken scum I think." He flicks an imaginary speck off his clean uniform, then stares at my creased clothes. "Did little Fish Boy try out the nightclubs last night? Can't little Fish Boy hold his drink?" He leans forward and winks. "Or has little Fish Boy been with a girl? His head shoots forward like a turtle poking out of its shell. "Was it worth it?"

Ignoring his sniggers of laughter, I pad across to the window and pull up the blind. Sunlight dazzles me. Virote was right about one thing: I must have slept in. I remember tossing and turning, not being able to rest — and now he'll never let me. His fins tucked in when Chaow was taken by the waves, but now Stonefish is ready to use poison again. He slithers into the room. "I'm

195

your line manager now!" His nostril twitches as he leans forward, smelling of garlic.

As the sun climbs the sky, Virote won't leave me alone. He has thrown a net to trap me and I am ordered to dump the slops into the garbage bins. I know where I want to stuff the disgusting rubbish and it's not there!

I am washing my hands at the outside tap, when he creeps up behind me. "What's this horrible smell? Oh dear, you've put fish skin and bones into the wrong garbage bin." He crosses his legs and his eyebrows crease in the centre. "What a shame, now you'll have to scrape it all out again." When he smiles, I feel like spearing him through the heart.

+++

KRISTA

I've done it! I can't believe I have swum this far. When I wade out, my legs are lead weights, like a robot powering down. But Sniff has enough energy for both of us: his little paws are whirling as he paddles towards me, then he runs around in circles: a spin dryer. I don't need more water — I've just had an ocean of it! I try to stroke him, but my hand won't do as it's told, so I sit down and he curls up in a wet ball beside me. Sniff is a life-saver. I was panicking when he kept barking and backing away from the side of the boat, but when I heard the water splash as he jumped in, it was such a relief.

The beach is littered with debris which seems to go on forever. "Can you see the fisherman, Sniff? We've got to catch him, or I'll never see Mum's locket again." The dog puts his head on one side, then shakes himself all over, spraying water droplets everywhere. "Thanks very much!"

He rubs himself dry, but I can't waste time stripping

off my wet clothes. Scrunching the blouse, I attempt to squeeze out the water. My arm twinges a little, but it's not painful. I'd almost forgotten about the wound; the leaves the old man pressed on must have been strong medicine. I haven't used the sling for a while now, and suddenly realise that I've left Jo's sparkly scarf on the Kabang. I wonder how long it will stay under the canopy, before the wind whisks it away. My step-mum must be worried sick not knowing where I am.

The old man's dressing is soggy, so maybe I should take it off. Wish I could ask the old man. Then I remember the locket and grimace. I put my arms around the dog. "Find him, Sniff!"

The dog rolls over, legs in the air. "Ha ha, very funny." I thump the sand, causing Sniff to bounce up, and I feel guilty for scaring him. Stroking his head, I feel his body tense. His tail is erect and his ears pricked; the short hair on his back rising in the centre like a Mohican hairstyle.

"What is it?" I whisper, putting my arm around him. I can feel the vibration in his throat as he starts to growl. His gaze is fixed straight ahead. There is a small crowd and I can hear shouting — or is it crying? Sniff has stopped growling, but his ears are still pricked.

"It's alright," I tell him. "We can go now." The dog starts nosing around, sniffing at shredded plastic bags.

"Not now!" Untying the rope from my waist, I creep towards him, my trainers slurping water; he darts away and digs his back paws in the sand. Then he puts his head on his front paws, inviting me to play. I lunge, but he bounces to one side and repeats the pose.

"Don't do this to me, Sniff, it's not a game." Remembering the empty sweet packet in the rucksack, I pull it out and rustle it. The dog creeps forward. I hold out my hand pretending to hold a sweet. "Please let me put on the lead. I won't hurt you, I promise." The dog raises an eyebrow, then flicks his gaze to my hands. "Mmm, come and get the nice sweetie…"

By the time I catch him, I'm sweating. He pushes a dry nose into my hand. "Sorry I had to trick you, but I'll find some food soon, I promise." Sniff raises an eyebrow as if he doesn't believe me.

Four ladies are resting against the sea wall, comforting an elderly woman who is crying. Their eyes expand as I approach. So what if I'm a white girl with sunburned cheeks, pulling a stray dog on a rope: haven't they seen anything like this before? I stare at the group of Thai ladies and conclude, no, they probably haven't. They are wearing veils across their faces, but their eyes are dark, mysterious.

One lady smiles and steps forward. "Engleesh?" *What a relief: someone to talk to someone at last!* I pull Sniff towards her. "Have you seen an old man on the beach? He stole my locket. Did you see anybody just now?"

The lady nods. "Engleesh."

"No, he's Thai I think." The woman smiles, so I continue. "I'm staying at The Green Turtle with Jo, but my Dad was in the tsunami, so I was looking for him, then I got lost in the mangroves, then the man found me." The woman is smiling, so I carry on. "But he stole my locket, my Mum's locket and I don't know what to do!"

The lady's eyes slant as she looks at her friends, then she gestures to me. "Engleesh!" With a sinking feeling, I realise this is the only word she can speak in my language. But she seems to like me, because she beckons for me to follow them onto the road. It is scarred with holes and a bicycle swerves to avoid us, nearly falling into an open sewer. I'm sure this is the resort, but I can't see my hotel; this must be a different part of town.

A scooter whizzes past and I wish I could hitch a lift, but I remember Dad's warning. Anyway, there's the dog. "I'm not leaving you, Sniff," I whisper, as a car passes us and parks further up the street. I'm desperate to find someone the old man.

One lady starts speaking fast and pointing at Sniff. The older lady raises her arm. "Engleesh," she says, holding her hand out to me. I walk next to her and the other ladies skip past to avoid being close to the dog. I look up at the buildings as we pass under their shadows, hoping one will be The Green Turtle. The basements are still covered in silt and dried mud is still pasted onto the walls like African huts. Sludge clings to the window frames, but many have no windows. I hope Sniff doesn't cut his paws on glass or get any splinters.

"Where are we going?" I whisper, when I lag behind the group for a rest. Sniff puts his head on one side and looks at me, as if he's thinking. "I know what you mean," I tell him. "I'm tired too, but these ladies are kind, they want to help." Sniff noses my hand, then licks me. "Yes, I'm sure we'll find some food... come on!"

+++

MARTI

I can't stand it any longer. When I see smoke curling in the air, I know Virote is taking a break, so I sneak behind his back. The ocean is calling, so down to the ocean I go. The sun is shining on the water like nothing has happened. I kneel down and a wave ripples through my fingers. Wish I could wash away Virote like that. He thinks he's so important, but if he was in my underwater world, I would flash past him like a stingray's tail. I would show him what real power is. He thinks he is better than me, but in the water, I am king.

When I took my first steps underwater, kicking like Papa taught me, he held my body and I flapped my arms. Then he guided me deeper, but I wasn't afraid. Why should I be? I was born on the Kabang; it was all I'd ever known. When the sun rose, we would sail between islands and dive for fish. When the sun set and the moon pulled the tide back, we would sleep. I lived and breathed the ocean.

I love her, yet I fear her. She is gentle, then she is fierce, snatching lives. A piece of blue tarpaulin is flapping like a flag, annoying me, so I run towards it and stamp hard. It won't stop fluttering, so I pull back my leg, about to kick it, when something catches my attention. A passport. After I've unstuck the pages, I see a faded photo: a young man with hair curling around his ears, not smiling. Poor guy, he must have been unhappy. I put the booklet in my pocket, then take it out again. He won't need it now.

Picking up a smooth stone, I aim high into the ocean. *Find your way home, find peace!* When it splashes, I try to picture the man being saved, not being sucked under by the Laboon's power. Perhaps I'll take the passport back to the temple; he might still be alive. I throw another stone and imagine it flying right to the edge of the ocean.

Further out in the bay, a low boat is sitting on the water. Why is a Kabang here? I walk closer, wondering if someone has brought their catch to sell. But all the boats need mending, apart from Grandad's. Is he here? Being curious, I strip off my clothes, tucking the passport under my shirt.

It feels wonderful to swim again. Taking a deep breath, I tuck my feet under my chest and pull the water towards me. Bubbles dance at my fingertips as I dive deeper. The water is clear and I can distinguish the colourful outline of the coral reef. A shoal of orange and white fish scatter when I swim closer.

My lungs are saying they want air, but I tell them to wait. I have seen a large spiky shell, the type Grandad likes. Kicking hard, I glide along the sea bottom and scoop it into my hand. I've got no bag strapped around my waist, so I hold the shell as I kick up to the light.

Heaving myself onto the Kabang, I realise that I am breathing heavily; I haven't dived in a long time. A smell hits me. Moken never use the boat as a toilet, so perhaps there is illness here? No-one is crouching under the roof, although I can see signs of cooking. Putting the shell on the deck, I decide to wait until someone returns.

If it was Grandad who sailed the Kabang, I must speak with him. The waves are washing over the hull, but I can't hear what they are saying. Wish I could read the signs of the wind and waves like Grandad. No longer do I feel one with the ocean: she is a part of me, but not the whole part.

The waves bring me his voice. An old man is standing on the shore, waving his cap. My toes curl around the edge of the boat, ready to dive, then I glance into the canopy, feeling like I am leaving home. Seeing the shell, I hook it over the wooden strut next to a string bag. Grandad will get a nice surprise when he swims back.

When I walk out of the waves, something shines so brightly that it almost blinds me. I squint through narrowed eyes to see Grandad swinging a necklace from his fingers. His gaze is glued to it, like a dog to a fresh piece of fish.

"Where did you find that: on the beach?" I ask. He looks like he has a head full of words, but they are fighting each other. Maybe he's just seen another body.

His rib cage stretches as he takes a deep breath.

"The girl, she's not well. I took the necklace while she was asleep."

"Looks valuable. You could sell that for thousands of Baht; have enough oil to last your whole life!"

Grandad shakes his head. "No, it is hers."

I'm confused. Moken girls like natural necklaces made out of twine or leather strung with beads, like mine. I touch the thin cord around my neck and finger the beads.

Coiling the chain in his hand, he points to the Kabang. "White girl."

"There's no-one there, and especially not a foreign girl." The old man must have had too much sun, he's gone crazy.

"Listen to me, Sky! I left her to sleep, because her body needs to heal." He frowns. "She is young. I couldn't leave her: the spirits brought her to me. I found some herbs to heal her of pain, but she looked whiter than the inside of a shell."

I look at Grandad, surprised. The Kabang is sacred, his home, his life, all he's ever known — and yet he was willing to share it with a western tourist. "If she really was there, then where is she now?" I ask.

A patchwork of tight lines gather on Grandad's forehead. "You must find her." He takes my arm, gripping it tightly. "I took the necklace to show you — she was asleep when light touched the sky, so I thought I could find you before she woke." He points at the concrete buildings, then hunches his shoulders into his neck and leans back. "Sky will know what to do, I told myself. Sky will tell the big bosses and they will find the girl's family."

As he swings the chain, I hold out my hand. The gold pendant is heavier than I expected and has little markings around the rounded edges.

"What does she look like?" I don't find out much; just that the girl is older than Petal and younger than Coral. Then Grandad says she has hair the colour of sunshine.

My stomach tenses like I'm about to dive into the bluest purest ocean. Jo's step-daughter has disappeared... Can the girl on the Kabang be the girl with golden hair? Excitement causes me to catch my breath. I have to find her!

31. Fear

KRISTA

Stone pillars rise above the houses: we have reached the temple. The older lady peels off from our group and stumbles across to the charts showing the latest death tolls. Another board is plastered with notes, corners flapping in the breeze. Messages and photos and names of real people... maybe, real dead people. Faces of toddlers, children, couples and elderly people, all smiling into the camera. Torn apart.

Has anyone seen Ellie Joy Hodges, aged 12, from Little Drayton, England. We love you so much, Ellie and we are praying for you to be safe. Please, please come back to us. Remember you can phone us any time day or night. We are at the hotel waiting. Mum and Dad xxx

I hope that they won't be waiting forever. I scan more messages, as I shuffle along in the queue.

Jonny, you are the life and soul of the party! We miss you so much, please get in touch, mate. Mike, Lou and Esther.

A wedding photo looks so out of place in all this misery. A young couple gazing at each other, holding hands. I pass by quickly. Some notes do not have photos, just words of love and a mobile number.

Then I stop. He is looking at me, his eyes crinkled with laughter. *Dad!* I reach out and touch his hair, his face and all the time he is looking at me and he doesn't blink. A message is attached to the photo, and my heart beats faster remembering Jo writing it.

My darling Rob, I know that you'll see this. You have only just come into my life and I won't let you go. Krista and I need you and love you so much. Jo xxx

The words go blurry. She really loves Dad. And she cares about me. I read the message over and over, tears running down my cheeks. I care about her, too. I wish I'd been nicer to my step-mum.

I wipe my eyes, trying to refocus. Then blink and rub my eyes again. A happy 'me' with glossy hair is staring at me. My pulse shoots off the scale.

Krista, please come back, I'm sorry if I... The next line is scribbled out, then she signs it *Love Jo.*

I sink down in the dust with the dog. A second later, he starts trembling and his body stiffens. His ears are pricked and his neck is straining. Following his fixed gaze, I see a man standing in the shadows of the temple. There is something about him I recognise. He's wearing shades, but I know that he knows I've noticed him, because he lifts his cap and smiles. And I suddenly feel scared.

A woman blocks my view, but the man side-steps. A low growl rumbles deep in the dog's throat. If I could growl, I'd join him. I glance at the board, at our photos. Dad is still smiling; he's not worried — but I am.

Having dragged Sniff along for about five metres, I

pretend to stroke him, but sneak a look between his ears. The man with the checked shirt is sliding his hand along the noticeboard, but his gaze is still fixed on me. My forehead feels moist and I can smell my armpits sweating.

Sniff won't budge. He is standing tall, his hackles raised, like he's on guard. *Run, Sniff!* When the man turns his back on us, I breathe a sigh of relief. His forefinger is sliding along the photos —must be traumatised because he's lost a loved one. But as his finger rests on my photo, I know it's me that's traumatised. He circles a ring around my face, then pulls it off the board. I feel sick.

He is holding my picture in his hand. His eyes aren't smiling, but his mouth curves. His foot starts tapping, sending shivers down my spine. The dog is straining, growling, in attack mode. I force my gaze away and try to catch someone's attention, but they are lost in their own worries. A woman walks straight past, eyes glued to the noticeboard. Her fingers skim over the letters and pictures, then her shoulders droop and she moves on. Then I yank Sniff's rope and run.

Footsteps slap the ground behind me. Can't think straight. Don't know what to do. I'm screaming inside as we tear round the corner of the building. *Got to get past this pillar... get away...*

Sniff's tongue is hanging out, then his little legs sink down and he refuses to move. *Pointed tan shoes! Don't look up!* But something makes me. The man takes off the shades. His grey eyes are dead eyes, no expression. My throat tightens; he's cast a spell on me.

Tipping back on the balls of his feet, he pulls something out of his jacket pocket. *My photo!* He raises one eyebrow, so it disappears under his cap.

Someone help me! The words are trapped in my head. Sniff growls, but the man's eyes don't flicker. He replaces my photo in his pocket, his gaze never leaving me. I shout, but it's like I've got a sore throat and my voice comes out as a whisper. He smiles and walks towards me.

A hand clutches my shoulder. Spinning around, I see the Thai lady with beautiful eyes, and I clutch the folds of her dress. Lifting her veil, she screams a volley of words at the man. He raises one eyebrow and slowly replaces his shades. Then he walks away. But my stomach is churning knowing that the man has my picture, he is touching me.

I'm still clinging onto her, but two monks are watching, their arms folded into flowing saffron robes. Their heads are close together like they are talking about me. I can hear the swish of material as a monk approaches us, a swarm of flies circling around his shaven head. My hair suddenly feels itchy.

Abruptly, the lady drops my arm and joins her friends, shuffling away from the temple. I wish I could join them, but Sniff is digging in his heels, straining as if the man is still there. The group of veiled ladies disappear — probably scared off by the monks. I'm desperate to follow, but Sniff's doing a tug of war.

"No, not that way!" He's pulling me back to the Missing Person's board. I manage to drag him off the path, then he leans against my legs and curls up in a tiny ball. I can feel his little heart beating; he must be exhausted. I'm desperate to get away, but I can't leave him.

I wrap my arms around Sniff's neck, resting my head on his. My photo is out there in the man's hands; he could be looking at me right now. And if he can do that, what else is he capable of?

+++

MARTI

She's not at The Green Turtle. Nor is Jo. And Sea View Hotel is still closed. I don't know why I'm searching; it must be a different girl whom Grandad helped. How am I supposed to find this kid when there are so many hotels and villas here? Maybe I should just sell the necklace.

But Grandad wanted me to find her; he didn't smile, but there was a light shining in his eyes that I thought had died with Papa. So I will look for the girl, even though the chance of finding her is like pulling a single krill out of a whale's mouth.

Further along the street, I spot a boutique. Its shop front is smashed and I'm walking past when I hear a shout; a woman is waving from the first floor window. "Come on in, we're open for business!" I walk into the ruins of the shop, then climb the stairs.

"We saved what we could," says the assistant. "What would you like?" When I say I'm looking for a young white girl, the lady raises her eyebrows. "You want a white girl and she has to be young?" she repeats slowly.

"That's what Grandad said," I reply.

The shopkeeper nudges an assistant. "His Grandad says…" She looks at me suspiciously. "I think we should tell the manager about this, he might want to call the police!"

Before they can catch me, I run. Perhaps that wasn't such a good idea. I decide to ask the aid worker for advice, but when I reach the temple, she's gone. Seeing an official, I offer him the passport, but he glares as if I'm a thief. Dropping it, I spin around and merge into the crowd before he can question me. Sometimes we are fortunate and the wind blows warm air and sometimes it blows cold.

I hide behind a pillar, feeling its strength. I will go back to Grandad and give back the necklace — it has brought me bad luck. I shrug my shoulders and look down the path.

And that's when I see her: the girl from the hotel, Jo's step-daughter. Blue eyes are looking straight at me. Through me. As she turns her head, her hair swings across her shoulders. It looks tangled, like it needs brushing, but I am sure it is her. But she is more interested in stroking a little dog, than looking at me.

I stab my foot in the dust. Of course she wouldn't notice a sea gypsy. I'm looking at the ground, when I hear barking and see a wild animal racing straight for me. I step out of the shade of the pillar to pick up a stone and raise my arm. The next thing I know, the girl is screaming at me.

Ducking one way, I dodge, but the dog is too quick. Tensing my body, I shield my face. I just have time to realise that a rough wet tongue is licking my hand, not biting me, when the girl flings herself at me like a human spear. "Don't you dare hurt him!"

You're the one who is attacking, I think. I grip the girl's shoulders, holding her at arm's length and she is twisting like a fish trying to escape a hook.

"Get off me!" she screams.

"But the dog likes me..."

The girl stops flapping and stares at the dog, who is looking up at me with big brown eyes. Wriggling free, she bends down and scoops the dog into her arms, her head close to his.

"I'm not going to let him hurt you."

I don't understand girls. Here I was, doing nothing, when she suddenly attacks me. And now she accuses me of hurting her dog, when it was just licking my hand.

The dog... I'm sure it knows me. It looks like the stray that sniffs around our hut. Petal loves it and gives it bits of fish or rice. Grandad does too; I've seen his hand

209

slipping down and stroking the dog when he doesn't think anyone is watching. My little sister once told Grandad that she knew he liked the dog, but he got angry and shouted at it, then Petal cried. She was the first person the dog came to, when we built the hut by the water. Petal even thinks that the dog saved her from the Laboon.

While I've been thinking, the girl has run to the Missing Person's board, and the dog has followed her. It can't be the same one; there are hundreds of stray dogs with short hair and spiky ears. But he wags his tail as I approach.

The girl hasn't noticed me. She is leaning forward, arching her neck. A man wearing a dark cap is watching them. He is standing as still as a pillar, but he is tapping his foot. I've seen him hanging around here before. I wonder who the girl is looking for. Has she seen death and is still living in a nightmare? I know she tried to attack me, but I still wish she would look at me again.

I must be crazy: I'm standing next to rows of corpses, death is all around, stinking in the heat, but all I can think of is the girl with golden hair. She's running her finger down the pictures, zigzagging, searching. Now she's touching one, but she's elbowed out of the way. I shuffle forward until I'm part of the crowd. I want to talk to her so much, but what can I say?

I'm Marti the sea gypsy who you saw diving for coins in the hotel pool?

I'm Marti the man who is going to make his fortune and fly like the tourists?

I'm Marti who would like to swim with you through the coral reefs.

My breathing is gearing up like an outboard motor. It's like my tip toes are perched on the edge of the boat ready for my first solo dive into the ocean.

The man's tapping has grown faster — he is

annoying me. His pointed shoes skid on something and he falls out of the shadows, stumbling against the girl, clutching her arm. She gasps and I can see the whites of her eyes. But he doesn't let go.

I dive straight in. "Can I help you, Miss?"

The girl shoulders drop as the man lets her go. He lifts his hands in mock horror and grins. Then he uncoils his body and leans on the noticeboard, crossing one leg. I watch him pull a cell phone out of his pocket, then he walks past us. The girl is rubbing her arm and I'm feeling angry. But what am I doing wasting time on him, this is my chance.

My lips feel suddenly dry. "Are you ok?" *Ok?* That's so pathetic — but it works because our eyes meet. I mean, really meet. It's like when you put a bait on a fishing line and the fish swims towards it and *bam!* it's hooked.

A crease forms between her eyebrows and she tips her head to one side. "I saw you by the pool, didn't I?"

I nod like a little dog, eager to go for a walk. "Yes. I work at the hotel."

A smile curls around her cheeks. "Ah, yes, I remember," she says. "Entertaining the girls!" Her blue eyes twinkle and I feel this blush sweeping up my cheeks. Stabbing my foot into the dust, I wish I could kick myself instead.

"Did you get much money?" she says.

I scrunch up my toes. "No." I look into her eyes. "I don't usually do stuff like that."

"No?" My stomach clenches, then I notice two little pools dancing in her cheeks. Teasing is good: teasing means she might like me. I manage to stop nodding and ask how she is. Her eyes fix on the noticeboard and her smile dies. And I feel stupid. She's looking for a relative — she's bound to be sad.

211

"What happened?" I point to the bandage on her arm.

She raises her eyes to the sky. "What do you think? We've just had a tsunami, right?"

Why am I staring at the ground when the girl is here, right in front of me? I force myself to straighten my back and ask if she'd like me to fetch a medic.

"It's fine. This old man did some kind of medicine and it doesn't hurt so much now."

"Looks bad."

She shrugs her slim shoulders. "Not as bad as some people." She nods in the direction of the morgue. "Like them."

Inside, I'm curling up in a ball like the dog. I need to find out if it was my grandad who helped, but it's like the ocean has swallowed my tongue and my words are stuck beneath it.

Then I hear an English voice. "Yes, yes, I'm still looking... of course I will... no, you don't need to worry..."

The man with the cap hasn't noticed me; he's scowling at the cell phone. "Well, in that case, I'll come and get you." His voice sounds warm, but his face looks hard and cold. Strange.

As he slips the phone back in his pocket and looks at us, the girl shrinks closer to me. The man lifts his cap and raises his eyebrow. I'd like to shave it off. Then he spins around on his heels and walks away. I'd do a rude gesture behind his back if the girl wasn't here.

My nostrils are doing this expanding thing they always do when I'm angry. The girl looks at me, then suddenly her mouth dances and little whirlpools crease the middle of her cheeks. Her sunburned face is spotted with insect bites, but she's the most beautiful girl I've ever seen. And she's smiling at me.

I'm like one of those western guys at the beach who jerk their shoulders back and suck in their stomachs when a pretty girl walks by. I can't breathe until she leans forward to read a message on the board. Her damp clothes are clinging to her body. And I can't stop looking.

Think of something else Marti, or she'll think you are a bad man. She's tracing a photo with her finger — I wonder if it's someone she knows. It couldn't be a photo of one of my people, as Moken don't own cameras. The only modern technology the elders accept are outboard motors, which are traded for fish, baskets, model Kabangs, or shell necklaces. These are better than the ankle bracelets and hundreds of jingling bangles girls usually buy, or those plastic Buddhas and Sand Mandala kits for trendy tourists playing at being Buddhists.

Like I'm playing at being a man. I should know what to say to her, how to act. I'm so close, yet I can't touch her. Her blue eyes are like the sea, changing shades as clouds dim the light of the sun. Her arms are slim and her hands look soft, but her nails are chipped, with odd patches of pink varnish. I look down at my own nails once made strong by the ocean; now they, too, are scratched and torn.

When I look up, she's gone white and her eyes are wide like deep sea fish. She's staring at the man who has reappeared; he is chatting to a short woman wearing a large straw hat and shades.

"Do you know that guy?" I ask. My question hangs in the air. The girl is gripping the noticeboard and her hands are shaking. As she sucks in a deep breath, I can see her ribs through the thin shirt.

Someone is shouting; a woman is running towards us. As she waves her hat, I recognise her: it's Jo. Striding past her is the man with the pointed shoes.

And the girl is running down the path, the dog

speeding in front of her. Long strands of hair are flying from side to side like a storm is sweeping her along. I hear a cry and see Jo clasping her mouth with both hands. She said her step-daughter had gone missing and she was desperate to find her, so why did the girl run away just now? Maybe they have argued and said things they regret.

I can't help thinking of my last words to Papa. I try to picture our hut in my mind and imagine telling him that I'll stay and sail the Kabang; but as soon as the words are in my head, it's like ocean currents are pulling them away, against my will.

Curls of dust sink into the ground. The girl has disappeared. This is the second time I've seen her here— but it's hardly the place for a date. *Stop right there, Marti! Remember your ancestors; marry a Moken girl. Yes, I know… but I can still dream…*

+++

KRISTA

I can still see his mouth slit open and his eyes devouring me. I feel sick thinking my image is locked in his possession. Even now I've escaped, he's still creeping me out.

And she was with him.

How could my step-mum team up with that man? I had begun to trust her, accept her, like her. I know she cares for me and Harry — or I thought she did. What's her game? If Dad knew about this, he'd tell that guy to get lost. But Dad may be lying in one of those body bags. I might never talk to him again, see him laugh or hear him say my name. I told him not to book the holiday — why didn't he listen?

If only we could rewind time, he'd be safe, The

Woman would be history and we'd be a proper family again. Mum would be sitting on the sofa, laughing, the locket swinging like a pendulum. Dad would be standing behind her, strong hands on her shoulders. I clutch my blouse, reaching for the chain, but my fingers grab empty air. It's gone — like Mum and Dad.

The old man left too. He pretended to help by treating my wounds, but he was a thief. That young guy didn't even help: he was going to throw a stone at Sniff. I'd never like anyone who could do that. He may be attractive and have the longest lashes, but I don't trust him. I don't trust anyone now — especially The Woman.

32. Revelation

MARTI

I'm pressing the locket so hard into my palm, that it's hot. Jo is squashed into an armchair, twisting a scarf around swollen fingers. I feel sorry for her; she didn't stop crying all the way back to The Green Turtle. The man with the checked shirt is with us in the lounge, tapping his feet on the floor. I don't like him, but if he's her husband, I'd better be polite.

Releasing my fist, I unfold my fingers like a lotus flower, revealing the golden secret. Jo gasps and leans forward, rubbing her eyes. As I swing the necklace, her head is moving from side to side and her hand is twitching. She's behaving just like the stray dog when I waft a piece of fish skin either side of his nose — she's even got a spit of saliva hanging off her mouth.

"Where did you get that? Did you find it? What have you done with her?"

I step back, surprised at her harsh tone. "Grandad gave it to me."

"Who? What? Where is she?" Jo flaps a tissue, then blows her nose loudly, while her husband stares at me.

"He said she had collapsed on the beach. Mother Ocean would have taken the girl, but Grandad brought her onto the Kabang." Jo's mouth is twisting to one side as she bites her cheek and stares at me with wide eyes. I

216

try again. "He looked after her when light faded in the sky." Now she is whimpering, so I speak quickly. "Then he gave me her necklace, so I can help find her family."

The woman's body expands as she stares at me, then her chest slowly deflates. She sinks back into the chair with a long sigh. "I've tried everything; I've downloaded more photos for the private detective." She turns to the man. "You've said you will find her, you've promised." She's strangling the scarf and I can hear pain in her voice. "She's my husband's only daughter, she's just fifteen. He's had a near-death experience — nearly drowned. He's recovering in hospital now, but if we don't find her, I think the shock would kill him." Jo's voice breaks into pieces.

I don't know what to do and I'm confused. *So the detective isn't her husband?* He murmurs something to her and she sniffs. "I know. I can't bear to think what might happen to her, all alone out there. What if...?"

The words hang in the air and I know what she means. I may only be a sea gypsy, but I've heard things. Bad people take girls and force them into the sex trade. Make them slaves.

Suddenly, she grabs my arm and the chain flies out of my fingers across the floor. Her scarf drapes round my wrist, colours merging, as she crushes my hand. "Help me find Krista, please!"

As the words hit me, my mind goes wild.

The girl with the golden hair is Krista, the Englishman's daughter! And I've just seen her, talked to her, the necklace is hers!

Unsticking myself from the clammy hands, I kneel down, feeling under the cabinet with a starfish hand. Touching the golden chain makes me feel closer to Krista. Jo shifts along the sofa, so I can sit down. The man pulls up a chair and sits opposite, his feet flat on the floor. I hope he doesn't start tapping them.

Jo talks about Krista so fast, that I can't understand it all. "... she's been gone for two days, then she suddenly turns up, then disappears again." She moves her hand violently, so I have to duck to avoid being hit, but this doesn't stop her flow. "It was such a stroke of good fortune that I met Tony."

The man raises an eyebrow. "Only too pleased to help. I'm off duty on holiday of course, but in an emergency like this, I felt it only right to step in and offer my assistance." He leans forward, rubbing his chin. "I certainly won't let your step-daughter slip through my fingers again, trust me."

"But how will you...?"

"Don't worry, I've got contacts. Being an ex-pat, I know people. Once you've been in the force, you know how to work the system, so to speak. I'll see what I can find out." He picks up his phone and dials, then says the signal is bad so he'll talk outside.

As the door closes, Jo tells me how she met Tony at the Missing Persons Board while he was looking for a friend he feared had drowned. They got talking and he volunteered to help find Krista, so she hired him as a private detective. She turns to me with tears in her eyes. "I felt so useless sitting here doing nothing while Rob's daughter is out there and he's...well, he's so sick." Jo's hands cover her cheeks and her chest rises up and down as she sobs.

I want to tell her how I found the Englishman on the beach, but her loud crying makes me feel uncomfortable, so I edge towards the door. I hear Jo blowing her nose, like waves crashing, then she stands up.

When I turn, she is wiping her face. "Please forgive me. I'll try not to embarrass myself like that again." She sniffs. "I've been so worried... not knowing... I mean, she just vanished..." She grabs my hand. "But now, I've got hope. She's still alive — and we'll find her." I nod, hoping she's right.

"Tell me everything about your grandad, anything you can think of." Before I can answer, my stomach rumbles. She looks at me. "Are you hungry, Marti? Come downstairs and we can talk while we eat." As soon as she says that, I realise that I'm starving. I'm desperate to find Krista, but I only had cold rice for breakfast.

Jo takes me to the restaurant and pays for a plate overflowing with rice — I'm not sure what's in the sauce, but at least it's hot. There are some stray tourists, but most have flown to safety. A group of aid workers is sitting in the corner, clustered around a map. Jo is distracted and keeps looking at them, while I'm eating. I'm about to explain how I carried her husband to safety, when she jumps up and strides across the room with a straight back. I hear snatches of conversion, then her voice rises. "And I thought you were supposed to care!"

She slams a spare chair against their table and storms towards me. "They said hundreds of people are out there needing their help." Jo's face is red and I think mine is too, it's so embarrassing. She won't sit down; she's hopping around like she needs the toilet. "But she's just a young girl, in a foreign country. Alone!" Jo spits the last word in their direction.

The charity people fold up their map. As they reach the door, one man looks back, lines creasing his forehead. "Sorry we can't help you. Good luck!"

I thank him, while Jo shouts into her phone. "Tony, where are you? I'm paying you to find my stepdaughter, so I need you here now!" She is gripping the phone like it's an anchor. I am looking for a gap to swim through.

"I'm glad your husband reached the hospital in time," I say. "He looked really bad and I thought he wouldn't make it."

"Yes, yes..." She looks at me, but her eyes don't focus. I can tell she's not really listening, as her gaze keeps darting to the window.

"I saw him," I say, "on the beach. He was..." Jo's phone rings, then she rushes over to the door. As the detective walks into the room, her voice rises like a monkey's excited chatter when a predator is near.

The detective is staring at me like he wants to scrape out information like fish guts. As his foot starts tapping, a shiver ripples through my chest.

"I'm going back to the beach," I tell Jo. "Thanks for the food." Pushing back my shoulders, I try to stay calm, but it's like the waters have been stirred up and I can't see clearly.

I'll tell Grandad about the English girl. It is not until I feel the sand between my toes, that I realise that Krista's locket is still in my pocket. Lifting it out, I flick open the catch for the first time. A woman is laughing at me, warm eyes sparkling with humour, as if I am important to her. She has golden hair like Krista, but she's older — must be her dead Mother. I stare into her blue eyes and promise to find her daughter.

I fix the chain around my neck; I'm not losing it again.

33. Escape

KRISTA

"No, we are not going back to the boat." I glare at the dog that is straining towards the beach. "You might like the old man, but he stole my locket and he might steal me next time." I hover at the crossroads, waiting for a chance to zip across. I'm terrified the man is following, but if I'm quick, I can grab some stuff at the hotel and be out of here before they spot me. Why was my step-mum hanging around with that creepy guy? I just don't get it. Her note said she loved me. I thought I could trust her. But he wants to do something bad, I can feel it.

I can't believe the Woman would get involved in anything like this— she likes kids. She's so patient with Harry and she even stops talking so much when she's with him; it's like he calms her. So why was she with that horrible man? Is she grabbing the first chance she can see now Dad's gone? Well, I've got news for The Woman, I'm not falling for her lies again. I remember when Dad first brought her home, she said *"How lovely to meet you, my dear,"* in a fake voice. Perhaps she doesn't care about me after all. I feel a sudden lump in my throat. No, I can't believe it. She's been kind to me, we were like a family when we were looking after Harry.

One thing I know, if she's with that man, there's no way I'm going back. I need to stay out of sight. If I can avoid him tonight, perhaps he'll give up. Not that I want another poor girl to be victimised — I'd hate that — I just don't want it to be me.

The lobby isn't busy. For a second, I think of the man with the bad leg, then push him out of my mind. My heart is beating so fast I am sure the receptionist will hear it. I try to stay calm as I ask for the room key, hoping that The Woman handed it in. *Result!* Clutching the cold metal, I smile at the girl, then walk across the lobby to the stairs. As soon as I'm out of sight, I run to my room.

Quick, see what's left in the man's suitcase. Raid the blue one as well. Grab a bar of chocolate and a packet of polos. I'll need that hoodie — don't want more bugs eating me. Two water bottles. Three? No, that's enough. A camera? I stuff it in a side pocket, then dash into the bathroom.

Toothbrush and toothpaste. A make-up bag. My hand hovers. *No, I don't need it.* I look at a pink razor and automatically feel my arm pit. Coarse hairs are sticking up like frozen stalks of grass. I'm about to take the razor, when I notice The Woman's present sitting on the shelf. I stare at the box. *There's no harm in looking, is there? A* silver bracelet! I can't help fingering the charms: an elephant, a dolphin and a turtle. *I love it!*

Before I can put it on, I hear a dog barking. *Sniff!* Dropping the bracelet, I race down the stairs, hoping I won't be spotted. He is still tied to the drainpipe in the back alley, and his tail spreads a cloud of dust. He stretches and yawns loudly. "Stop it, Sniff, we've got to be quiet," I whisper. I untie the rope but he refuses to move. I rub his hairy ears and he rolls over and kicks his back legs, moving his bum in the dust.

"Not now!" I can't believe that I'm going to be caught just because my stupid dog wants a tickle. I have an idea. "You like polos?" The dog jumps up, wagging his whip-like tail. I hold out a sweet and he moves forwards, head low to the ground. I step backwards and he follows. "There, that wasn't hard was it?" He looks at me expectantly. "Not yet. First, we need to get out of here. We're going to find my dad."

The dog noses my hand. "Another sweet?" I hold a polo in my fist and Sniff trots next to me, trying to catch it. We walk along the boulevard, keeping under the shade of the palm trees. The dog strains towards the sea wall, but I am not crossing the road to the beach. I rustle the sweet wrapper. "You know you want them, don't you? Mmm, tasty!" He looks at me and wags his tail. "Here you are!" He jumps up and catches the sweet in his mouth. A moment later, he puts his head on one side and looks at me.

"You can't have finished it already?" He licks his lips. "You're supposed to chew it!" A long tongue slides around his mouth and his eyes sparkle, then he noses my pocket. "No, you'll have to wait. Just get us out of here and you can have the whole packet!"

"What shall we do, Sniff? Shall we walk along the coast road? We might get to Phuket town where we can find help." I tug the lead and sigh. "But we wouldn't get there without transport. Perhaps we could hitch a lift?" Sniff refuses to budge.

"Ok, not a wise move."

Sniff wags his tail, then trots along the street. I'm staring at the beachfront hotels, but he doesn't like the idea of climbing over the debris and keeps pulling towards the beach. Brakes screech and horns blare and a taxi driver swears at me. I've nearly caused a pile-up!

A soldier patrolling the sea wall glances at me, then blows his whistle. Pulling hard on Sniff's lead, I drag him onto the boulevard. "Forget the old man, it's not happening," I tell him in an angry voice. "We're going this way — come on!" Sniff is standing with his paws splayed out. He is doing a Mohican again: a line of coarse hair standing upright along the centre of his back. I grab the scruff of his neck, then feel his throat vibrating, so I let go, fearing he'll bite. I can't hear his growl above the traffic noise, but I can feel it. Then I see what he is looking at: the creepy man is striding towards us.

Sick leaps into my throat. I don't know whether I pull Sniff or he pulls me, but we're speeding down the boulevard. We duck down a side-street, then I risk a backwards glance. *There he is!* My throat is hurting, but we can't risk stopping. I'm panting as hard as Sniff when we tumble out at a T junction. We're back on the main street.

Which way? A gap in the traffic. Quick! We made it!
But it's too late: the man is right opposite.

I've never been so thankful for a traffic queue before. It's a bit like one of those TV adverts, the one on a railway station, with a girl and guy are on different sides of the track. A train blocks the guy from view as it rushes past, then when the track is clear, he's gone. In the advert, he reappears on her side and they fall in love. Except this is for real and the guy is a psycho.

I'm not waiting to find out. If he's patrolling the streets, we're not safe. I grab Sniff's fur, my arms around his neck. "Come on!" My heart is pounding. I know we haven't got much time. We have to lose him completely. And that only leaves one thing… I look up at the steep wooded hills.

By the time we have disappeared into the forest, I am not sure who is in charge. Sniff seems to know where he wants to go and he's leading me up a leafy path, thick with undergrowth. I've only got three polos left, so I hope it's not far.

The forest is steaming, far too hot to wear the

hoodie; so I've constructed this head-covering thing with a shawl I found in the street. Someone must have dropped it, because it's stuck with dirt, but I've peeled off the worst bits. I've wound the shawl around my head like a turban and it's hanging down my back, covering my neck. I don't like to think of the last woman who wore it.

That's so untrue: you can't stop thinking of the poor woman and wondering what happened to her!

I guess it's a survival instinct to run; just wish I'd focused on those TV programmes that Dad loves. He's so into bush craft, he'd dig up roots and chew them – he'd be fine. I try to remember some survival techniques, but all I can think of is the disgusting bugs I might have to eat. When we last watched a jungle programme, The Woman wasn't sickened by them like I was. Creepy crawlies and my step-mum must have a lot in common.

My thighs are aching with the strain of climbing, but at least there's no sight of the man. Or anyone. We're in the middle of a forest. Trees and more trees. No mangroves, thankfully, as the water is far below us, but I'm dripping in sweat. *Water!* I take a long gulp and feel the liquid sliding down into my chest. The poor dog is panting, so I pour some water in a large leaf, forming a pool in the centre — but Sniff laps so fast that he spills most of it.

We don't halt for long, because Sniff scents something and pulls me over roots and leaf mould. I yank the rope. "I've only got two legs, remember." He puts his head on one side and blinks. "Alright, but when we get to the top of the hill, I need a proper rest, ok?" He wags his tail. "Go on, then, you're the boss!"

The scenery is amazing: large thick green leaves, like the evergreen indoor plants we get in the UK, but ten times the size. Vines are trailing down from the trees: real Tarzan vines. When I see a monkey swinging between branches, I stop for a moment. "Look Sniff, did you see it?" Another monkey jumps onto a long thin branch and I hold my breath, worried that it will crack, but the monkey curls its tail around and sways in the breeze.

Calls of the wild echo from the trees and all the time, the droning hum of insects — like the radio has been left on. You'd think those insects would get sick of singing the same tune the whole day, every day. Occasionally, something slithers across the path and disappears into dense undergrowth. I'm glad I'm with Sniff, but I'm not sure he'd be much use against a snake.

I put my arms around the dog and force him to stop. Large brown eyes watch me drain the bottle, and I feel guilty. "You need another drink, don't you?" If Sniff could nod, he would. I unscrew the second bottle and drip water into a spiky leaf, squeezing it like a funnel. The dog jumps up, putting both paws on my thighs. "Don't spill it!" I shake the drips onto his muzzle and he licks his lips. "You'll have to find a stream if you want more. Sorry, this bottle's mine."

It's ok for a dog, but I don't want to drink water with the risk of parasites. I'm glad Dad made me have those immunisations now, although I wish I had some mosquito spray. Thankfully, my arm has stopped bleeding and there's less risk of infection. The old man's herbs should be marketed, they work like magic.

What am I saying? I'm praising a thief!

The rucksack is sticking to my back, so I take it off and sling it over my shoulder, but I'm still boiling hot. I can hear my stomach rumbling, so I pull out the chocolate — it's melted onto the silver wrapper. I try sucking it off, but it tastes metallic and I've got this horrible taste in my mouth. I stuff the chocolate back in the bag, feeling panicky.

What have I done? I'm stuck on a hillside in the

middle of a forest in Thailand! And my step-mum has teamed up with a foot tapping psycho!

I refuse to think about her. I'm not a kid she can manipulate: I'm a survivor. I look back at the undergrowth that I've trampled, then at the path weaving up through the trees.

What would Dad do? Or Izzie? Stupid question: she'd go back to the spa or the local beauty spot, waiting for news of her family.

Suddenly I know what I have to do: think of good things, of home and how it used to be. We always had a stock of ice cream tubs in the freezer: raspberry ripple, butterscotch, vanilla… Mum probably knew it was bad for me to eat too much, but she let me, all the same. She used to laugh and say you only live once, so a treat every now and again was fine. And if it was more than every now and again, she didn't seem to mind. Mum was the kind of person who'd do anything for you. Fetch you from anywhere — even the end of the world, I guess. Except she can't, not now.

She used to sing to me when I was little: nursery rhymes and her favourite tunes from when she was a child. Granny probably sang them to Mum, as did her Granny before her. I like that: songs and stories passing down through generations. It makes me feel connected to those people I've only seen in black and white photos; part of my past.

The dog doesn't even look up when I start to sing. And I don't care if I'm way out of tune, if this is going to help me survive. Get out of this forest and find Dad.

+++

MARTI
The Kabang is still moored in the bay. I strip off my shirt

and kick my sandals onto the sand. The girl's pendant looks odd lying on my bare chest and the metal feels cold. I prefer my faded leather necklace; it's part of me and I usually forget it's there.

When I climb aboard, I find Grandad crouching under the low roof. He lifts his head, but his face does not light up. "Soldiers came, they told me I have to move on shore." His lips go down like the moon is dying and wrinkles collide under his cap. "They say I cannot live on the Kabang and I can no longer dive for fish."

Shadows hang under his eyes and they no longer reflect the sky. "The ocean is my life. I float with the waves, but without the Kabang, I am a broken sail. Can a fish swim without the sea? Can a bird fly without the sky? I was born on the ocean, I am part of her and she is part of me. I will die if I can't stay living free."

It is the longest speech I ever heard Grandad say. We sit together, yet apart, bare feet touching the bamboo decking. They can't take all this away from him; the Kabang is part of Grandad. He would feel trapped without the sea and the wide skies. Our forefathers sailed these seas; it's what Moken do.

So why are you working at the hotel?

Crawling out of the canopy, I try to push the thought away, but I know that if the soldiers take our Kabangs and force Moken to live onshore, the underwater world is lost to us. I look at the old man, hunched up like a crab hiding under its shell. The decision isn't hard to make. "I will speak to the elders: they will know what to do."

Instantly, his head lifts. "They have the totem poles, Sky; they will consult the spirits. Our forefathers will give us wisdom." I shrug my shoulders. What can dead spirits do against soldiers with guns?

Grandad has joined me and he is gripping the mast. "They will not find it."

"What?"

"The Kabang. I will hide it in the mangroves." He pushes back his shoulders and his back straightens. "I will row into a place only I know." He taps me on the arm and points over the roof canopy, towards the headland. Then he smiles and nods towards a rolled up bundle. Together we unravel the sail and fix it to the mast. "Sky, you must go to the hills and talk to the elders, while I sail back to the lagoon."

As I lift my arms ready to dive, the necklace moves against my chest. *The English girl!* I've forgotten to tell Grandad about her. But what can I say? *I saw her, I know who she is, but I let her slip through my fingers like a fish.* The Englishman asked me to find his daughter and I failed. I've failed Papa and I wasn't there to save Rune… so how can I save my people?

Grandad is mouthing something when I resurface, so I tread water, waiting to hear what he's saying. "Talk to the land people, Sky." I glide towards the smooth edge of the boat and his wrinkled fingers close over mine. "Tell them to leave us alone."

When I reach shore, Grandad is standing tall, his back to me, facing the ocean. The sail curves, collecting the wind and the wooden boat flies like a bird skimming low over the water. The Kabang was made for this, as Grandad was made to sail the ocean. As I watch the Kabang shrinking in the distance, the wind snatches my breath.

What was I made for, where do I belong?

34. Danger

KRISTA

Sniff is on a mission. He is alert, scenting the air. I'm hot and tired and I must have sung '*She'll be coming round the mountain*' a million times! I'm fed up of the mosquitoes. It's like every step I take, more are waiting to attack me. I could be a model for some mega zit cream — before, not after.

I have no idea where we are, and I wish I'd never let the dog take me into the forest. Knowing Sniff, he's probably taking me on a sneaky, roundabout route back to the old man: climbing up through the trees, then down to the bay on the other side of the headland. I can see glimpses of blue over mountains of green. The sea is way off, but I can hear the sound of water. Sniff pulls me closer to the edge of the steep slope and I yank the rope. He digs in his claws and whines. What has he got: a death wish?

"If you want to be off the lead, fine, but you are not taking me with you." I slip the rope off the dog's neck and he stands for a moment, head on one side, then he's off, running through the undergrowth. A minute later I hear barking somewhere below me.

"Sniff!"

He has disappeared in the dense bushes that cover this side of the hill. Beyond them is the sea and the curvature of the earth as it meets the sky. Somewhere out there is home. My bedroom with the posters of Levi's band. The white chest of drawers with my clothes spilling out. My desk piled high with school files. And the shelf with all my favourite photos of family and friends.

I need to see Mum smile again. Pulling the chain out of my shirt, I reach for the locket. The world shrinks around me as I stare at my clenched fist. *How could I forget?* Losing the locket feels like losing my last link to Mum.

She was there for me when the waves roared. She was there for me in the darkness of the mangroves. She was there, helping me survive. Mum used to say everything would be fine, even when her hair was falling out in sad little clumps. Dad and I were worried sick, but Mum still said, *"everything's fine."* It's not! You've gone and I'll never see you again. Or Dad.

This is crazy – I can't stay here, clinging onto the side of the hill. Suddenly, I catch sight of Sniff. He seems to be heading towards a depression in the landscape, a gulley. Bracing my legs, I start to zigzag down the hill like a crab in slow motion. I'm leaning into the hillside, pulling myself along, clutching anything I can find. My legs are trembling. My feet are on such an angle, that if I slipped, I'd have no chance.

The gulley is closer now and I hear the sound of rushing water. And laughter. Other people! Tearing open a curtain of leaves, I see water gushing over a rock face, splashing into a pool below me. Three girls are bathing, sunlight sparkling on the water. I can hear barking, but I can't spot Sniff. *Do a runner if you want. I need real people to talk to, not just a dog who does his own thing.*

Climbing down the edge of a slippery gulley isn't the wisest course of action, but what choice do I have? My calf muscles are putting on brakes, tensing with each step. Not far now. Suddenly, I hit moss, then I'm sliding on my bum, out of control. The mountain is rushing towards me. *A tree!* I grab the thin stem as I skid past. It bends. I scream. I know I'm going to fall. Then it lashes back, relaxing like a bow.

My breath is being cut into pieces. I'm hovering above a ten metre drop. *Don't look down, don't look down!*

Someone is shouting, but I can't answer. I can't move. My toes are curling in the trainers. I slowly stretch out my left arm, feeling for a stronger handhold. *A branch!* My fingers curl around it and only then, do I turn my neck. Slowly. Ever so slowly.

Praying that the branch will hold my weight, I grasp it and pull myself away from the edge. *Phew!* My heart is hurting, it's beating so fast. Want to see if the girls are still there, but can't face leaning over the rock.

A rushing ball of fur almost throws me off balance. "Sniff!" I wrap my arms around the dog. "Don't ever do that to me again!"

The dog's body sways as he wags his tail; it's hard to stay angry with him for long. I'm stroking him when his ears prick up and he pulls away, scrambling down a hole between two rocks. This time I'm not going to let him get away. Squatting to get a better view, I can see it's some kind of cave, but light is touching the sides so there must be a way out. Taking a deep breath, I lower my body into the gap. Pulling with my fingertips and pushing with my toes, I wriggle through. For once I'm glad that I'm skinny. I slide out hands first.

And there, lying on a flat rock, is the dog. And beside him, sitting cross legged, is a young Thai girl. She is wearing a creased yellow dress and staring at me with the deepest brown eyes I have ever seen. When I approach, she flinches and wraps her arms around Sniff.

He starts making happy noises. Does he know her? I say hello, but the girl won't look at me. She glances through lowered eyes and has the longest lashes. Izzie would die for them — she is always buying extra thick mascara and fake lashes.

I try again. "Hi, I'm Krista." I touch Sniff, but the girl pulls him closer.

"Lucky!" Her voice is soft and high-pitched, almost like a bird call. Why is she shouting she is lucky; she is obviously confused. And where are the other girls? She jumps up and darts down to the pool, Sniff scampering at her heels. I catch my breath, but she doesn't seem scared of falling, just of me.

I always wanted a little sister. And a dog. Sniff was my friend, but as soon as someone else comes along, he deserts me. Like everyone else. When Mum died, I wanted a sister so much, someone to talk to. I could tell Dad some stuff, but not everything.

Sniff and the girl have gone. The pool is glowing with sunlight, but I'm alone. Again. I look up at the steep cliff. There is no way I can climb back up. I'll have to go down.

White mist sprays as the waterfall crashes into the pool. Sinking onto a smooth rock, I take off my shoes and dangle my feet in the clear water. Feels wonderful to splash the sweat off my face. Droplets fall into the water, rippling out in circles. I stare until they merge into nothing, wondering how I'm ever going to get to safety. Then I see myself looking at me. I don't look happy.

A reflection overshadows mine in the water. Heart pumping, I swivel round. I am looking up at a young woman with her arm around the young girl. Another girl is hovering behind them. Sniff dashes towards me, bouncing into the pool. Water cascades all over me and I wipe my face for the second time.

The oldest girl is smiling and holding out her hand, but Sniff chooses that moment to shake, covering us both with another fountain, then wags his tail like he's enjoying himself. She laughs and pats his head. "Lucky like you!"

Now I understand. *Sniff likes you too!* I say in my mind.

The girl pushes her long hair out of her eyes. She's only a few years older than me, with such clear skin that I bet she's never had a spot in her life. Around her neck is a shell necklace, tiny amber shells strung together on a twisted fibre. She sees me watching. "You like?" I nod, telling her the necklace is beautiful.

Before I know what's she's doing, she has taken it off and is fastening it around my neck. I bite my lip, unable to believe she has given me such a gorgeous gift. "No, it's yours."

She shrugs her shoulders. "I make more!" She laughs and I join in. I know I've just met her, but it feels like she's already my friend.

"Thank you so much, but..." I pull out the pocket in my shorts. "I haven't anything to give you in return."

Hair flies around her shoulders like a shampoo advert. She puts a finger on her lips. "No. I give." She touches her mouth. "You want eat?"

At that moment my stomach growls and we both laugh. I follow the girls under the waterfall and we walk along a hidden path. It doesn't take long before they are chatting and asking me questions, but I can't understand them, as only the oldest can speak English.

Smoke drifts into my nostrils. More people. When I edge closer to the oldest girl, she takes my hand and leads me to the camp fire. A woman brings a bowl of some kind of soup. As I drink, tension drains out of me. I know everyone is looking at me, the children curiously while the adults are more reserved, but it's not scary like that horrible man. No, these people are for me, not against me.

It's not like the first day at school when you feel small, and even smaller if the teacher speaks to you.

It's not like a club when people are assessing if you're a threat — more talented than they are.

It's not like joining senior school when everyone is seeing how chatty or attractive you are and if you'll fit into their group. I always failed that test.

I am lost in a foreign country, with people I've never met. But I feel safe.

+++

MARTI

There's that noise again. I stop. It stops. I walk a few paces, then freeze. What is it? A gibbon perhaps or a wild boar? I've kept on hearing the crack of branches being trampled, ever since I left the beach. If it is a wild animal, I wish it would find what it's looking for and leave me alone. I need to find the elders and tell them what the soldiers are planning.

Soldiers! My stomach feels as if someone is digging into me with a knife, rooting around for a shell. Soldiers could easily track me. The forest is dark, full of hiding places; it is not like my world under the waves where I can swim free.

What are you saying, Marti? Your world is bigger, faster, more exciting now!

Is it?

I don't know what I want any longer. I'm in that place where the ocean meets the sky; you can't see where one ends and the other starts its journey. I had it planned, I thought I knew what I wanted, but the waves have swept everything away.

Grandad said this track weaves up around the headland and leads to our camp. When I deliver his message, the elders will consult the spirits for wisdom. But how can the spirits fight soldiers? Spirits are made of air; they cannot defend us. Like I couldn't help the girl with golden hair.

Krista! I wish I'd known who you were. I wish I'd told you about saving your father. I would have seemed like an eagle in your eyes, not a common sea bird.

Another twig crackles. If they come with guns, what choice do we have? Moken are peaceful: our spears are for fish, not people.

My clothes brush against the branches and thick leaves. Huge tree trunks shoot up into the forest tops, with strong roots anchoring them to the ground. Kabang trees. *Don't look up; keep running!* But I can't stop the memories... Papa explaining the technique of hollowing out a tree to build a Kabang; demonstrating how to make a small fire under the boat to seal it. I know he wanted me to find a Moken girl so I can build my own Kabang.

Smoke! Wisps of mist are curling through gaps in the trees. The smell of cooked fish touches my nose. I hear laugher. Running towards the sound, I push waxy leaves away from my face.

And there in the middle of a clearing, I see her.

The girl with the golden hair!

She is sitting in the middle of the Moken women as if she is one of them. I blink. It's like the horizon you can never reach, which goes further away as you sail closer. Impossible to reach. But when I open my eyes, she is still there, smiling at another girl who is cuddling a dog. My little sister. I'm home.

+++

KRISTA

This is unreal. I'm sitting in the middle of these tribal people, in the middle of a forest in the middle of Thailand...when this lad suddenly appears like he's the next contestant on a jungle reality show. What does he think I'm going to do: jump up and kiss him? I don't think so! He is the guy who attacked Sniff. He is the guy who just stood there when The Woman and That Man were at the temple. He is the guy who showed off diving into the pool while those stupid girls were eyeing him up.

Now he's hugging these girls like a right player. I can't believe that I nearly trusted him and fell for his act. The friendly girl with glossy black hair has her arm around his waist like she loves him.

Oh no, he's walking over to me, asking if I'm alright. I stare into the fire. Anger is flaring up inside me and my stomach has clenched into a hard knot. How dare he follow me here, then pretend he's concerned with my safety? Where was he when I needed him?

A small hand touch mine. It is the little girl wearing the yellow dress. She lets go of the dog and pulls me away from the fire. To the guy.

"Krista!"

As he speaks, I know I'm blushing. I look down quickly. *How do you know my name? Who are you?* Then something catches the light as it swings in front of my face. My eyes are fixed on the chain as it moves back and forwards. I gasp as I recognise it. Reaching out, I grab the locket. "That's mine!"

We are either side of my chain, like a tug of war. If he breaks it, he's dead. Why is he saying he knows it's mine, how does he know? He must have taken it from the old man, or bought stolen goods.

Now he's backing down and letting go. He hands back the locket and I make sure my fingers don't touch

237

his. Like when he gave me back my postcard. I bend down and put both arms around the dog. *Sniff, tell him to go away!* Sniff noses under my arm, pushing my head up. The guy hasn't backed off; he's laughing at me. So is the little girl — they all are.

"What's so funny?"

"I've come all this way to give you back the necklace…"

"It's a locket!"

"Ok, locket…but I've been trying to find you for days and now I have, all you can do is storm around like a tiger."

My arm feels hot; my whole body does. My face is burning. I thrust the chain in his face. "Where did you get it?"

"Grandad said the white girl was still sick, so he swam ashore…"

"He stole it! The old man pretended to help, then when I was asleep, he stole it!"

"No, he showed me the necklace and…"

"Locket!" I snap, interrupting him.

He smiles and holds up both hands. "Grandad was trying to find someone who could help, so he showed me the n…" He pauses as I suck in a deep breath. Then his eyes twinkle as he opens his mouth: "…locket!"

+++

MARTI

She is like a tiger, prowling around the fire, ready to pounce at anything I say. She's gorgeous, fiery, hot. I know it's wrong to think like this: I'm a sea gypsy, my destiny is a Moken girl. But as I see my sister putting an arm around Krista's shoulders, I can't help it. She is here, isn't she? Right now, she's one of us.

The fire is dying down when she relaxes. Petal is the one who convinces her. Not by words — although she does chatter like a flock of sparrows — but by her smile. Krista's cheek bones have stopped clenching and her hands are no longer in tight fists. She is smiling at Petal, so I hope she will smile at me too. I sit down next to the girl with golden hair. "Would you like to meet my mother? She is over there with Coral, my older sister."

Krista's face is so funny: she looks like a deep sea fish with massive staring eyes. "Your sister?" she repeats, staring at Coral. "But how…?" Pink colour washes up her cheeks. "I mean, how is it you work in the resort, while your family live in the forest?"

"They don't." Krista wrinkles her nose and tips her head on one side as I explain. "We are Moken, sea people, we don't live in forests."

"Then why are you at the hotel?"

I sigh, then lean towards Krista, my back to the elders. "Because I want a better life. I want to be someone, achieve something, not just sit on a boat in the ocean."

I am trying to explain about my dream of moving to the west, when the dog starts to growl. A man is standing behind Coral: a white man wearing a cap the colour of a storm cloud. Jo's detective has slipped into our midst like a slimy eel. He mouths something, but his words are lost in the crackle of the fire. Krista is leaning away from him like a tree pushed by a strong wind. She's frightened. He is standing over us like he thinks he is a god.

Pressing my hands flat on the ground, I spring up and face him. "Was it you following me?" He rubs his stubble with his thumb, but doesn't answer. I can't see his expression as he's wearing dark shades. "What do you want?" I ask.

He steps closer to the fire. "I've come for Krista." I

hear Krista gasp and then everything happens quickly. Coral rushes forward and puts her arms around the girl with golden hair.

Stepping in front of the girls, I stare at the detective. "I don't think she wants to go with you."

The man isn't moving, but his glasses are flickering with reflections of the fire. Then he takes off his shades and raises one eyebrow. "What would you know? I've been given authority to take the girl, but who are you? Just a garbage boy. Trash. A nobody."

"I'm Marti."

The man's lip curls. "Just Marti? Not a policeman or a detective who has been paid to find the poor girl and bring her safely back to her stepmother?"

He's trying to squash me into the ground. The man sidesteps, attempting to reach Krista, but I block him. Straightening my back, I look the detective in the eye. "I'm Moken and these are my people."

Coral and the elders crowd around me. Mama holds out her arms for Petal, then cuddles her into her chest.

The man's nose twitches and he swipes his hand across his stubble. "Well, Moken, I'm here to take the girl." He pushes back his shoulders and pulls a note out of his pocket. "And this proves it!" He wafts a piece of paper at me, then holds it with both hands so Krista can read it.

She looks at me, a crease between her eyebrows. "It's from my step-mum."

The man nods. "That's right, darling. Everything will be alright now. She's given me authority to bring you back." He looks at me down his nose. "Safely." I grit my teeth; what's he implying?

He waves the note, but I ignore it. I've seen the man with Jo and know he's telling the truth. Krista looks at me like I'm a swordfish, about to pierce her heart. I don't

240

want to let her go, none of us do, but he's the big white man and we have no rights.

Coral links her arm through Krista's and pulls her close. The man's gaze moves from one to the other and he smiles. "You girls will make some man very happy one day!" The hairs on the back of my neck are standing up; something feels very wrong. Cloud must think so too, for the small thickset man emerges from the edge of the crowd and puts a strong arm around Coral's waist, claiming her. I stand and watch as the detective grabs Krista's hand. The look she gives me could spear a barracuda.

And I'm back on the balcony looking into the jaws of the Laboon. But this time, I can't jump, like I did for Harry. I have to let her go.

35. Desire

KRISTA

Fingers press into my wrist like handcuffs. *Help! Why won't someone help me?*

Marti knew I didn't want to go, I heard him. But he just stood there, they all did — except Coral. I feel sick. Afraid. I'm alone with the man and I have this terrible feeling. *Dad! I need you!*

Branches claw my face. I'm dragged through bushes, the rucksack strap digging into my neck. Suddenly, I cannon into his sweaty body. Fear leaps into my throat. He grabs my shoulders, his breath hot on my cheek. Beads of moisture glisten above his lip. "Far away enough I think, don't you?"

Far enough for what?

Arching my back, I kick as hard as I can, but he just laughs. "Trying to get away are we?" One eyebrow lifts and his lips smack. "Punters will love you."

Terror squeezes my body. Every sinew is screaming, tearing to get away. I feel his fingers sliding down to my breast. "Not much here," he squeezes me, "but your hair is to die for." I scream, twisting to get free. He curls my hair around his hand, pulling harder. I smell his vile sweat and spit in his face.

He swears, then yanks my hair, so my neck falls back. My scream is cut off as his face touches mine.

MARTI

Something tells me to follow. Like the call of a shell in your ear; a faint murmur of the ocean telling me her secrets. I know I should have gone with them — protected the girl with golden hair. Krista's father asked me to find her and now I've let her go. If anything has happened... My heart starts hitting me like a fierce monsoon. I run.

There's only one track down, so where are they? I knew I couldn't trust him, but I just quivered like a jellyfish in the shallows. *While he is taking her into the deep.*

I'm tearing through the trees. Nearly reached the waterfall. But it's not the water that's screaming. *Krista!*

Sick shoots into my throat. A spear is jabbing into my brain. Grabbing a stick, I explode with anger. Everything happens so fast. It's like the spirits are controlling me, I'm possessed. I stare at the man's crumpled body as I swing the branch again.

"That's enough!" Krista is stumbling towards me. Dark tangled hair. Eyes huge in her pale face.

"Enough?" I stare at Krista. "He was trying to..."

She is biting her lip, trying not to cry. Then she looks at the man's unconscious body and shudders. "Please, just let's go."

Bending over the monster, I place my hand in front of his lips. "He's still alive, but I think he'll be sleeping all night."

She looks at me, her mouth trembling. "He won't...?"

"You're safe now. We'll go back to my people — Mama will look after you." Krista starts to walk, but her face turns as whiter than a piece of cooked fish. I hold out my arms. "Here, I'll carry you." She is shaking her head; her whole body is shaking.

"Krista, I'm not like him, I'm not going to hurt you." She stumbles and holds a tree for support. I step towards her. "Please Krista… your father asked me to find you! I saw him on the beach."

Her chin juts out. "You're just saying that to trick me." She spits into the dust. "Like him."

"No I'm not! We used a door as a stretcher and carried him. He's in hospital and they are doing all they can for him. I hope…" I swallow and can't look into her eyes. "I mean, I'm sure he's going to be alright."

She grabs my arm, forcing me to look at her. "You're lying."

"No! He was there, this tall man lying on the beach. He asked me to find his wife and daughter…"

"Dad…? My dad is really alive?" Krista's mouth is wide open and her lower lip is trembling.

I nod, hoping the Englishman will survive. "Yes, Jo told me."

"That Woman!" I look at Krista, surprised at her angry tone. She is glaring at the man on the ground. "She can't be trusted. She's in it with him."

She shivers and I long to give her a hug. "We should go back to the camp," I say, but Krista shakes her head and backs away. Her body suddenly crumples and I catch her before she hits the ground. I hold her tightly and it feels like we're swaying together to the sound of the waves.

"I'll carry you. I'll take you anywhere you want," I find myself saying, and then think, how pathetic she'll think I am. When she wriggles out of my arms, I know I've lost my chance.

She sinks to her knees, her fingers scrabbling in the undergrowth. "I nearly forgot this," she says, picking up her rucksack. I watch as she opens the flap and lifts out a camera. "I knew this would come in useful." She tries to take a photo of the man's crumpled body, but her hands are shaking, so I stand behind and steady her.

"These photos are a gift from me," she says, glaring at the side of the man's face. "To the police."

Then she twists her head and looks at me through her eyelashes. "Now, how about that lift, Marti?"

36. The Night in the Trees

KRISTA

I can feel the warmth of Marti's body behind me as I nestle into his chest. His hands are clasping my waist and his legs are stretched out, braced against branches to protect me. It feels like a Titanic moment, except we're not Rose and Jack standing on the bow of a great liner, arms outstretched; we're balancing six feet up a tree in Thailand. We're wedged into the fork between three branches, like a seat. It's close enough to jump down if we needed to, but high enough to be safe if the man regains consciousness and tries to find us. Marti says we'll be safe here for the night; he thinks the monster will be out for a long time.

It was horrible, terrifying, I felt like I was suffocating in evil. Then Marti appeared and after that, the trafficker hadn't got a chance. He collapsed on me; his shoulders were so heavy, I couldn't breathe. Then I could see daylight. Marti must have dragged him off me. I can't recall exactly what happened. But the man went out, just like that. I felt faint, so Marti offered to carry me, but I suddenly thought of the camera. As soon as we get back, I'm showing the photos to the police — I hope the disgusting paedophile gets locked up for a long time.

We didn't get as far as the Moken camp, because I kept feeling dizzy. My arm has started to bleed again where the man grabbed me. Marti said his arms were breaking carrying me — I *think* he was joking. Most of the trees are like telephone poles, but Marti found a thicker one with low branches that we could climb. He said that the spirits will keep us safe. I hope so — the forest is alive with screeching insects.

I've never been so conscious of anyone, but I don't dare turn around. I know I'm blushing and my heartbeat is so rapid, he's bound to feel it. My mind is racing, saying a thousand things, but my voice is clamped at the back of my throat — he must think I'm such a baby.

A high pitched noise starts buzzing around my ears. I jerk my head trying to avoid the insect and feel Marti's arm tighten around my stomach. He laughs. "Don't worry, it's just a cicada." He swings his other arm, sweeping across the top of my head.

"Ouch! What did you do that for?"

"Just trying to catch one." His hand hovers in front of my face. "Look!" A fly-like insect is swinging between two fingers, fairy wings stretched above its body, full of tiny veins — except one wing is now squished.

"You didn't have to do that," I tell him.

"What?"

"Hurt it. It wasn't harming anyone."

"So why did you scream?" I clench my teeth and say nothing. "Krista, it's only one little cicada, there are millions of them. They'll stop singing when darkness steals the light."

"That one already has." I hear a sigh and feel his breath hot on my neck, but it's not frightening like the man's. I watch the cicada flutter down to the forest floor.

We're silent and I look up to where stars flicker on

and off, as silhouettes of trees shift in the wind. I hear the rustle of leaves and imagine millions of cicadas folding their wings for the night.

"I shouldn't have done that." The whisper is soft in my ear and his hair brushes my cheek. I nod. His hands tighten and his thumbs trace semicircles in the soft flesh under my ribs. I arch against his strong arms and breathe out slowly. It is the sexiest moment of my entire life. But when his fingers lace around my waist, I suddenly feel a giggle wanting to jump out. The more he tickles, the more I start shaking, trying to keep the laughter inside.

A warm hand touches my neck, turning me to face him. Tingles of excitement are dancing in my mind, but all I can do is splutter, "I'm ticklish!" Dark eyebrows rise and with a hot finger, he traces a line from my nose to my mouth. My heart is going wild. I look into his eyes and know this is the moment I've waited for all my life: a guy I really fancy is going to kiss me. I'm shaking inside, but it's not from lust.

Gazing into his deep brown eyes, I'm trying to control myself, but I can't stop the laugh shooting out of my mouth. Worse, I spray him with spit. His eyebrows jump — have I ruined everything? Marti's nose twitches and his mouth starts to dance. The nervous pressure is too much and we both burst into giggles. The more he laughs, the more I do. I only stop when my ribs are aching and I nearly fall out of the tree.

+++

MARTI

I can't believe my luck! I'm holding a beautiful girl and we're all alone. I've told her we're staying here to be safe from wild animals, but the most poisonous beast in the forest is that evil man. If he wakes, I'll be ready for him.

Krista is trembling: she's either afraid, or she wants me as much as I want her. But I can't let myself think stuff like that, I just need to bring her back safely to her dad after the next tide, when morning opens the sky. It's strange, but for the first time in my life, the forest is my friend. I used to feel scared if we ventured into dense trees to collect wood. This is the dark place of the spirits, but tonight I feel they are on my side — hope I'm right.

When Krista starts laughing, I feel hurt. Then something takes hold of me; I can't explain it, but her laughter catches me and pulls me along so fast I can't stop. It's only when I see her long legs starting to slip, that I manage to control the spasms digging into my stomach. Pulling her back onto my lap, arms around her waist, I never want to let her go.

"Sorry about that," she says. "It's my second most ticklish place." I say it doesn't matter and can't help wondering where the other place is. I feel her body relaxing into mine, like when I'm holding Petal. Then she starts asking me all these questions, expecting me to answer, when all I want to do is kiss her. She asks me if he will come back — but if he does, I'm ready for him.

"Marti, do you ever think: why did it happen?" Her voice is musical, rising with the question.

"The waves?" I ask. The back of her head nods against my chest. "The Laboon hadn't eaten people for a while, so it was hungry."

"Yeah right! I mean, for real: what caused the tsunami and why here, why us?" I explain that the Spirits needed to rid the land of evil, so we can start again.

"But those people weren't evil!" As Krista turns her neck, her voice rises like a monkey spotting a predator. "All those bodies — some of them were just children — what had they done?" I look down, I don't know what to say. Those people didn't deserve to die. And what about

249

Papa: he wasn't bad, he was trying to save me. I'm only half-listening, as Krista says something about God wiping people out with massive waves at the beginning of time.

"So you think the tsunami is like that: sent because everyone's sinned?" she asks. I stay quiet, what's the point. "But at least God saved Noah in the Ark, with all the animals."

"Even cicadas?" I say quietly.

"Even cicadas. Two of every kind, like us," she says. "But we're in a tree, not an ark." She twists her head, so her hair touches my cheek.

And then it happens. And I'm diving past vibrant colours, whirling and spinning. I can't believe that an English girl wants to kiss a Moken boy; that a western girl would fancy a sea gypsy. It's unreal... it's amazing... she's amazing! I reach for her hands and clasp mine over them.

But when I try to kiss her again, she pulls away and starts chattering like a tree sparrow. She wants to know all about Moken girls: what they wear and if they free dive and fish. "Do girls braid their hair or have long fringes?"

Feeling suddenly conscious of my untidy hair, I push it away from my eyes. "I'll cut it."

"No, don't — I like it." Swallowing the sudden lump in my throat, I gaze into her eyes. And lean forwards, hoping to kiss her again. But she starts talking. Wants to know how it's possible to hold my breath for so long — I wish she could! What is it with girls — why can't they just stop talking? She thinks free diving is some kind of trick.

"I was born to swim," I explain. "It's easy, I don't think about it. I dive into the shifting light, to where the turtles weave in and out of the coral reef and large crabs crawl on the seabed. I don't need another breath."

"Turtles are cute," she says.

"I am glad; they are sacred to my people." Krista's face is so close that I can feel her breath on my neck. I know that her eyes are as blue as the ocean on a clear day, even though the sun has slipped below the trees and dusk is closing out the day. She's the first girl I've wanted to look at me like that; plenty have tried, but this is different — she is different.

"Swimming with turtles is like swimming with the gods," I tell her. "You feel stronger, bigger, more alive."

"I'd like that," she replies. "But I'd be frightened."

I shake my head. "Fear is on land, not in the water."

"But how can you walk along the bottom of the pool; it's impossible!" I smile to myself — so she was watching when I collected the coins those girls threw in.

"How do you learn to walk? You just do!" I try to explain what I can't explain — that you learn to dive from your parents and will yourself to stay down." Krista looks at me and moonlight dances in her eyes. I'm amazed she's interested in our customs, but if it gets this response, I'll tell her all I know!

"Sometimes we make a raft out of palm leaves and stay motionless in the water, blowing bubbles to pretend we're fish. Other fish swim past, then *bam!* they're hooked with our harpoons. Straight through!"

She shudders. "Sounds scary."

"I'll teach you. There's nothing like it! You're flying through the water with beautiful colours and coral reefs and shoals of tiny fish scattering at your fingertips. You can go anywhere, do anything; there are no rules, no boundaries."

Her hand squeezes mine. "I like the sound of that! But I thought, working at the hotel, you weren't into that lifestyle …" She smiles. "You're more Sea Gypsy than you think, Marti!"

"No I'm not!"

"If you say so…"

Krista thinks it's funny, but she's wrong. I'm never going back. I try to pull my hand away, but she's gripping it; I'm hooked. She giggles. "Marti, have you ever seen a starfish? I'd love to see a real starfish in the water."

"Sure, I've even seen them mating." Her hand tenses, then slips out of mine like it's swimming away. I know I've said the wrong thing, but I don't want to stop talking. I tell her there are lots of other fish in the sea and diving is fun, but I'm never going back to the flotilla. "If I do, Rune would have died for nothing."

"Rune?"

"My friend. He taught me to speak Thai and English. He was so kind and he never moaned, although sometimes I could see that his leg was hurting."

"His leg?"

"He had to wear straps around it or he couldn't walk." I hear Krista suck in her breath, so I try to explain. "I know it was difficult for Rune not being able to bend his leg, but without the calliper, he wouldn't have had a job. He could sit down in reception, you see." Krista's back stiffens and she sits as straight as a spear. What have I said now?

"It wasn't my fault," a little voice speaks into the air.

"What wasn't?"

"Jo said the man who saved me had a calliper."

I can't breathe. *Rune died saving Krista. He is only dead because of her. If only he had saved himself instead.* I clench my teeth, then let out my breath in a long sigh. *No, I don't mean that. Rune wanted to help others; he wouldn't want me to be angry.*

Fingers lace into mine. "Have I said something to hurt you?"

"No, it's just that Rune was kind, I miss him. He never mocked me for who I am, he accepted me. He even suggested I adopt a Thai name to fit in."

"Isn't Marti your real name?" My mouth zips shut, then she elbows me in the ribs. "What is it?"

"Don't you dare laugh. Moken call their children anything they see — things they like around them."

"Like?"

"Hook, or Crab, or Rain," I say quietly.

"Tell me you're not called Crab!"

"My name is Sky."

"Sky," she repeats. "I like that: full of stars and clouds and red sunsets."

"Yes, and thunder and lightning and monsoons — bad spirits."

"Not that again. You don't honestly believe all that stuff, do you?"

"No... of course not. We're in the 21st century and Moken are stuck in bamboo huts on stilts, peeing into the water. Our culture has no place now; we have no voice."

Krista grabs my arm and I'm scared we'll fall out of the tree. "No, we're the ones who have got it wrong — GCSE's are pathetic! We get these things called predicted grades, but that just makes kids panic or get stressed if they don't achieve them. It's rubbish. Exams can't predict a tsunami can they, or warn people to escape? What's the point of learning geometry, formulas and square roots? There should be less pressure and more time to do what we want!"

"That's right! I want more out of life than foraging from the sea like my ancestors. That's why I'm trying to get out, become someone. A sea gypsy drifts where the sea takes you — I can't even read properly."

"You can't read?" I curl up inside; why did I tell her that? A minute later, I'm surprised when her back melts into me again and she twists her head. "Look, I'll do you a deal: if you take me to the coral reefs, I'll teach you to read." Bubbles of excitement shoot around my stomach. When I agree, little lines crease the sides of Krista's eyes. I'm smiling too, telling her once I can read, I'll be able to teach Petal and she'll get an education.

"Is she your girlfriend?" Seeing the smile slide from her face, I try not to laugh. "Would it bother you if she was?"

"Of course not. If you're with someone, that's fine." Her voice is cold and she turns away. I let her believe it, but I am trying not to laugh.

"She's my kid sister!" Krista swivels around, pretending to hit me, but I grab her arm. "And for your information, I'm never getting married — who would want a sea gypsy?"

She looks me straight in the eyes and doesn't look away. I'm suddenly shy and don't know how to act with her. Does she really like me? As I hesitate, her cheeks deflate, her eyes drop and she yanks her arm away. And the moment's gone. She clasps the locket in her fist.

Disappointed, I push my back into the branch, giving her space, then look at the ceiling of leaves above my head. How can someone be so close, yet feel so far away? It's going to be a long night. I can almost hear her crying out for her Mum and Dad. "I'm glad you've got the locket back," I speak into the darkness.

Her sigh is stronger than the wind. "I was terrified the picture would get ruined if it got wet, but I managed to protect it." I suddenly think of the locket around my neck as I swam out to the Kabang. I hope I haven't spoiled her treasure.

The chain tightens, as Krista cradles the locket. "Mum died four years ago." The words seem to echo around us. I don't dare say anything — it feels like a moment for the spirits.

Then Krista starts talking and she can't stop. "She

had cancer. I kept going into her room that week. Every night, I was afraid I'd wake up and she wouldn't be there. So that night, Dad said I could sleep in the big bed. I snuggled in between them and held Mum's hand. It felt warm. My cheek was next to hers, so I knew she was still breathing. In the morning, I woke up to find she'd stopped and her hand was cold and hard."

"And you wish she was still with you."

"But she's still here in my locket."

"Like a spirit?" I ask.

She shakes her head. "Not really, but ever since Dad gave me the locket, I can feel her more. And now I don't feel so alone."

Or perhaps it's because you're cuddled up to me, I think, as her breathing becomes more rhythmic and her body is heavy against mine. I keep thinking of how she must have felt, her mother dying like that. Dad's death was quick, so he wouldn't have been in pain for long. If only he had followed the elders' advice and not gone looking for me. If only he hadn't cared, he would still be alive — it's all my fault.

I hug Krista's sleeping body and gaze into the darkness. The leaves have stopped rustling and the cicadas have gone to sleep. I wish I could.

37. Freedom

31st December 2004

KRISTA

It is still dark, but I know a massive blush is covering my cheeks. I can't believe I slept in his arms. My back is nestling into his chest and his breath is hot on my neck. I can see his hands crossed over my waist and his legs encircling mine to stop me from falling. I'm wide awake, so it feels like it should be morning, but the sun isn't up. I wish I had a mirror and some make-up. My face has got spots and my hair feels itchy and greasy. I am with this gorgeous guy, but I'm covered in mosquito bites and I've got hairy armpits. It's so embarrassing.

"Hello."

My heart starts racing as I twist around to face him. I feel myself blush again. "Hi. Did you get much sleep?"

He smiles. "You sure did."

"How do you know?" Marti's eyes twinkle and he pretends to snore.

"I don't!"

I elbow him, but he catches my arm. "Say you snore, or I'll let go of you…"

"You wouldn't dare!"

His fingers touch my rib cage. "Say it or I'll tickle

you!"

I decide to jump down. Bad move. I fall onto my bad arm.

Marti drops down beside me. "I was only joking. Please don't be angry."

"I'm fine. Just hurts a little."

"I'll take you back to Mama; she will find healing leaves."

Marti's family are kind, but that man may still be somewhere in the woods — he may be waking up – we can't risk it. When I beg Marti to take me back to the resort to find Dad, he puts his arm around me and leads me into the darkness. I hope he knows the way down to the beach.

We walk in silence, but inside, I am asking Marti a hundred things, wanting to know all about him. Being a sea gypsy sounds exotic, exciting. Perhaps he can hold his breath for even longer than the old man. I'd like to ask, but Marti is busy trampling on vegetation, as the path has petered out. The bushes and trees are so densely packed, that I'm getting scratched whichever way I turn. It's hopeless: we're hemmed in.

Marti is wrestling with a branch; it squeaks as he twists it, then cracks. I hear swishing noises as he uses it to hack away at vegetation. He makes a gap for us to squeeze through, then holds the thin stems back so they don't whip against my face. I can feel the ground dropping away. The forest floor is so uneven, it's hard to keep my footing. My knees jar as I miss a foothold and my ankle nearly turns over. I stumble against Marti, but he doesn't seem to mind. I don't either.

"Tell me more about your friend," I say, when the slope evens out.

Marti's hair falls over his eyes as he nods. "Rune was always there for me and he offered to let me stay in his bungalow." Suddenly he raises the stick, swiping a large bush.

"But he sounds much older," I say.

"Only forty-three."

"If he was that nice, you'd think he'd be married."

"Perhaps he didn't find anyone."

"Or perhaps he did."

Marti lets go of my arm and faces me. "No, he didn't. He told me there was someone, but she probably went off with someone else, or perhaps she died."

"Perhaps…"

Marti walks away from me. I don't know what his problem is. As I watch his figure disappearing, I realise my eyes are becoming accustomed to darkness; either that, or it is getting lighter. The moon is still shining and I can see the tops of the trees. What if the man has tracked us and he is planning another attack? Suddenly, the trees seem creepy and every sound I hear scares me. I start to run.

I'm relieved to find Marti waiting for me. He takes my hand without speaking. The sky has lifted, washed with a lighter colour. The ground feels softer under my feet. "It's sandy!" I shout excitedly. "We must be near the beach."

Only another few paces and a vast expanse frees us from the claustrophobic forest. I feel like running to the shoreline, but I'd probably cut my foot on a piece of debris. Then I notice something. "What's that?"

"Where?"

"Over there... look!"

Turtles! Lots of turtles, are heading for the highest point of the beach. We creep closer and see some digging large holes with their flippers. I can't control my excitement as I grab Marti's arm. "That one's laying hundreds of eggs!" It's incredible. All around us, turtles are covering their eggs with sand. Our turtle has finished laying, but it doesn't have a break; its head is low to the ground and it is pulling sand towards the eggs, with its front flippers, like a dog burying a bone. I've never seen anything like it.

Something brushes past my leg. A black shape crashes onto the sand, right onto the turtle's babies.

"Stop it! It's taking the eggs!"

Marti claps his hand over my mouth and pulls me back, his arms around me. Eyes glow as the animal moves closer; suddenly I'm not just afraid for the turtles.

"Keep still," Marti whispers so softly I can hardly hear him. I'm desperate for the eggs not to be eaten, but I don't want it to attack us. Our turtle is scrabbling in the sand, desperately trying to cover them.

When I hear the animal padding away, I breathe out in relief. "What do you think it was?"

Marti lifts me to my feet. "Let's go before we find out." The moon slides out from behind the clouds and I see our turtle moving down the beach. The eggs are safe. For now. I hope that horrible animal doesn't dig them up if it reappears from behind those two palm trees. As I look up, their branches seem to be touching.

Turning to face Marti, I look into his deep brown eyes. "Can we come back? I'd love to see the turtles hatching."

He squeezes my hand. "I'd like that."

+++

MARTI

Early morning light stretches out and a pink line is highlighted with gold. I would love to be on a plane high in the sky. Krista is sitting next to me, our knees touching. Soon, she will fly away, but I will never forget her. Or the

259

night in the trees. An orange glow touches the faint clouds. We sit on the beach until the sun shines red gold, powerful, dominating the ocean.

But we need to walk to the sea wall and I need to let her go. The wall is a barrier between our worlds. When we cross it, she will become a tourist again, a westerner, a hotel guest. And I will go back to being a sea gypsy, a garbage collector, a street rat. Out there under the wide sky, watching the turtles or sitting under the trees, we were free to be who we wanted to be. I felt I could be more than I am. I would love to lie on the beach with the girl with the golden hair while she watches the turtles hatch; seeing her eyes light up with wonder. But that's only in dreams. When we walk up the steps, we will cross into our old worlds.

"When will I see you again?" she asks.

I look into her blue eyes and give her a last hug. "I'm going with you to the hotel. We're going to find Jo, remember." Her mouth dips at the edges and I want to kiss it. "But I'll still be working here — you can still see me." I look at her. "If you want to…"

Her throat moves as she swallows. "I know." Then she says my name and squeezes my hand. I rub my thumb over her tiny veins, wishing we could stay like this forever. I don't know who lets go first, but our hands separate.

38. Reunion

KRISTA

For once The Woman can't speak. She can't stand either: her legs have buckled. Her shoulders are shaking against the carpet and tears are wetting her dress. For a second, I forget she paid the trafficker, I just need a hug. I sink down beside her and she throws her arms around me and gives me a slobbery wet kiss. *That's enough!*

Shuffling backwards, I sit on the floor opposite her. She is gulping big breaths and gearing up to say something, but I can't wait. "Where's Dad?"

She leans forward and grabs my hands. "I've...I've found him. He's alive! I was trying to tell you at the temple with the detective, but you ran off...."

I shake The Woman off at the mention of that monster. She starts flapping her arms as she talks rapidly. "Rob's so much better — he's out of intensive care now — he's going to be fine."

But Marti thought Dad was dying; he couldn't look at me and it was the way he said *I hope*. I clench my fists. "You're trying to trick me." I pull away from her, and spit out the word: "Again!"

Now she is the one shaking her head. "No, love, it's true. And now you're back, too — it's like a miracle!" Her cheeks are glowing, like she's telling the truth, but then I think of the 'detective' and I back off.

She grabs my hands, forcing me to look into her eyes. "Krista, believe me, your dad is alive! George Skelton drove me around all the field hospitals; we even went as far as Phuket town in case Rob had been airlifted there, then we went back to the first one I'd seen." She shakes my hands. "Rob was there all the time! His poor body had been so swollen — like a cartoon character — that I hadn't recognised him when I'd walked around the wards after the tsunami."

She lets go of my hand to wipe her eyes. Then she sniffs loudly. "That was the day you disappeared..."

I rip my other hand out of hers. "No, you're lying! You and that man, you're in it together!"

"What man? What are you talking about? I don't understand."

"I bet you don't! You'll try to deny everything now, won't you? Well, I've got photos to prove it and I'm going straight to the police."

The Woman is doing a convincing impression of being puzzled. "I thought the policeman must have found you and brought you back here?"

"If he's a policeman, he should be locked up."

Her mouth drops open. "What are you saying?"

"You know."

I suddenly realise that she doesn't. Colour has drained from her face and her lower lip is trembling. This performance would win an Oscar and I don't think she's that good an actress. Her neck has disappeared and her shoulders are level with her ears.

"But he told me he was an off duty policeman when I met him at the temple." I watch her lip trembling and bright spots of colour sprout in her cheeks. "If he's touched you..." Her chest is rising up and down like waves. Her pupils are two dots in a sea of white. "Oh Krista, love, I'll never forgive myself if he's harmed you.

I believed him, I gave him all your details... I even downloaded some photos..." A harsh cry comes deep from within her body. She covers her face with shaking hands, digging her elbows into her chest.

I'm not sure what happens next, but one moment I'm as rigid as a ruler and the next, I'm squashed against her chest. "If he did anything..." Jo leaps up and starts pacing around. "If he hurt you, I'll kill him!" The thought of my 5' 2' step-mum facing up to that disgusting trafficker with a set of curling tongs is crazy. I start to giggle, and soon I'm laughing so much it aches. Then suddenly it turns into tears and I can't stop.

"Can you ever forgive me?" she asks. I sniff, wiping my nose on the back of my hand. Jo passes me a tissue and I notice the box is half empty. She sees me looking and her lips lift a little. "It's my second box. I was in such a state, and I didn't know what to tell Rob — why you weren't coming to visit him. I had to invent another hospital that you were in, because he..."

"I want to see him! Please can I see Dad?"

Her face creases in the biggest smile. "I'll ring for a taxi. Your dad has been very sick and it was touch and go for a couple of days, but he's going to be alright. It feels so long ago, now, I can't remember which day I saw you at the temple, but you ran off before I could tell you I'd found him."

The dizziness is turning into bubbles of excitement. Jo is holding my hands and, even though her eyelids are rimmed with red, her eyes are shining. "His poor body was still swollen, his face was bruised, almost unrecognisable. But there was something about his eyes... Could this be your dad? When I leaned over the bed, my heart started shaking. It was him! Under all the mess, it was Rob." She breaks into sobs, punctuated with words. "His poor face..." My step-mum doesn't even notice that snot is dripping down her chin – it's not a pretty sight. But Dad sounds much worse.

While we're waiting for the taxi, I ask her about his injuries, but she says I don't need to know.

"Tell me!"

She coughs and blows her nose. "He had taken in a lot of water, but not just water, you see: sand and grit and sewage. His whole body was full of it and for the first two days, they thought he wouldn't make it. His organs nearly shut down."

I clutch the locket. "But you said he's alright?"

Jo pats my hand and nods. "He will be. It's just that he had inhaled so much mud and silt, that it had affected his lungs and he was very tired. When I first spoke to Rob, he didn't move. I kept talking all that afternoon and then — oh Krista, I couldn't believe it — I saw his eyelids flicker. It was the best moment of my life!"

Saliva is working over-time in my mouth and I keep swallowing. But my eyes are fixed on my step-mum's face as she tries to control her breathing. "Then I saw his lips move and I know he said my name." She reaches out a hand. "Come on, the taxi's here." I jump up, then she takes a deep breath. "But be prepared, he isn't like he used to be.

A knot tightens my stomach. "W...what do you mean?"

My step-mum looks at me without smiling. "Just be prepared, that's all."

39. Love

KRISTA

It's like walking through a war zone. So many beds with so many hurt and dying people. So many shattered dreams. It's not fair. Life's not fair. I hear words like septicaemia and pneumonia as I follow Jo along the corridor. She takes my hand, gripping it as we approach a bed at the end of the ward.

My heart starts thumping. I can't do anything except stare. *Dad?*

His nose is squashed in by wide cheeks and his arms have expanded like The Incredible Hulk. But his eyes are still the same and they are locked onto mine.

"I thought Shrek used to be your favourite film," jokes this faint voice. His mouth doesn't smile, but I know my dad is still there beneath the swollen body. I lean over the bed and press my body against his, my tears wetting his cheeks.

"I'd been knocked unconscious," he tells me, after the deepest, but gentlest hug ever. He talks slowly and I know it will take a long time to hear the story, but I'm not going anywhere.

"Mangroves... you know I went to see the mangroves... I was jogging back along the beach when suddenly I heard a noise like a jet engine...then this massive black wave was coming for me ... I ran for my life."

He pauses and I can hear the breath fighting to get through his windpipe; when he sucks in, it sounds hollow like sucking the last dregs out of a bottle. I reach out and hold Dad's hand and he squeezes it ever so slightly. "When I came to, I was in the water. It was like being trapped in a washing machine full of metal belts whipping me."

"That's horrible."

Dad doesn't respond; he is looking into the distance. "Things kept cutting into me, then I was pinned down... the weight of water was crushing me... I knew I wasn't going to make it. In my mind I was repeating: I love you, I love you..."

"Rob, don't..."

Dad looks at my step-mum like they are the only two people in the room. I feel a dart of pain, then Dad squeezes my hand. "Krista, you are my life and I couldn't bear to leave you."

Jo's lower lip is trembling again. "You don't have to tell the rest."

Dad looks at me and I nod. "I want to know." He opens his mouth, but spasms of coughing rock his body. I break away, because I know he's going to be sick. A horrible smelling gunge spews out of his mouth, soaking down the bed and onto the floor. It's gloopy and thick, and I clap my hand over my mouth, gagging.

A nurse rushes over and tips him onto his side. More slimy gunge pours out. It's vile, gross, disgusting. When Dad stops retching, I uncurl my fingers and see red marks in my hands. The nurse is spraying disinfectant and mopping the floor while Jo is wiping Dad's face and neck. She is touching him so gently that I can see how much she loves him. In the middle of this disgusting, filthy mess, she is there. This massive lump is blocking my throat. She's been so kind while I… well, she must have known some of the stuff I've been thinking.

Stumbling past hospital beds, I grip the door frame. It's like the waves are crashing over me again. Waves of pain and guilt and fear. I've swallowed the sick feeling so much, that my mouth tastes disgusting — like the stuff coming out of Dad. It kept pouring and I didn't think it would ever stop — like the empty feeling when I lost Mum — it went on and on. Now Dad looks like he is dying too. All the time I was searching for him… when I was lost in the mangroves and sleeping on the old man's boat… all the time, he was here. But now it may be too late.

Dad's eyes flicker when Jo says I've returned. I don't care if he's sick, I need to be with him. I place my hand over Dad's scarred one and his milky eyes blink; he looks so weak and tired, I don't want to leave him, but my step-mum says we'll come back later, after he's rested.

"You need to build up your strength, Krista, you've been through quite an ordeal." We find a street vendor but the smell of the red spicy sauce nearly makes me puke; I can still see the gunge pouring out of Dad's mouth.

I manage to sip some juice, and even though I'm worried sick about Dad, I can't help giving a little smile as I watch my step-mum trying to use chopsticks. The sticks look like they're tackling in a hockey match! She gives up and uses a spoon. Through a mouthful, she asks me how I escaped from 'that evil man.'

I smile, as Marti walks into my mind. "This lad rescued me and we spent the night in the trees."

Jo splutters and the bar stool rocks as she leans forward. "Tell me you didn't, Krista… you're only fifteen." I don't answer; I'm enjoying this. She is going manic, waving the spoon. "You spent the night with a strange boy? Oh Krista, how could you? How old is he? I'll kill him!"

I can't help laughing, because it's the second time she's said that in as many hours. "It's not what you think, we didn't do anything."

Her neck disappears into her chin as she looks at me under her eyebrows. "You said you spent the night with him…"

"Yes, but we only talked and …" I feel a blush creeping over my face.

"And?"

"And nothing. He's a sea gypsy, we're from different worlds; he wouldn't want me, I can't even hold my breath underwater."

"He wouldn't want *you*!" Her eyebrows are going crazy — she really needs a manicure. "I hope you wouldn't want *him*! What is a sea gypsy, anyway? A scavenger, some kind of wanderer?"

My elbows slide until my chin is resting on my forearms. "The Moken people have wisdom we don't understand: they were born on the sea and can hold their breath for over five minutes." Jo is staring at me, so I try to explain. "They are like fish underwater, swimming through the coral reefs."

"He really didn't touch you?"

"Well, he had to hold me, so I didn't fall out of the tree." She gasps and I push my shoulders back, looking down on her. "That's allowed, isn't it? You wouldn't want me to have fallen and That Man to find me, would you?" I've got her there; she backs off. Her jaw is no longer clenching, so I keep talking. "The Moken elders knew about the tsunami and they predicted the Laboon — that's what they call it." Then I explain about the crabs and the cicadas. Marti would be impressed — I bet he didn't think I was really listening.

The noodles have gone cold, but Jo is still holding her spoon. "So they are a kind of nomadic people? Indigenous?"

I don't know what that word means, but I'm not letting her know that. Instead, I describe the Kabang. But I don't say how special it felt waking up under the roof of the wooden boat; how peaceful and free I felt without people organising me all the time and telling me what to do. Free to be me.

She wouldn't understand: it was one of those times you had to be there and experience it for yourself. "I swam!" I tell her as I finish the story. "See, I'm not scared any longer. I survived three nights in the open and I swam in the sea!"

Her mouth falls opens and she puts her head on one side, looking at the window. Then she holds up three fingers, puzzled. "Three?"

I nod. "The first night was the worst." I see her catch her breath and enjoy telling her where it was, as I want to see her reaction. I'm not disappointed.

"A mangrove swamp? You were in a swamp? Alone?"

"But the next day I was rescued by this fisherman and he put some herbs on my arm, so it stopped throbbing."

Her spoon is hanging in mid-air between her nose and her mouth, "A fisherman...a man?"

"Yes and I spent the night on his boat."

"Alone?" A bubble is struggling to go down her throat.

"Well yes, unless you count Sniff." Her mouth is about to crack open, so I save her from breaking up: "He's a dog!"

We link arms as we walk back to see Dad. He's had a good sleep, the Thai nurse says, when we spot her in the corridor. She seems exhausted, but still manages to look beautiful. I smile and thank her. It's still a shock when I see Dad's face, but this time, I keep the fear inside. He is lying on his side with his legs propped up under the sheet. Something looks wrong, but I can't work out what. It can wait, because I need to know the rest of his story.

New lines are etched on Dad's forehead, as he starts talking. I know he's in pain, but he's determined not to show it. "I tried to hold on, believe me, I tried… but I had to breathe, I had to. When I opened my mouth, the heaviness disappeared and everything went white. I knew I was drowning…"

My calf muscles tighten and my body goes rigid, staring at Dad. He reaches out a hand. "I thought of you, Krissie — you and Mum — your faces flashed through my mind."

I hear a strangled moan and see half of my step-mum's face hidden beneath her hand. Dad's touch is like magic. Her fingers open like flower petals as he pulls her hand down to his lips. "And yours, Jo...I knew I'd never see you all again." Jo is shaking her head, but I am staring at Dad: I have to know everything.

"What happened?"

"Another wave must have hit the thing trapping me."

"What was it?"

"I don't know and I don't care!" Dad's eyes come alive for an instant as he looks at me. "It was one of those times when your body takes over. Suddenly my head was above water. Then I heard the sound of my own body gasping for air. I was alive!" I breathe out a sigh of relief and Jo blows her nose loudly.

"Were you on the beach?" I ask.

Dad stares at the end of the bed. "I fought to keep my head above water and I was swept onto a pile of debris."

My step-mum faces me. "We know now, that Rob was deposited a mile along the beach..."

"Every breath hurt, I coughed up mud and sand. My shoes and shirt were ripped off..." Dad reaches out his hand and I lace mine over his, as if I'm the parent. I can feel his fingers trembling as he looks at me. "I was so tired, but I knew I couldn't fall asleep. If the water came back..."

"Please Rob, don't... you're exhausted."

Dad ignores Jo and his eyes fix straight ahead. "Then there were people, I think they were people, but I only saw shapes and heard vague noises. They lifted me onto something hard. My leg...pain shot through my leg. I must have blacked out. The next thing I remember is this face. I tried to tell him to look for you... to tell you I was alive."

"He did!" I whisper as Marti slips into my mind.

"Oh Rob!" Jo is hugging Dad while I am picturing Marti, strong and tall, carrying him to safety. She turns to me. "Your dad is improving each day with the cocktail of drugs they give him." I look at her, puzzled, but she nods. "The doctors say it's to clear his sinuses and ear canals of silt." Dad lifts his hand, but she waves it away. "No, you can't stop taking them. You need the drugs for the pain and the aftershock."

Dad wrinkles his nose. "If I must. I guess they must know what they're doing. They tell me that when I could speak, the first words I said were my wife and daughter. They asked me where we were staying. Then they went quiet. I saw people mouthing things and I knew they were saying that you were dead."

"But Dad..."

"I couldn't think straight, love. I was like a zombie, just following orders. Get up. Eat. When I saw visitors

271

wandering around, I couldn't focus on their faces. I couldn't stop thinking of you...I was going crazy with fear."

"But we're here now, Dad, we're both here."

Dad doesn't smile. "It was like I was churning around in the waves all over again. I had been going to meet you, but the waves were massive... the waves... I kept having nightmares about the waves." His body starts to shake and his breathing is faster. "Krissie, you were waiting for me in the café... on the beach." I try to shush him, but he won't stop. "And even if you survived, news headlines kept flashing in my mind about human trafficking."

Jo gasps and her body starts shaking. I bite my lip to stop myself bursting into tears. Dad lifts his shoulders a fraction and touches my cheek. "But you're here, love, so nothing happened."

"You're going to be alright, aren't you Dad?"

He pretends to punch my cheek. "You betcha! A few more weeks of rehab and I'll be as right as rain." He smiles, but his lips are pressed tightly together. I see a look pass between him and my step-mum.

"Then we can all go home?" I ask hopefully.

"Yes love." I tuck my hand into his larger one and he squeezes my fingers. "They do great things with prosthetics nowadays, I'll be running before you know it." I see Jo's gaze dart to the sheet covering Dad's legs and I have a sinking feeling.

He lifts my hand to his lips. "You mustn't mind, darling, I've got used to it now. It will be fine, honestly." He smiles. "I might not be doing the half-marathon this year, but at least I'm alive and I've found you again, Krissie." I burst into tears.

We're all crying now. The physio must think we're crazy — it's not like one of us has died. He rolls Dad onto

272

his side. "I hear you had a good cough. Let's try to get rid of the last bits of sand and mud. He starts to rub Dad's back and Jo pulls me away from the bed.

"We're lucky they managed to stop the infection and save the rest of your dad's leg…"

My eyelids roll back into their sockets as I stare at her. "Lucky?"

She nods. "I know it doesn't feel like that now, but when the wound has enough muscle and tissue growing on it…"

"Skin grafts are amazing," says Dad. "I'll be like a pirate, on crutches for a while, but I'll be fine."

As Jo smiles at him, her whole face lights up. *She's beautiful; how did I never see it before?* I look at her wild frizzy hair and for the first time, decide it suits her personality. If she had it cut short and tamed, I don't think I'd like it. I blink away the tears that threaten to roll down my face. I feel a gentle nudge and accept the tissue that she passes me.

"Everything's going to be fine, Krista, honestly. The doctors and surgeons here are great; the whole nursing staff are incredible." She smiles at the physio.

I look at The Woman. My father's wife. My step-mum. Jo. And I believe her.

She kisses Dad goodbye. "See you in the New Year, darling." Dad and I exchange a raised-eyebrow look. The Woman sees us and smiles. "Today is New Year's Eve, didn't you know?"

That means tomorrow is the start of a new year. Dad has a second chance — we all do.

EPILOGUE

Do not lose the ancient wisdom
or it will sink beneath the waves
and you will become less than yourself,
like a sponge without water.
We were made to be free.

– The Old Fisherman

40. Sunrises and Sunsets

1st March 2005

MARTI

Many sunrises and sunsets have passed, but the scars of the Laboon remain. The ocean's vomit has left hurts, and some may never heal. New moons bring hope to some, but misery to others, as more bodies are washed up on the shore or others identified. Harry's mum still hasn't been found, so they can't move on and they can't say goodbye. At least I saw Papa's body. I will never be able to tell him the decision I've made, but perhaps his spirit can see beyond the western seas.

Do the spirits see us? Do they know the paths we take? Does the moon look upon the earth and know where Krista's attacker is now? She gave the photos to the Thai police, but she's heard nothing. I'm not surprised; the country is in chaos and the snake must have slipped away. I hope he shrivels up and sheds his evil skin, or someone stamps on him.

But there is some good news: her dad is strong enough to walk with a stick. I've seen him as many times as fingers on my hand and I have grown to like him. He is kind, like Rune. Jo is often there, looking like a bougainvillea bush in her bright red dress — but never letting me be alone with Krista.

The first time I saw him was the first time I ever rode in a car. But I couldn't step inside until Krista took my hand. Then there was this roar and it felt like the ocean floor had dropped into nothing. I was flying faster than a bird soaring in the air; faster than our Kabang when the sail catches the wind and we race across the waves.

Jo was sitting in the front with the taxi driver. I could breathe her scent, but stronger was the fresh smell of Krista's hair as I snuggled next to her. Slowly, I relaxed, and dared to look out of the window. Then a telephone pole was whizzing towards me. I clung onto Krista and heard her laughing. When I opened my eyes, we were still racing through the street. People's faces zoomed towards me, then were torn away. A truck flashed past faster than a marlin. Trees and hotels and signposts were all eaten up by our speed. I loved it!

And I loved holding Krista's hand. She was leaning into my shoulder like she was made to fit there. She was wearing a new bracelet, a silver twisted chain with charms on. When she moved her hand, the silver decorations tinkled like chimes. I saw Jo turn her head, a glowing sunrise on her face.

The taxi stopped, but the ground was still flying past me and my feet didn't know how to stand. I was still shaky when I met the Englishman. He was sitting, one spindly long leg stretched out on the bed. He was wearing a green shirt and looked like a mangrove tree, half in the water.

When he thanked me for saving his daughter, I didn't know what to say. I felt like a crab, tucking into its shell. Here I was, a Moken lad, standing in a hospital being thanked by a white man. Then he smiled and teased Krista that she had brought along a nice young man to meet him. The girl with the golden hair looked at me, and her eyes traced circles in mine. I felt a great hope suddenly rising: had the Laboon brought us together for a purpose; were the spirits smiling down on us?

Then Krista's dad offered me a job: he's going to write 'a paper' about the Moken people and he wants my help. I thought paper was something you wrote on. It seems I've got a lot to learn about English customs. This was my chance to get away, live a new life When Krista smiled, my dream was so close I could touch it. I gave her dad the gift Grandad had carved, but as I held the wooden Kabang, I could feel the call of the ocean. And when I let go, I felt I was letting go of part of myself.

Rob held the souvenir against his chest and his eyes filled with tears. I thought he was in pain, so I said sorry about his leg, but he shook his head. "No. The tsunami has given me a gift. I don't know why I was spared when so many were taken. But I do know that I won't take anything for granted any longer — my whole life is extra time." He clasped my hand. "If you want to come to England, my home will always be open to you.

I didn't cry until I was alone looking out at the ocean under the stars. I know I will stand here again when two tides have washed the beach and I say goodbye to the girl with golden hair.

41. Shadows Crossing in the Moonlight

2nd March 2005

KRISTA

We should have left last week, but that would have only been fifty-six days. I made Dad promise to stay until the turtles hatch. Cambridge University said he can start lecturing whenever the doctors pronounce him fit, and when he feels up to it, he can prepare lectures at home. Dad was keen to leave, but I begged him to wait. "Just four more days, that's all they need."

"They?"

"My turtles. They take sixty days to incubate, I've searched the internet in the hotel."

He smiled. "So that's what you've been doing. And I thought you were revising Maths and Physics."

"I can do that when I'm back home."

"It's your GCSE year — you've lost a lot of time as it is..."

"And you nearly died. Life is worth more than exams. Anyway, this is geography, isn't it?"

Dad laughed. "You've got me there!"

"So you agree? Please, I really want to see the

turtles hatching."

He smiled. "Well, if it's that important to you..."

I nodded. "It is."

Straight away, I text Izzy with the new phone Jo bought me. I've got used to calling her Jo all the time. She only feels a bit like The Woman when she's bossing me around and telling me to do my homework, but now I realise it's because she cares. When I feel *The Woman* coming into my mind, I imagine pressing Delete, then inserting *Jo*.

Izzy says it's freezing back home and she wishes she was here. She's just doesn't get it. The beach is still a mess and so many people have lost loved ones. I met this poor lady who had lost all four of her children. And Izzy is whingeing because she never received her postcard.

Dad can walk along the hospital corridor now, so the doctors are happy with his progress. He needs crutches of course, but I've got used to the sight of his trouser leg ending half way. We're staying at The Green Turtle again for our last night in Thailand. Marti's hotel. I haven't seen him much, as we had moved to The Golden Lotus to be near the hospital.

Granny and Grandad flew out the week after the tsunami and fussed over Dad so much I think he was privately relieved when they went back to England. He said he wanted me to go with them, so I wouldn't miss out on "*a vital term for GCSEs*" but I don't care about that stuff. He only gave in when Jo said she'd found an online tutoring service, and she'd make sure I didn't miss out on my studies.

I miss my friends of course, but Dad has set up a Facebook account for me. I feel pretty cool, because the website only started a year ago and Izzy said most people at school don't know much about it. She has an account of course; she posts all the time. Well, maybe once a week. Loren said Izzy's seeing Jack now.

Jo has bought me a new denim jacket and I wear it a lot. I've gone shopping with her several times and we've bought some really cool stuff. I even let her buy me a patterned scarf! I wore it when we went elephant trekking. It was amazing! Our tour guide drove us into the national park and we saw this huge waterfall. Then we hiked along a trail and heard a barking deer – that's what the guide said, but Jo and I thought it was a dog! I wish Dad could have been with us, but he promised we'll come back one day.

Dad's not coming with us tonight either. "But I will be thinking of all those little turtles racing down to the shore," he said. I told him I'm going to find the exact place our turtle laid her eggs: under the shadow of two tall palm trees that arch over the beach.

Dad looked at me, his eyebrows dipping in the middle. "You know they don't all survive, don't you?" he said.

"Ours will!"

The moon is lighting a pathway along the beach. If you don't look at the debris sloping up the seaward side of the wall, you could almost believe that nothing has changed and this is the beach in the brochure. Jo has arranged everything. The Skeltons are with us. George Skelton went a bit over the top when Jo mentioned the expedition — said she's the best babysitter he's ever known. She looked after Harry and the girls when the family flew back to Thailand last month — except it was a false alarm and the body was some other poor woman, not their mum. When they flew this week and Mrs Skelton's body was identified, it must have been horrible.

George said his wife had always dreamed of seeing the turtles, so he and the girls would see them for her. I thought they would be too sad, but soon as they arrived,

Harry ran straight over to Jo and tugged her hand. "Turtle!" he shouted, causing everyone to laugh.

I wish Dad could come too, but he said negotiating the beach in darkness, even with a torch, would be one challenge too far. "There may be other people wanting to see turtles hatching and I'd only get in the way." Jo reminded him she's organised a wheelchair for our flight tomorrow, but Dad gave me a look, so I know he won't be using it. "I'll be running in no time, just you see," he whispered behind her back. We both laughed. I watched his eyes crinkling at the edges and I felt I'd never been happier. Until I remembered about Marti.

Jo wouldn't let me tell him tonight's the night. When I mention Marti, it's like she doesn't trust me — she just can't forget about the night in the trees.

I can't forget either.

Every time we'd go to the beach, I would wander past The Green Turtle hoping to see Marti. But whenever we did meet, Jo popped up like a bodyguard. Yesterday, Marti told us the Moken have been herded on shore. I wanted to ask about Coral and Cloud, but Jo said it was time for my lesson. "We can't fish without Kabangs," Marti called as Jo dragged me away. "Petal isn't even allowed to pick up shells on the beach."

Dad likes Marti; I know he does. When I told him Marti wanted to live in the west, he offered to help, even though George Skelton had already offered a job in his factory. Dad's eyes lit up as he looked at my friend. "While I convalesce, I would like to write a paper about the Moken people and your input would be invaluable. I am thinking of focussing on the impact the tsunami has had upon your indigenous way of life." I can't understand why Marti didn't answer — it's a great opportunity.

We follow the unsteady line of light: shifting circles of sand lit up by our torches. We have passed the other

281

tourists and the officials who are helping to protect the turtles. They were holding some kind of ceremony with little flags strung around a gazebo. Lucy and Olivia wanted to watch, but we are heading further up the beach.

Somewhere beyond us are the two palm trees. I remember how their shadows kissed on the sand in the early morning light. Then I hear someone calling and I see a little girl running towards us, her bare feet skimming the sand. It's Petal! She tugs my hand, her brown eyes sparkling with excitement. "Krista, look. Sky!" And I see him walking towards us with the old fisherman.

With every step that brings him closer, I feel more nervous and excited. I can't look at him. The others are making a fuss of Petal, but Jo is looking at me and nodding her head, her shiny hair swinging around her shoulders. *You must have told him!* I can't believe it, it's like Jo has given me the best present ever.

Does this mean Marti has changed his mind and he's coming with us to England? I'm disappointed when he walks straight past me and leads us up the beach, but I know where he's heading. The old Moken man walks beside me, his face creasing into happy wrinkles; his missing tooth no longer bothers me.

Petal is holding both our hands and, as she skips, we lift her like a swing – just like Mum and Dad used to do to me. I smile and a strong sense of peace washes over me. Strength is passing through us: the old man, the young girl and me. It feels like it's coming from deep in the past; ancient and yet new.

Marti has stopped and he is looking up. I shine my torch, flickering light over the two tall trees. I can just distinguish their branches hanging over the beach. He doesn't look at me, but I remember standing here with him, watching the palm leaves swaying in the breeze, looking down to where their shadows touched. Like us.

One of the girls — I think it is Lucy — shouts and dashes forward, but her dad catches her arm. "Shush, it's essential we're quiet as possible once they start hatching. We don't want to scare them, do we?" We sit down in a group and wait.

I'm desperate to talk to Marti, but he's sitting next to George Skelton, their heads close together. I can't help watching, although I know I should be examining the sand for little movements. The girls soon get restless and Harry pokes the sand, trying to find a turtle, so Jo tries to distract them by a guessing game. I notice Marti arching his back and he stands up. He takes a small step back, then another. I catch my breath. Jo and George don't seem to have noticed, but my mind is going wild. *Please sit next to me.*

The space between us feels so far, yet I can feel the heat of his body. My pulse must be over a hundred; I can hear it drumming in my ears. I can't stop thinking of the night in the trees. Marti is here and I want to touch him, to be touched. But I keep my eyes fixed on turtle territory — I'm not making a move until he does.

Then Harry squeals. Following the direction of his pointed finger, I see a little hat of sand lifting and tiny flippers peeping out. They are starting to hatch! Suddenly, everywhere around us, baby turtles are pushing up from their beds, flapping to get their sense of direction. One moment they were hidden, and now the beach is alive with little creatures making their first steps. Then it's a cavalry charge: you don't know where to look next.

Marti nudges me and I realise I am clutching his arm — when did that happen? He smiles and my heart does a somersault. He leans towards me, then someone says something and he retreats.

Fine, if you care more about them, than me, I'm not

bothered. I walk away and take lots of photos of the tiny hatchlings. It's quite dark, so the images will probably be grainy, but I don't care. If Marti doesn't want me, at least I'll have some turtle photos to wow my friends.

He's near me. I can hear his breath getting faster, then I feel a firm grip of my arm. "Haven't you taken enough?" I push my feet further apart and press the shutter release. He grabs my hand. "Sit down!"

He sinks to his knees and pulls me down with him. And it's suddenly magical. We are lying on the beach watching the turtles. It's awesome, like a wildlife programme, but there are no camera crew and reporters. It must seem like a huge journey for the turtles, even though we could run down the beach in seconds.

Please Marti, make up your mind — come to England — you know you want to!

Harry and Petal fall flat on the beach, copying us. Their heads are close together: her dark one and his blonde. "I think Harry's found a girlfriend!" jokes George Skelton; and Lucy and Olivia giggle. I don't know how they can laugh now they know their mother is dead — perhaps it helps. Marti grins as if it's a big joke, but I can't smile. We are still worlds apart.

Suddenly I hear a shrill voice. "Get off, leave them alone!" A flock of birds are swooping out of the darkness, hovering above the baby turtles. The girls are waving their hands trying to scare the birds. I shine the torch beam straight at them and they flap off, but soon they're back, with reinforcements. The girls tiptoe around the turtles trying to guard them, but Mr Skelton stops them. "Don't! You might tread on one, you have to leave them to fend for themselves."

"But they'll be eaten. We have to do something!" cries Olivia.

Her dad shakes his head and looks sad. "You must

let nature take its course. Birds need to eat too."

"Leave it alone, bully!" Lucy shouts at a bird who swoops down and flies off with its prize. She glares at her dad. "I'm taking some turtles down to the sea."

A large hand covers her smaller one. "We'll go back right now if you can't behave." Lucy sits down and hugs her knees. I feel the same; I'm willing the tiny creatures to reach the sea. *Just a bit further, come on!*

When we see the first little turtles being lifted up by the gentle waves, silent tears are falling down my cheeks. I'm not the only one: Jo's in floods, and I see Mr Skelton rubbing his eyes.

Marti leans closer to me. I stop breathing as his hand touches my chin, catching a tear before it falls. I can feel the tiny hairs on my upper lip, as his fingertips touch the corner of my mouth. I feel the sweep of his fingers as he brushes tears over my cheekbone, smoothing them off my face.

I can't speak; I'll tell him how I feel if I do. I keep my eyes fixed on the turtles scrambling down the beach. We sit fused together in silence. It feels like we're meant to be together at the start of new life, just as we were there when the turtle hid her eggs in the sand. I don't want this evening to end. Tomorrow means going back home and tomorrow means saying goodbye.

+++

MARTI

I want to stay like this forever: hearing the scratching of flippers as turtles race down the beach. Feeling the sand under my feet. Touching her bare toes. Sitting next to the girl with golden hair. I breathe her breath. I touch her tears.

Her bracelet jingles as she tucks a strand of hair

behind her ear. Krista sees me looking and smiles. "Do you like it? Jo gave it to me." Then her cheeks turn red and she touches the tiny amber shells around her neck. "I love Coral's necklace too. Please tell your sister that when we come back, I'll bring her a present from England."

But are you ever coming back?

I have no chance to ask, because Petal runs up and hugs my arm. "We go now?" I look at Krista, and as we move apart, I feel part of me is dying.

Nearly everyone is saying goodbye to the turtles, but Grandad is crouching, his hands wrapped around his knees. I kneel down, a question in my eyes. I sigh like the wind rustling through palm leaves, but already I know the answer. He looks at me and I notice new wrinkles clustering around his eyes. "The waves are calling to me, Sky."

I've known that for a long time. Ever since they found him and marched him to the camp. Seeing him hunched in the corner of four bare walls, I knew. Seeing him tracing his finger on the dirty floor, I knew. Seeing him holding a bottle of cheap beer, I knew. "Do not become friends with alcohol," he told me. "It bites like a snake. I cannot see the ocean; fog has clouded my mind."

Grandad touches my shoulder. "The Kabang is mine, they cannot take that from me. I will sail with the next tide. I will head for Surin, where our ancestors lived. The wind can take me where it will, I will be free."

"But the soldiers may come for you…"

"The spirits will protect me. The waves are calling and the stars shine. I cannot sleep without hearing the sound of the ocean. I cannot live without the sky above me and the breath of the salty air. "

I say farewell and gather the group. Our torches shine the way back along the beach, but something makes me turn.

Grandad is standing, his arms open wide. "Do not forget your forefathers, Sky," he calls. "Do not lose the ancient wisdom or it will sink beneath the waves and you will become less than yourself, like a sponge without water. We were made to be free. You can't hear the birds sing, or feel the rain touch your cheek if you are shut inside man's dark buildings; but when rain falls on the ocean, it dances like shoals of fish bubbling just under the surface."

As I lift my hand, the moon shines a silver line on the two trees, their shadows crossing in the moonlight.

42. Kiss of the Tsunami

3rd March 2005

KRISTA

It's time. Dad calls my name, but I don't move. I can't. If I let go of Marti's hand, I'll never see him again. I'll be packed away in the taxi and a line will be crossed through our lives. I'll be back at school, taking GCSEs and Marti will be working in the chaos, helping to rebuild the hotel. Or perhaps he'll live in the camp and protect his mother and sisters. Forget all about me. Marry a Moken girl one day and raise a family.

Last night was magical, lying on the sand. Marti's chest was so close to mine that I could hear his heartbeat. I wanted him to kiss me and I'm sure no-one would have noticed, because they were watching turtles hurtling down the beach — but he didn't. And now there is no chance, no time.

I squeeze Marti's hand like I never want to let go. His hair is brushing my face and he reaches out and touches me. I look deep into his eyes and speak inside my head. I wish I could say the words aloud. I've dreamed of him ever since that night in the trees — to be honest, ever since that time at the pool. Looking so fit with his brown hair shining with reddish blonde streaks. As soon as I saw his deep brown eyes and he teased me, I knew. But I tried to fight it, thinking he was just a flirt.

If only he would say yes to Dad's offer. Dad and Jo are from different backgrounds, so why shouldn't Marti and I be together? He doesn't need formal education; he knows important things, like how to protect people. All I know is facts and formulas and rubbish stuff I'll never use. Marti understands the sea and how nature works.

"Dad thinks the world of you, he really does. I thought you wanted to make a new life…and I…"

Marti looks deep into my eyes. "And you…?"

I open my mouth, but no sound comes out.

"Krista, you are like a bird that flies away, but I need to stay on the ground. You know I can't come with you."

I squeeze my eyelids together to stop the tears falling out. Fingering the bracelet, I feel the turtle charm and hold it tightly.

Then his hand curves around mine and I hear his voice. "Whenever I walk to the two palm trees, I will sit on the sand until I can see the shadows crossing in the moonlight."

When I look up, Marti's's eyes are moist. "The stars shine in the west as well as in the east." He pauses. "I will dream of you, but my destiny lies here with my people. Grandad is living on the ocean again, but if they find him, the soldiers will take his Kabang."

"Why? You have as much right to fish as anyone else."

He nods. "I know. You can't put people in boxes and close the lid so they can't see out."

The taxi hoots. Jo and Dad are calling. And I know I have to go. Then an electric shiver ripples through me. Marti's arm stays perfectly still, but his thumb is tracing tiny circles over my fingertip. As I look into his brown eyes, I feel we're talking without words. And I know what he is saying.

+++

MARTI

She's gone. Spirals of dust are evaporating and I'm standing alone outside the half-eaten wall of the hotel. Soon she'll be in the air, lifted out of the chaos, away from the sea's vomit. Far away from me.

Last night, we said things, but they were just dreams, stolen by the morning mists rising out of the forest. Challenge was like fire in her eyes and heat was burning me up. Life was waiting to be explored, everything I have always wanted — and more. But when I woke, I knew where my destiny lies. Papa has gone to the spirits — I am the man now. Mama and my sisters have to live in the camp, and I am worried the soldiers will pester Coral. Cloud is drinking a lot and he might get angry and throw a glass bottle. So many lives have already been lost — I have to protect my family.

Krista said I'm proud to be a sea gypsy. She's right. Our elders have proved our traditions make sense. Westerners, rich tourists and the government didn't know about the Laboon, but Moken did. Without our knowledge, deep back through time, the Laboon would have swallowed us all.

Maybe I'm a 21st century sea gypsy: New Moken. *"Honour your family, but make your own way,"* Rune always said. *"Respect your traditions, Marti, don't fight them. Learn to use them in the modern world."*

Now the anger of the spirits has been appeased, I'll use the languages Rune taught me to help Petal and her friends. Maybe she can be the first of our family to go to school and get an education. We can keep our traditions *and* have education: start to live again.

But not with Krista. All I'll have is images tucked in my mind, memories to click open like a locket:

When I first saw the girl with golden hair as she stepped off the bus.

By the pool when she was wearing a flowing see-through shirt and a black bikini.

Finding her by the temple, like a fish out of water.

Dragging her away from the poisonous trafficker.

The night in the trees.

Lying with her on the sand while the turtles fought to reach the waves.

And just now, when Rob thanked me for saving his daughter.

Krista was standing in the hotel gardens on the freshly washed lawn; it rained in the night and the fragrance of new grass and salt from the ocean filled the air. The tall man was leaning with one arm propped up by a crutch, the other around his daughter. Jo joined them, buzzing around like a honey bee. When she smiled at her husband, fresh colour touched her cheeks and she seemed to glow. They looked like a happy family: Rob, Krista, and Jo in her long dress with red and yellow flowers, the material billowing out around her.

Waves of shiny hair flowed down Krista's back. She was wearing pure white shorts and her legs were tanned and longer than ever. The locket was touching a tight blue strapless top which matched her eyes. She showed it to me once, so I know that her Mama is still inside it, just a bit blurred because of the water. The silver charm bracelet sparkled on her wrist and the Moken necklace looked so right around her neck. I couldn't take my gaze away.

But I didn't approach — it felt like a sacred moment for the spirits. I wanted to hold a shell up to my ear, to know what they were saying. It was as if I could see the sun shining through the water, but I was swimming below the surface. If only I could glide up into the light and join Krista's world, but for now, I must stay.

I watched Krista twist her hair around one finger, so different from the dull matted strands after the Laboon tore into our lives. I longed to smooth it away from her face and run my fingers through the silky strands. I longed to be still lying next to her, watching the turtles. I longed to be able to say yes.

Perhaps she heard my mind calling. She smiled and waved me over. Her dad thanked me again and again, then Jo hugged me and the adults drifted to the car.

Leaving us alone for a moment.

A message spun between us, without words. My heart was pounding, as she stepped towards me.

We were standing so close only a tiny fish could dart between us. I wished we were alone under the water and I could show her my world. If only we could have a few more days — or a lifetime to swim through rich coral reefs and dance with the fish. I could feel my body drifting towards her like a gentle wave, swaying until the hairs on my arms told me we had touched. My fingers tensed, not daring to kiss her with her dad and step-mum around. So close yet a whole world away.

When Rob called Krista's name, she didn't move, but a fiery sunset spread over her cheeks. Then an electric shiver rippled through me. Her arm stayed perfectly still, but her fingertip was tracing tiny circles under my palm. I watched the coral shell gently swaying against the silver turtle charm. Blue eyes sparkled like sunlight on the sea, as her head tilted towards me.

The taxi hooted and Jo called softly. I felt Krista's fingers slipping away, and for an instant, thought of Rune, of life torn away too soon. Then the girl with the golden hair said my name and I looked into her eyes. They weren't shining any longer and a little crease crinkled her forehead.

No longer caring who was watching, I pulled Krista towards me and wrapped my arms around her slim body. Clinging onto hope. As our lips touched, this current passed between us, so strong that we could both feel it. Speech wasn't necessary: I was telling her not to go and she was saying come with me. We were tumbling in the waves, daring each other to dive deeper. Dancing to the song of the sea.

Then I felt her pull away. And I knew it was time. Tears shone in Krista's eyes. Soft hair brushed against my cheek. Our last kiss, was gentle, not like our kiss in the tree, hiding under the canopy while the cicadas sang and the night curled about us.

This was the kiss of goodbye.

*Thank you for reading Kiss of the Tsunami.
On the following pages I've provided further
information about the Moken Sea Nomads,
and the Indian Ocean Earthquake and
Tsunami.*

*If you've enjoyed this book, I would love to
read your review on goodreads.com*

*You can contact me at
facebook.com/rachelriversporter
or tweet me @RiversPorter*

blog: rachelriversporter.com

THE MOKEN SEA NOMADS

Austronesian speaking tribes, who live on or around the islands in the Andaman Sea, between the west coasts of Thailand and Myanmar (Burma.) The Moken are also called Sea Gypsies, a generic term that applies to a number of people groups in South-east Asia.

The ocean is their universe. For over 3000 years, these nomadic people have sailed from island to island in small hand-crafted wooden boats called Kabang, where they live, eat and sleep, only coming on shore during monsoon periods.

They can dive to depths of over 20 metres on a single breath and stay there for several minutes, walking across the seabed or remaining motionless, ready to spear a fish. Moken children learn to swim before they can walk and their vision is excellent underwater. The Moken have developed techniques for attracting fish, like blowing a stream of bubbles to lure certain species, or lowering rope with leaves attached, creating a natural reef.

When the tsunami hit on Boxing Day 2004, sea gypsies read the signs in the sea and recalled ancient folklore predicting the 'Laboon,' so most escaped unharmed and were able to save others. The islands where the Moken live received much media attention in 2005 during the South-east Asia Tsunami recovery, where hundreds of thousands of lives were lost in the disaster.

Their free-diving abilities have ensured their survival through the ages, but after the tsunami, the authorities wanted to keep the beaches free for tourists, forcing many Moken into permanent camps. Without a nationality or citizenship, the Moken are powerless and many are exploited, while at the other side of some islands, wealthy tourists are enjoying tropical island holidays. Without the ability to construct a Kabang and pass on ancient knowledge and skills, the Moken indigenous seafaring lifestyle is threatened.

+++

PROJECT MOKEN

"Project Moken was founded by a creative team of film-makers and designers, whose main objective is to inspire and generate enthusiasm about the Moken Sea Nomads. Through films, interactive productions, and ecotourism, we work towards a sustainable future for the Moken lifestyle. Invited to view the world through Moken eyes, we focus on the unique and fascinating nature of their 3500-year-old culture as being one with the ocean."

projectmoken.com

Norwegian film director, Runar Jarle Wiik, has made an acclaimed documentary about the Moken people called *No Word for Worry.*

INDIAN OCEAN

EARTHQUAKE AND TSUNAMI

also known as The Boxing Day Tsunami

On 26 December 2004, an earthquake measuring more than magnitude 9 triggered a series of devastating tsunamis along the coasts of 14 countries bordering the Indian Ocean. It was the result of the Indo-Australian Plate moving below the Eurasian Plate and was one of the deadliest natural disasters in recorded history, killing over 230,000 people. The tragic death toll and widespread devastation prompted a worldwide humanitarian response.

In the open ocean, the swell was just 50 centimetres high but travelling at over 500 km/h. As it entered shallower water, the tsunami started to slow and build, and waves of up to 15 metres high hit the coastlines of Indonesia, Thailand, India and Sri Lanka; with some estimates being considerably higher. Many coastal communities were decimated, with estimates of two million people left homeless. In places where trees had not been cut down to make way for developments, the mangrove swamps helped to act as a barrier to reduce the energy of the water.

ABOUT THE AUTHOR

After graduating from St Andrews University, Rachel Rivers Porter completed a PGCE at Durham University, then she taught English in schools in the north of England.

Writing has always been a passion. As a teenager on summer holidays, she would be tucked into a sand dune, scribbling in a little red notebook, while her family played golf on windswept seaside courses. She enjoyed using unusual place names to create characters and new plot twists. Reading that evening's instalment to an enthusiastic audience, increased her desire to entertain through writing.

When her own children were young, Rachel enjoyed creating short stories at home, whilst writing plays for pupils to perform at school. Following a successful course with Penguin Random House Writers' Academy in 2015, she is now writing full-time.

She has bought a stock of little red notebooks and always carries one in her handbag!

rachelriversporter.com